I0676323

My Sweet Saga

By

Brett Sills

ADMIRAL J PRESS

LOS ANGELES

Published by Admiral J. Press
www.admiraljpress.com
Disclaimer page art by Jayne Dickens

ISBN: 0615532136
ISBN-13: 9780615532134
LCCN: 2011907704

To my parents who are nothing like the ones in this novel; I hope I don't embarrass you at book club. To my friends for all their encouragement and support, I can't thank you enough. And to my Saga: You know who you are, wherever you are.

My Sweet Saga

You are about to read a memory of something that never happened. Please excuse any inconsistencies or bending of the truth.

Flight 4

All I wanted to know was what she said.

It was a reasonable request completely obscured by my lack of ability to distinguish space and time. But I needed to know. To put my mind at ease, to put everything that just happened, the craziest couple of months of my life, into some kind of perspective. They say a picture is worth a thousand words, but Michelangelo's entire body of work said far less than the few unknown syllables she uttered.

I just wanted to know what she said.

I thought it might be a coffin. But it couldn't be; coffins generally weren't equipped with no-smoking signs and vacuum-flush toilets. But it sure felt like a coffin.

Either way, as if rising from a grave, I popped out of the cramped airplane bathroom, not with the grace of a phoenix or even the vigor of a zombie; a zombie's current popularity might render such a comparison as cool. No, I exited the bathroom more like an exhausted jack-in-the-box owned by an impatient three-year-old who wound me up, tossed me aside, and found a paper bag more interesting than my one, boring trick. Only, upon my release, I fell flat on my face with a heavy thud, the oversized boxers and pants that were not even my own flapping around my ankles.

Face down on the ground. Again. My bare ass as my representative to the world. Again. Complete shame. Again. This had become an all too familiar position.

"What'd...she say..." I softly mumbled, as I instinctively touched my already fat upper lip and black eye while attempting to fight the residual grogginess from the small tranquilizer administered to me only a few hours before.

I tried to gather my thoughts, but it wasn't easy when they fell from my mind like dancing snowflakes that disappeared before they hit the ground. The second a clear one came into focus, it was effortlessly replaced by something absurd in comparison. Kind of like if two plus two equaled strawberry cheesecake. And no matter how hard I grabbed my head, I couldn't catch a fleeting memory or emotion long enough to make sense of it. Apparently, being repeatedly pummeled by various fists doesn't quite have the same effect as a shiatsu massage— who knew? But despite the clouded confusion, there was one thing that stuck out with clear lucidity: My God, I wanted to know what she fucking said.

A female voice crackled to life on the PA: *"Mina damer och herrar, kapten ber er sätta på er era säkerhetsbälten på grund av turbulens i området."*

There it was again.

I finally picked up my exhausted, teetering stack of a body and noticed the sight of an angry, muscular blond man with a crescent moon for a face quickly bearing down on me. Again. This time I smiled for no good reason, as I looked down at what appeared to be the diamond pattern in the carpet moving like electrons around an atom. But while I pondered my disoriented state-of-mind, the blond bull expertly circumvented the flight attendant's drink cart, like a gymnast might a pommel horse, and grabbed my shoulders with what I thought were bear claws.

"What say did she?" I slurred, with what I can only imagine was putrid breath.

"You're pathetic," Fabiochin said bluntly, with a thick accent. He pulled me back toward my seat, like a petulant child, as other passengers gasped at the sight of my wobbly, half naked body. I protested by allowing my arms and legs to go limp, but he easily dragged me down the aisle like I was a broken marionette doll. I couldn't even give the horrified audience much of a show.

"Haven't you been publicly naked enough today?" he asked, as he forced up my pants, threw me in my seat, and slammed my face into the headrest, re-opening my busted lip. It's not very often someone gets asked that question, and I don't even like looking down at my own naked body in the shower, so I assure you, it was not by choice.

I tried to re-gather myself for what seemed like the billionth time and let a few more seconds go by before his rhetorical question registered in my porridge brain.

"WHAT?" I asked as loud as my old deaf grandmother used to. He didn't bother to answer because, you know, the question didn't actually require one. He just stared at me with what can only be described as disappointed disgust. Like I'd failed at being a human. And he had a point.

I slowly gazed at him, probably because I genuinely wanted him to repeat himself, but I got quickly distracted by wondering whether or not he'd be offended if I put my finger in the cleft of his nutcracker-like chin. I did my best to curl into a fetal position because I thought if I contorted my body just right, I might be able to hide in that deep chin crevice. But my pondering was interrupted when he informed me that if I had to pee it was "tough titties as you Americans say." I actually had never heard an American say that, but, regardless, it appeared I'd be holding it in for the remainder of the flight.

The cabin calmed as the passengers soon realized that I wasn't a terrorist and, instead, just dazed and half retarded. But ouch, was propelling my already Jackson Pollack of a face into the seat in front of me really necessary? Count: a fat lip, two black eyes, a broken rib, maybe a concussion... or sixteen. And God knows what else was metaphorically injured. Strangely, the only thing that remained unharmed was my large Jew nose that dominated my mangled face. A Jew is never too sedated to escape irony.

After the first moment of silence that I could remember since this bullshit began, a panicked flight attendant gently tapped my new, violent friend on the shoulder.

"Is everything OK?"

"Yes, it is fine," he responded in a professional tone.

I laughed like someone told me a really funny joke. I could feel their judgmental eyes settle on me. I just shrugged my shoulders in response; I didn't know what was funny anyway.

"Is your friend mentally disabled or is this something we will need to alert ground authorities about?"

"Definitely the former," he responded.

The man dug his muscular fingers into his pocket and, in one smooth motion, flashed a badge.

"My apologies for falling asleep. I won't let it happen again," he continued.

The flight attendant tensed at the sight of the badge. "Is he a fugitive?"

"No, he's no danger. He's just...odd."

I just stared at the headrest and played mental connect the dots with the newly splattered blood on the stained blue fabric. It seemed like the most productive thing I could do.

"He was deported this morning and the government is having me see to it that he actually goes back to America. For good," he continued.

The flight attendant gasped. "What did he do?"

"Things. *Unspeakable things,*" he said dismissively, as if he was tired and I was just a stupid nuisance that kept him from a weekly poker game.

But *Unspeakable things?* Had I really? I quickly realized that my absurd actions over the past several hours probably only seemed appropriate, due to the heightened reality that my life had become, but *unspeakable* seemed dramatic. But instead of fighting the accusation, I sunk into my seat and, through my sedated haze, raised my hand like a child in first grade and asked for one more request, even though I was barely cogent enough to form a complete sentence.

"Wha'd the…she say…?" I said in one final moment of sad, yet calm desperation while pointing to what seemed to be nothing in particular. But I was really pointing at something neither of us could see.

"She said there is turbulence and to buckle up," Boxchin finally relented.

How fitting. I thought about the events of the last few months until I poured the memories into an emotional high-speed centrifuge and subsequently passed out from the dizziness. Let me be absolutely clear: none of this was typical. I was not James Bond. I was hardly a man of mystery. I was just your garden-variety, inherently boring, thirty-year-old who stupidly decided to take a chance.

So, how in the world did this all happen? Perhaps my father was on to something and wasn't so crazy after all. I thought about the Saga that led me to this exact moment as I considered my life before and wondered what it would be like now. The things we do for love. Or whatever you want to call that.

Moments before, my "caretaker" referred to me as "odd." I always found it bizarre that a human could ever judge another by that word. For something to be weird or odd, something had to be normal. But no two humans are exactly alike, not even identical twins. Sure, we share similar thought patterns and physical attributes, but the beauty of humanity is that we are all 100 percent unique. All our decisions are formulated by an inimitable thought process that provides one-of-a-kind solutions. Therefore, no human on Earth could be odd, weird, normal, or otherwise because every single human being on planet Earth is, in most ways, completely different from the one standing next to him—or her.

That said, four years ago, before pretty much every single thing changed, I, my life, was well...completely fucking normal.

PART ONE

Several Weeks Earlier...

Welcome to My Life

(Not Exactly the Normal Part)

"I just want to thank everyone for coming, really; this promotion just means the world to me," a teary Clarissa cried while addressing the table of ten that were present in honor of her big promotion to senior publicist. Her nine co-workers, including her boss, hung on and smiled at her every word while I suddenly became enthralled with an episode of *The Amazing Race* that was playing on the television only a few feet away.

Clarissa wore this tight black dress that matched the color of her hair and made her body into visual flypaper.

When I saw her like this, it reminded me of the first few months of our relationship: those dates where we couldn't even make it halfway through dinner before we'd sneak away to the bathroom and fuck loud enough for the entire restaurant to cheer, as if a waiter had just dropped ten plates. Actually, I couldn't even remember if we really did that or just thought it; we probably just considered it; it seemed like so long ago. Regardless, the memory quickly dissipated once I disappointingly learned that seven of the eight teams, which were currently racing (amazingly!) through St. Petersburg, Russia, had no clue who Anton Chekhov was.

My trance was broken by the sound of applause (I guess Clarissa had just finished her speech) and the serving of dinner, which, for me, was the plainest taco known to man, literally a white tortilla with some lettuce and tomato. For the record, I did not order this dish because I loved it; I ordered it because it was probably the only thing in the restaurant that wouldn't kill me. Clarissa and I had discovered this place after her trendy Toyota Prius ran out of gas for the third time, which is really difficult for a hybrid. The first time, Captain Impossible told me she didn't realize the gaslight was on; the second time she claimed she was talking on the phone and failed to notice the tank was low; and the third time she just blamed the car for not getting the gas mileage it promised. Or maybe she circled "D" for "all of the above" each time. I can't remember. The third time it occurred, she stalled right in front of this hole-in-the-wall Mexican restaurant on the corner of Beverly and Martel and was so distraught when I picked her up (over something that was entirely her fault) that she demanded, for once, we eat Mexican food, even though I was deathly allergic to cilantro, and this place stopped just short of infusing it into their ice cubes. Apparently, the greasy food calmed her nerves to such an extent that she dragged me back repeatedly and, though I protested each instance, she'd flippantly tell me to "quit being a baby" and to "just get something plain," as she'd "check in" using FourSquare to preserve her mayoralty. So, of course, this death trap was the place she picked for her promotion dinner, and that's why I had to deal with her annoying co-worker, Dave, staring at my plain taco like its blandness personally offended him.

"That's *all* you're having?" Dave asked. "You should at least put some Pico de Gallo on it. They make it so good here; you'll love it, trust me. If I could marry it, I would."

Dave attempted to heap a pile of the poisonous slop on one of my tacos as he laughed way too loudly at his own lame joke, but I firmly grabbed his wrist to ensure that he wouldn't. Though I was in a crappy mood, I didn't really feel like dying.

"Well, *excuuuse* me," Dave said with his hands raised to mockingly signify he meant no harm.

Dave might have been in love with the sauce, but the only thing I would have loved was to tell Dave to suck a bag of hard dicks, or maybe I should have accepted his offer for the yummy Pico de Gallo only to vomit it all over his tacky red shirt once the cilantro reacted with my allergy. But since this was Clarissa's big night, I ultimately felt it was inappropriate. Dave dug into his enchilada, thinking of his next question that was bound to piss me off.

"So what do you do, Brandon?" Dave asked while shoving the cheesy mess in his mouth. He succeeded. I hated that question, yet it's the only question people in Los Angeles care about, and is often requested before your name. Sadly, this was the third time I'd met Dave, the third time he asked me the question, and the third time he gave the same response to my answer.

"*Oooh*, that's cool," Dave said in a tone that was an octave higher than his normal one, clearly giving away the fact that he *didn't* think it was cool.

After Dave took the hint and decided to leave me alone, I briefly paid attention to the cacophony of publicity-related stories being told by the rest of the group, which were all equally narcissistic as much as they were non entertaining. If Hollywood jobs were diseases, publicists would be the gonorrhea. Every time I've broken bread with these people, their conversations always entailed two things: 1) the first name of a celebrity, but never the last and 2) the funny thing said celebrity did.

"So last night at the Clairol event, Ashton did the funniest thing…" Clarissa said as she addressed her eager coworkers who salivated like hungry puppies at the word "Ashton."

Ninety-five percent of Clarissa's stories started this way. She'd often follow up with some lie detailing how she didn't care for celebrities and some bullshit about how they were just like everyone else, followed by some cliché regarding putting on pants one leg at a time. After the sixth time she used this line on me, I made sure to put my pants on both legs at a time, right in front of her, for two whole weeks. She never noticed.

"OMG, and then he TOTALLY grabbed my ass; I think he just has an Asian fetish."

And that's how ninety-five percent of her stories ended. Clarissa was of Chinese descent and usually weaved this into most of her reasoning as to why people treated her the way they did. Those who knew me best probably found it odd that I ever dated a Chinese woman. After all, I didn't even like Chinese food beyond sesame chicken. In fact, when I was five years old, and all I wanted for my birthday was a Cabbage Patch Kid, I cried for hours because my aunt bought me a Chinese one. I sentenced little Yu Fung to five years solitary confinement in my closet, and released him years later when he "volunteered" to be the mummy for my fifth grade history project on ancient Egypt. But around the time I met Clarissa, I had recently finished a fascinating book on the Ming Dynasty, which spawned an eight-hour Wikipedia tear on that big communist country that could. I suddenly became fascinated with the Chinese. But it turned out that dating Clarissa was not nearly as informative as Wikipedia, plus Wikipedia never said OMG.

"OMG, Clarissa that is *so* Ashton!" one of her co-workers screeched in some horrific Valley girl accent. It doesn't even matter which one.

I excused myself to the bathroom and washed my face with cold water while listening to a muzak version of Madonna's "La Isla Bonita." It was in this moment I wished I had some kind of hard-core drug problem, because this was usually the time a movie protagonist would light up a joint or snort a line to help him or her cope with a sticky situation. But since I barely even drank alcohol, I just gripped the sink with both hands and looked directly into the mirror, staring at the droplets of water that fell from my cheeks and eventually onto the white porcelain sink. At least I finally had a moment of silence. *If I could only find a way to stay here for the rest of the night,* I thought, *that might be perfect.* Actually, maybe dying wasn't the worst alternative after all.

I re-approached the table and knelt next to Clarissa while donning my most convincing face that suggested I might be ill.

"Hey, I'm not feeling so well. I think I'm gonna bust outta here."

Clarissa looked genuinely disappointed, though I wasn't sure she had even spoken a word to me the entire night.

"What, you can't leave! Are you OK?"

"I think I might have eaten a little cilantro by accident."

"Oh," Clarissa said with a hint of guilt. "Didn't you just get the special lettuce tacos?" Clarissa stated this as if "special lettuce tacos" were actually on the menu, and that explaining my order to the waiter, who could barely speak a word of English, wasn't a huge chore.

"Yeah, but I think Dave might have put some Pico de Gallo on it when I wasn't looking."

"Well, do you want me to go with you? Because…"

"No, no…you stay with your friends. It's your night."

"Oh, OK…well let me walk you out."

Clarissa excused herself and, while grabbing my stomach and wincing, I made some half-assed apology to the table that could have earned me a spot on one of those Pepto

Bismol commercials where they danced and sang about having an upset stomach and diarrhea.

As Clarissa accompanied me toward the door, I couldn't help but wonder if this was the feeling a traitor had while walking the plank of a pirate ship.

"Oh, I forgot to tell you, you have to pick up your blue shirt from the dry cleaners. We're having dinner with my parents tomorrow night and you know my father finds blue soothing."

My face sunk slightly and Clarissa immediately noticed. She often picked up on the slightest of movements; maybe it was some ancient Chinese secret.

"Brandon, they're paying for our entire wedding and they want to discuss some things. We have to go. This is non-negotiable, OK?" Clarissa said, as she full well knew she'd get her way. "I know my parents make you uncomfortable, but the blue will help. They love you, Brandon, I promise."

Complete Bullshit.

Clarissa took her dainty hands, cupped my face, and looked directly at me, softly, yet seriously with her unusually round, light brown eyes.

"Do you love me?"

When she did this, she always looked so beautiful that I convinced myself that I did. I broke her gaze and nodded slightly.

"Then trust me. OK, now go home and get some sleep. I'll be there soon, 'k?"

Just as we were both about to turn away, there was a question I had to ask: "Hey Clariss...do you know who Anton Chekhov is?"

Clarissa quickly scanned her mind while scrunching her forehead, her go-to face while searching for bullshit to say when she had zero clue what the other person in the conversation was talking about.

"Oh wait, your college roommate? From France, right?"

"Yeah, that's the guy," I said with a hint of disappointment as I turned toward the door to leave.

"Brandon!"

I turned back again, this time with a little less enthusiasm.

"You didn't congratulate me. I mean, this is the night my dream came true."

My head was suddenly infiltrated with the image of a naked Ashton Kutcher lying face down as Clarissa undid his soiled diaper and, with a baby wipe, cleaned his anal crevice with such precision that Ashton couldn't wipe the shit-eating grin off his fucking face for the entire shit show. What does it say about a person when something like this is their dream come true?

"Congratulations," I said softly as I kissed her on the forehead.

I walked out of the restaurant, exhausted. But I wondered whether or not I still had time to go to Yogurtland before it closed.

Dreams

Lately, I've had this recurring dream where I'm roaming the crowded halls of my old high school in a state of panic because I can't find the classroom to take the final exam for a class I hadn't attended since the first day of school. Sure, it was a textbook anxiety dream, but this one featured a twist: I strolled the halls accompanied by a pure-white, baby polar bear. And believe it or not, he was really well behaved. I didn't need a leash, he never made much noise other than the occasional squeal, and he managed not to shit on the floor. Win! Strangely enough, either no one found it odd that I was flanked by an endangered species, or no one cared, but after a futile search for the elusive classroom, I decided, like the conscientious bear owner that I was, to take him back home because he looked hungry. I assumed I had slabs of meat in the fridge, because if this were happening in reality, he'd be the only polar bear in the world surviving on Cap'n Crunch. But as we passed through the library toward the exit, two security guards confronted me demanding I turn the bear over to the authorities at once. After I calmly refused and attempted to quell the escalating situation, one pulled a gun and shot the bear point blank, causing my little fallen friend to bark one last dying squeal. As if the bullet pierced my heart, I dropped to my knees, scooped the little snowball in my arms, and watched the crimson blood infiltrate his white fur until it resembled the color of the Haagen-Dazs vanilla raspberry swirl frozen yogurt I normally enjoyed while watching television on boring Sunday nights. Fury built from head to toe, and with revenge streaming through my veins, I'd...wake up. Always at that exact point.

Once I realized the latest installment of the dream had ended, and that I was fully awake, I noticed Clarissa peacefully sleeping next to me with a curious grin plastered on her face. Sometimes I thought she knew when I had a nightmare and secretly enjoyed it.

Believe it or not, the apartment where Clarissa and I lived had been my bachelor pad only a year before. When Clarissa's old lease expired, she convinced me that we could both save money if she moved into my one bedroom. In the old version of my apartment, the white walls were bare save for a framed print of a sad clown playing baseball with the Chicago Cubs, originally painted by John Wayne Gacy.

Yeah, that John Wayne Gacy. Apparently, when Clarissa first saw this piece of "art," it almost sent her running for the hills, but I was never actually moved by the painting; I just found it to be an interesting conversation piece. But now the sad clown on the white walls had been replaced by bunny prints on what she called taupe walls, enclosing furniture that was actually purchased at a real store and not found for free on Craig's List. In fact, the day we bought that furniture at Ikea was the day I realized this relationship was real and, as a result, became arguably the most terrifying day of my entire life. But it didn't stop at the furniture and re-painted walls. She purchased a doormat with our names on it, demanded the landlord replace the carpets, and the top shelf of my bookcase, which used to feature some classics by Shakespeare, Dostoyevsky, and Orwell, was replaced by a black wooden placard that said, "And they lived happily ever after...All because two people fell in love." And that was the only thing on the shelf. She relegated my books to the back of the closet because she claimed they were "old, smelly, and dusty" and needed to replace them with that thought provoking statement emblazoned on cheap balsa wood. But I didn't hate the message because of its questionable nature or even its faux sentimentality; I despised it because it was purchased from Target. You'd at least think that kind of sap was the product of the blood, sweat, and tears of some hippie who hadn't showered in three days and chose to peddle them on Venice Beach to support his weed habit. But a multi-billion dollar conglomerate? Clarissa did not care about its origin and felt it was thoughtful. I often thought of cracking it over my knee to prove some kind of point, but I never figured out exactly what the point was and, anyway, I'd just get yelled at.

Despite all the annoyances, Clarissa was still a functioning female with warm working parts that slept next to me every night. And when I soon realized the morning had taken hold of my nether regions, I wondered if, for old time's sake, I should wake Clarissa in the manner I would have two years ago. I'd sneak up behind her and wrap my arms around her tight little body, pressing my warmth against her ass. She'd slowly wake up, release a soft moan and pull her pajama bottoms down just enough to reveal her pink thong. I'd pull my dick from the confines of my boxers, press it against her while rubbing her pert tits through her tank top, and whisper some kind of morning poetry about how bad I'd like to fuck her from behind. She'd grab the back of my head, force my lips to her neck, pull down her thong and demand that I feel how wet her pussy was. Before I knew it, I'd be balls deep. Two years ago, this was 100 percent, foolproof, always worked. Now, we hadn't had sex in three weeks and both of us offered a litany of excuses as to why.

But suddenly inspired by my own thoughts and memories, I spooned her and softly kissed her cheek down to her neck. But instead of nuzzling into me, she pushed my arms away as if they stung her.

"Not now..." she sleepily muttered. "I left my tampon in by accident last night and I think I'm out. Can you run to the store to get some?"

She sure knew how to kill a boner.

"Now?"

"The sooner the better. You don't want me to get Toxic Shock Syndrome, do you?"

Good question.

She turned over again and resumed her slumber, while I was left trying to remember what kind of tampons she used and how humiliating it would be to buy them. Not because I was a guy buying tampons, but I was a guy buying tampons at six a.m. I could feel the cashier laughing at me as she made the whipped sound in her head.

And fuck, did I hate that sound.

But, sadly, I was used to it.

Work

"Good morning, black people!"

Gladys, the office's matronly receptionist, announced this every morning after she arrived, like a school bell signifying the start of homeroom. I was consistently one of the first people in each morning because Clarissa insisted I get there a half hour early to give the appearance of hard work. Appearance being the key word as that thirty minutes was usually occupied by checking the statistics of my moribund fantasy baseball team and giving the "thumbs up" to random Facebook statuses. Like clockwork, Gladys popped her bright chubby cheeks, which somehow emitted a rosy glow despite her dark skin, over my cubicle.

"And you too, Brandon!" she said, in what I would think was a flirty tone if she wasn't a sixty-five-year-old woman.

"Ah, I can't hide from ya, Gladys!"

She laughed at my comment, though it was incredibly lame and I said it each morning. Just to clear any confusion, I was employed by a predominantly black television channel, and by predominantly, I mean exclusively, and worked in a predominantly African American office, and by predominantly, I mean I was the only white person there. Simply put, my job was to find rental space around Los Angeles to place our terribly offensive billboards for our god awful programming.

Bryan Lomax, my only office friend, pulled up alongside my cubicle and sat on the mountain of Diet Coke that acted as a makeshift chair for people who never stopped to talk to me. He slouched and sighed.

"My baby still won't fuckin' shit in the potty."

Bryan was built like a tank, had a head the size of an industrial refrigerator box, and excelled at coming up with creative ways of telling me he had to take a shit. But arguably, the most interesting thing about Bryan Lomax was his work e-mail address. Since our company's e-mail prefixes consisted of the first initial, followed by the last name (with no space), Bryan's e-mail appeared as Blomax@aic.com. I'd never call him Blomax to his face, but in the epic poem otherwise known as my inner thoughts, he would forever be Blomax. Believe it or not, Blomax was also the person in competition with me for a promotion that would present a once-in-a-lifetime opportunity to be incredibly ordinary. Clarissa felt this should be the most important thing in my entire life.

"Yeah? So the potty that plays congratulatory music after you shit isn't working?"

Bryan shook his head in disbelief.

"You know what he does? It's the strangest thing. The little shit actually walks into the bathroom, backs into the corner like he's a cat in a litter box, and pushes one out in the diaper. So he knows to shit in the bathroom, but refuses to use the potty. Dia-fucking-bolical!"

"You gotta think it's something he'll just learn eventually. It's not like he's gonna back in the corner of his high school locker room and unleash hell," I retorted.

Bryan shrugged.

"Just wait till you and Clarissa have kids. You'll see."

Believe it or not, that was the first time anyone mentioned my future children. Or at least the first time it had hit home. No family or friends ever broached the subject, and Clarissa's parents were still in disbelief that she'd want to marry a guy like me (and by that, I mean fiscally challenged…and white) when a perfectly good Chinese dude, Ronald Fong, had been in her grasp only a few years prior. What the hell would my kids even look like? Certainly not like me. Then again, half Asians were an attractive bunch, but why would I care if my children were sexy or not? Fuck, I never wanted kids.

"Anyway, more importantly, we have a bit of an issue," Bryan stated in his best "getting down to business" voice.

"What's the problem? They change the soap in the bathroom to that foam shit again?"

"No, we're still good there, but we have to take a ride. Don't worry. I cleared it with the bosses. You're gonna love this."

Sweet, a field trip.

The majority of my job involved sitting in my cubicle and only moving to get that pathetic excuse for coffee that I was convinced was actually dirt, or to walk to the bathroom. This seriously endangered my ultimate weight goal of being able to see my dick by the time I was forty. So any excuse to get out of the office was a welcome one, even though Bryan's car was kind of cramped and smelled like baby vomit.

Bryan was only twenty-six years old, but he had already lived a lifetime worth of experience. He was the product of a broken home in the Los Angeles suburbs where his mother literally would have sex with a different man every night. Bryan was pretty sure that she was a prostitute, but couldn't rule out that she just might have been a slut. After his crime-filled teenage years that featured a little robbery mixed with a couple of DUIs, he found solace in the military where he, as he put it, "learned to be a man." That's what happens when you shoot an Iraqi in the head and watch it explode like a watermelon. Soon after he came back to the States, he met a nice girl, Marie, who grew up behind a white picket fence. A few months later, they conceived little Bradley. Not that I cared, but I found it humorous that someone with no college education and a lengthy record was competing with me for the same job.

Bryan turned left on La Brea Avenue from Wilshire and found a parking spot a few blocks up with a broken meter.

"So are you gonna tell me what we're doing here? Or are we just going to Yogurtland? 'Cause I'm cool with that."

Bryan pointed to the top of a nearby building and, more importantly, at a billboard for our ever-popular show called *Honey Buns*. Except this particular billboard was severely torn and covered with splotches of red paint, as if Goliath had used it as a napkin while eating some real saucy noodles.

"Ah shit, look at that. What happened?"

Just then, a small Persian man approached Bryan and me in a fury, waving a piece of paper like it was damning evidence.

"I tell you what happen! Look!" the man said.

"That must be Ali, he owns this building and called me about this," Bryan said with a smile. "Isn't this cool?"

"You fucks pull that board down right now! Look at this!" Ali said, while handing me the note that read:

"If you put up this billboard again, I will find out who is responsible, hunt you down, and bomb this building to the ground."

"Hey, that's me!" I said with fake exuberance. "Sweet, I don't think I've ever been threatened before."

The billboard featured a big black ass in a tiny little thong with the principle characters of the show laughing hysterically at some unknown source of humor in the background. I had never watched the show, so I did not know the significance of the ass or who or what had *Honey Buns*, but judging by the maniacal grins on the people behind her, perhaps Honey Buns had farted.

Ali was still shaking with anger. I took off my sunglasses like David Caruso to show him I meant business.

"Any clue who did this?" I asked Bryan in my best detective voice.

"Well, it is Beverly and La Brea, you know; it's kind of a Jewishery area."

"A Jewishery area? Nice. You think some old Jew did this?"

"Well, don't you think the billboard would offend those dudes who wear wool coats when it's ninety-five degrees out?"

"A smile would probably offend those people," I offered. "But a Jew didn't do this."

"No Jew! A black do this!" Ali added to the conversation. "They rob my store two times and look at note, they rhyme like Snoop Dogg."

"Ah, come on, man," Bryan said, like he'd heard it a hundred times before.

I nodded, suddenly finding humor in the situation.

"He's got a point, Bryan. Plus, this guy might know something about terrorists."

"Please, when have you ever heard of bombs goin' off in the ghetto? This was the work of a militant Jew. I'll bet you twenty bucks."

"Who give shit! Just get down!" Ali screamed again.

Bryan and I did not flinch and kept looking at the billboard, as if it held some kind of answer.

"Perhaps if the note was written on law stationery or a doctor pad, I'd buy it was a Jew," I said.

"I'm telling you. I was fifty feet away from a pipe bomb in Baghdad. I know those Israelis are a nasty bunch. This is the work of a Jew."

"Oh yeah? A lot of Jews are parading the streets of Baghdad?" I asked.

"What, you think a black guy did this too?"

"No, probably an Arab dude. They probably hate big black asses even more than Jews. Now, if the ass was white and the woman's hair was blond...then maybe some old Jewish woman might have done it."

"Why would an Arab guy threaten to bomb a Persian guy's building?"

"Haven't you ever heard of Sunnis and Shi'ites?"

"Do you have any clue what you're talking about?" he asked, in a condescending tone.

"No," I shrugged to show I actually didn't give a shit. "By the way, why are we even here, shouldn't the police be handling this?"

"Oh yeah, definitely, but I thought this would be more fun," Bryan said, while looking back at the billboard.

He was right.

"What do you want to do about it?" Bryan added.

"I dunno, I guess we'll take it down and find a new space."

"You sure? You want the Jew terrorists to win?"

"It would be nice for once."

I took some pictures of the billboard with my iPhone, just in case anyone would need to see it while Bryan attempted to calm Ali down by assuring him we'd be taking down the billboard as soon as possible. Although I was sure nothing would come of this incident, I knew a story that involved me being threatened by terrorists would succeed in making me seem important. After Bryan finally assured Ali, he cracked his knuckles and stretched like he had more work to do.

"Let's get out of here, " Bryan stated. "I gotta catch the brown express two train to Deucetown."

Work indeed.

If nothing else, this killed half the day. Plus, I had forgotten to pick up my blue shirt from the dry cleaners, so I'd retrieve it on the way back to the office and wouldn't have to do it during lunch. The small victories in life.

The Phone Call

Not one of my superiors mentioned the vandalism incident and, honestly, I had mostly forgotten about it after lunch. I was coasting through my usual afternoon routine that consisted of reading CNN and ESPN.com, while quickly opening an old Excel sheet when someone walked by, to perfect the illusion that I actually did something with my time. I even mastered a concentrated stare and sigh that I learned from George Costanza in that Seinfeld episode where he tried to trick his bosses into thinking he was overworked.

I loved when my office phone rang while my boss was in close proximity, because it really gave the appearance that I was getting some work done. He was your typical annoying boss that spoke in platitudes and often exalted the benefits of Friday, while denigrating the horrors of Monday. I always cherished our conversations in the elevator about the weather.

Imagine my delight when I had to excuse myself from this afternoon's conversation, about his being tired and looking forward to the upcoming weekend, to answer a call from a blocked number.

"Get those signs up, baby," he said, while snapping and firing off the finger guns before he walked away.

I answered the phone, but it was hardly someone selling billboard rental space.

"Brando! How ya doin', kiddo! Guess where I just came back from?"

Oh shit.

"Not now," I responded, deflated.

"Oh stop, c'mon and guess!"

I wasn't guessing.

"Hong Kong! Now guess how many bitches I fucked in the past 100 hours. C'mon, guess, I dare you."

"Dad, I'm not in the mood. I'm at work."

"Sixteen! That's right; I skied those slopes sixteen times. And only had to pay for two of 'em!"

Four years ago, my father was the sole winner of a $350 million dollar Powerball jackpot. After a lump sum payment just north of $180 million, he paid my mother $20 million to leave town, bought himself a huge mansion in Beverly Hills I had yet to see, a new black Maserati, a pottymouth, and the personality of a tremendous racist. Any conversation with him was somewhere between a messy enema and a messier abortion. Thankfully, he only called about once every six months.

"Dad, seriously, I'm at work. I'm busy. I'm getting married soon, and I'm up to my ears in—"

"You're getting married?"

"You knew this."

"To the gook?"

"Gooks are Korean or Vietnamese, pending on which war, Dad. Clarissa is Chinese, for the hundredth time."

"That's a mistake," he said through a condescending belly laugh. "Now, fuckin' a chink broad is fine, but marrying one? You're askin' for it."

"Duly noted, nice chatting."

Just as I was about to hang up...

"Just wait a second. Don'tcha got a second for your old man? I have a story for ya. You're not gonna believe this one."

My father was rich beyond belief but had told me many times that I would never see a penny of his money. He always made some allusion to wallpapering his coffin with thousand dollar bills instead of giving it to his only child. He seemed to think he earned his lucky fortune through perseverance and hard work and was more than pleased to rub his wealth in my face. This was how I became officially convinced there was no God.

"If you hang up, I'm gonna keep callin' ya till you pick up."

This was strange. I hung up on him constantly and it usually took six months for him to realize.

"Why?"

"Would you just listen to the story?"

Fine. I really had little else to do anyway.

"So a month ago or so," he said, "I'm at this auction, waitin' to bid on that spic Pele's jersey from the 1970 World Cup, when before I even had the opportunity, they announced a surprise new item, a round of golf in Dubai with…guess who?"

Silence.

"Guess!"

Silence, I would not guess.

"No guesses?"

Genius.

"Tiger fuckin' Woods! Can you believe that shit? I had this beautiful image of Tiger and me on the links in the land of camel humpers and, you know what, I had to have it. So, I outbid the entire room for it, and two weeks later, I'm on a flight to Dubai for my match. What a crazy city that is! I didn't know those oil slurpin' towel heads could make somethin' so modern. Anyway, when I got to the course, I found out I'd have to share Tiger's time with some tall Kraut who looked like a blond Alec Baldwin; apparently he won a similar auction. So we're out there on the links, right? The course is beautiful. It's a little hot, but I got some new special deodorant recently, so the pits stayed dry. You know how I am about my pits (sensitive). The first seventeen holes, ya know, I'm playin' pretty well and we're all shootin' the shit about whatever, but me and this tall Hitler-loving cocksucker are tied going into the 18th, so this cocky Gerry (he did a good job of keeping the insults fresh) suddenly wants to make things interesting. So he proposes a bet and that nigger Tiger…half nigger Tiger? (quarter actually, Dad) Anyway, he's all for it and tryin' to talk me into it. So you know, I'm a man's man (debatable), I'm not gonna back down. I'm gonna take him down like we did in World War Two. So, anyway, he let me go first and I hit this fuckin' beautiful ass shot, right down the fairway, and I scream "tits baby!" as this thing lands. You know, to psych out this marble-mouthed, beer-guzzlin' pussylip. My best shot of the day, I mean, they shoulda made a video of this shot and put it in a fuckin' tutorial or something. But you know what happened next? This sausage-chewing piece of shit saves his best shot of the day for that moment. Can you believe it? He'd been Sir Shanksalot all day till then."

I guess Dad couldn't have played too well up till that point, either, if they were tied.

"So, our balls are like two feet from each other (hey now). And now fuckin' Tiger is laughin' cause he knows it's on. So, in two more shots, both of us are on the green, pretty much right next to each other. Remember it's tied. So this Nazi tankbanger (kinda a funny image) waltzes up to the ball there and does this weird-ass wiggle thing...no it was more of a shimmy, for concentration or something and knocks in a twenty-foot putt! Can you believe it? So, I get up there and measure my shot. I ask Tiger for some advice, but now he's sayin' he can't get involved because of the bet, and I'm pissed because I dropped 250k, for what? No advice? Just that smug toothy grin and receding hairline? So, I line up my shot, take a few practice swings with the putter, and just as I'm about to hit the ball, you'll never guess what happened. C'mon guess!"

Still won't guess.

"Fine, Tiger's desert darky of a caddy fuckin' sneezes! Right in my backswing! So my ball goes flyin' away from the hole to the ass end of the world, and I'm callin' for a do over, but they're not giving me shit. I fuckin' lose by a stroke, and I get so mad that I chase that carpet pilot around the course with my putter all ready to make him into a popsicle, while Tiger and Adolf have a good laugh over the whole thing. Between you and me, I think that rich spearchucker wanted me to lose."

I wonder why.

"Can you believe that story?"

He was finally done and only one response came to mind: "Why did you want to buy a Pele jersey?"

"What? I just told you this entire incredible story about golf with Tiger Woods and that's all you can say?"

"Why are you telling me this?"

"Well, because of the bet. We bet that the loser buys dinner."

"What, you need a couple bucks?"

"In Stockholm."

"Sweden?"

"Yeah! That's where this asshole was from. Loser buys in the other bastard's home country."

"I thought he was German."

"Why would you think that?"

"I dunno, something about you calling him a Hitler-loving cocksucker and a, what was it, Nazi Tankbanger?"

"The point is, I need you to come to this dinner with me."

"Right."

"Oh come on, it'll be good. I haven't seen you in forever."

"Not since your last girlfriend flashed her big fake breasts to our entire extended family."

"You're still angry about that? It was a party. And they were nice."

"It was Grandma Sylvia's funeral."

"Well, there were hors d'oeuvres and music. I told him I'd bring you; he really is curious to meet you."

I quickly thought about why he suddenly wanted me to join him for a trip. He'd never invited me anywhere before, even though we lived in the same city.

"Dad, you haven't offered to take me anywhere or give me anything in four years. The one time I asked, you told me to 'get fucked' if I recall."

"Well, this is different."

"Why?"

"Because I told him you worked for NASA. That you might train to become an astronaut."

"What?" I asked with genuine befuddlement and a hint of anger.

"I may have mentioned it. Trust me, I considered hiring someone to play my son, but it would just be a clusterfuck."

"Why in God's name did you tell him I worked for NASA?"

"Why are you so nosey?" he responded.

This incredulous question gave me pause. There really was no answer to that query.

"Great conversation, Dad, I'll talk to you later."

"Fine, but a car will be outside your apartment tomorrow at five a.m. I expect you to be in it. This trip will be all expenses paid."

"Give me one reason why I should ever go anywhere with you."

Finally, my father seemed exhausted by what he would have considered petulant antics, but what I would have considered well-deserved doubt.

"Because I'll make it very worth your while, OK?"

A long moment passed, and I could still hear him breathing on the other end of the phone. Silent, for once.

"Brandon. I don't ask much from you, but I'm asking you to please go." Suddenly, for the first time in years, I heard something different in his words: sincerity.

I bit my cheek and looked at the phone receiver as if it provided a window into my father's eyes. But all I saw were holes.

I hung up.

The Pleasure
of Dinner with
My Future
Non-English-
Speaking
In-laws

C larissa took my hand as we snaked through the
myriad of shoppers at The Grove toward the Italian
restaurant where we planned to meet her parents. Her
parents always selected The Grove for our meals, a festive outdoor mall that constantly pulsated with mediocre
music from local bands and had an elaborate water fountain that danced to Lionel Ritchie's "All Night Long"

every thirty minutes. I'm sure they chose it because it was walking distance from their house, but I always found it funny that two people who never smiled would consistently choose a mall that was second only to Disneyland in manufactured happiness. Not to mention, they seemed to love riding the large green trolley that transported shoppers throughout the mall even though the venue was no longer than a football field. I figured that people who actually chose to ride the trolley and had full use of their legs just sucked at life.

"My father's been having foot problems lately and Mom says he's been grumpy," Clarissa said as we approached the hostess.

"Is that his new excuse for riding the trolley?"

"Would you just be nice?"

"When am I ever not nice?" I responded.

"Brandon, stop."

"OK, I'll ask him if he needs a foot massage."

Clarissa gave me a disapproving glare.

"You know, they don't have to pay for this wedding; they're doing it because they love us."

Clarissa located her parents who sat motionless at a table in the rear as they waited. You know in those spy movies where the hero picks out the terrorist bomber in a crowd because he looks too quiet and reserved? Well, if this hero existed in real life, he'd tackle Clarissa's parents every time.

Clarissa smiled and waved, but her parents barely moved, their still expressions not budging. They really had perfected the ability to be impervious to fun. As we approached, I extended my hand to her father.

"How are you tonight, Mr. Chang?" I asked cheerfully. "I hear the old dogs have been bothering you?"

I felt Clarissa jab me in the side. Mr. Chang looked confused and mumbled something to his wife in Mandarin who groaned.

"Good to hear," I responded with a smile. He jerked his hand away from mine.

As usual, her mother barely acknowledged my presence. We sat down, and I buried my head in the menu, hoping there was an item that would magically make this night end early. They always seemed to last forever. But there was a reason I despised dinner with Clarissa's parents beyond the normal list provided by anyone who suspected his fiancée's parents didn't like him: Clarissa's mother's unusually large hands.

Now, I do not suggest that they were simply big for a woman, or even large for a man, I'm insinuating that something was medically wrong. Mrs. Chang could not have been an inch taller than 4'11", and I would have been shocked if she were 95 pounds soaking wet, yet she appeared

47

to have stolen her hands from the StayPuft Marshmallow Man. And I could never stop staring at them and openly wondered if they would slowly lift her off the ground much like a hot-air balloon would. Then, my mind would wander to whether or not Mr. Chang had ever received a hand job from her, and, of course, I tried to figure out if his wang got lost in those skin oven mitts like a normal hot dog would in a foot-long bun.

I knew her beast hands were an unapproachable subject within Clarissa's family because the one time I broached the issue, Clarissa evaded the question like it was infested with germs and muttered something about a long story. I wanted to tell her I had all day to listen to it, but I assumed she wouldn't have appreciated the insistence. However, I did scour WebMD for clues, but the only symptoms I found led me to believe I had cancer, so I quickly closed the page and forgot it ever happened.

On a side note, whoever taught Mr. Chang his limited English must have told him that every English sentence should be punctuated, not with a period or question mark, but the words "support my daughter."

"So, we agree to pay for wedding, but have you figure out way to support my daughter?" Mr. Chang always delivered his sentences in a formal manner that made it seem like dinner was always some kind of political summit.

"Actually, Daddy, Brandon is up for a promotion at his job. He has worked very hard," Clarissa quickly stated, as if this would impress him.

Mr. Chang slowly nodded and muttered something to his wife. Mrs. Chang looked at me with the only expression her face knew how to make and mumbled gibberish back to her husband. I knew she was talking about me because I heard the word "*mian bao*," which means "bread" in Mandarin. Clarissa informed me that her mother called me this because, during our first dinner together a couple of years ago, I ate the entire breadbasket at the Olive Garden before anyone else could have some.

Clarissa quickly noticed the uncomfortable silence and tried to strike up banal conversation, while I searched for the singing waiter whose voice was so loud that he drowned out any conversation with his Andrea Bocelli covers.

"Brandon, you should tell my father what you do at work. I think he'd be very impressed."

I didn't see how that was possible. The interns at work weren't even impressed.

"Well, I work for a television station and find locations to place our advertising billboards," I stated matter of factly.

"So, all of LA can see them, Daddy. Without Brandon's help, no one would know when to watch the TV shows."

49

"That's right. Because of me, all of LA now knows *Honey Buns* is on Thursdays at nine."

Mr. Chang appeared confused as Clarissa nearly spit out her water.

"Honey Buns? What Honey Buns?" he stated in his broken English.

"Daddy, it's just...nothing."

Clarissa punched me hard in the leg again. Mrs. Chang growled like a wolverine and placed her hands flat until the puffiness spread like puddles over the tablecloth. Apparently, the blue shirt wasn't working.

"And this work help you support my daughter?"

Clarissa actually made three times what I did. But I assumed this would be lost on his traditional values.

"Because my daughter is princess. Pure, nice girl. Need to be treated like princess and supported. Like Ronald Fong do."

Ronald Fong was Clarissa's last boyfriend. Now, with a name like Ronald Fong, one would probably picture a geeky Chinese guy who worked at Bank of America and loved to do math problems on the weekend. Well, that couldn't be further from the truth. Ronald Fong looked like the Taiwanese Tom Brady, straight down to the manly chin. He led Harvard to two winning football seasons as its starting quarterback, and founded an incredibly successful law practice in downtown Los Angeles. Clarissa's parents loved The Fong more than they loved their own daughter. I could just picture dinner with the Changs and Ronald Fong. Cracking jokes in Mandarin, handshakes where Mr. Chang shook with the right while patting Ronald's shoulder with the left. I bet Mr. Chang even smiled during these occasions. I knew Ronald had asked Clarissa to marry him, but only after he agreed to spend two years helping starving children in Africa. True story. But he never anticipated that Clarissa wouldn't wait for him. And I often thought I was her proof to Ronald, her parents, and even herself that she didn't need to. Though, she actually cheated on me with him during the outset of our relationship, but somehow spun it into a positive when she claimed her guilt proved that she had true feelings for me. Or something like that. Regardless, I bought the excuse because, well, I don't know why. But even two years later, she would have these longing daydreaming spells that were always punctuated by her muttering the words, "I was just thinking about something from a long time ago." I always just figured it was about Ronald. (Oh, and for the record, each time Mr. Chang referred to his daughter as a "princess," I had to bite my tongue and refrain from telling him that, when we first started dating, she'd constantly scream "fuck me long time" in the midst of doggy style. She thought pretending to be a Chinese whore would turn me on and, though I could understand why, it actually did nothing for me. Regardless, those days were long gone, but were hardly the actions of even metaphorical royalty.)

Ronald and Fong were the only two words in the entire world, in any language, that actually made Mrs. Chang crack a smile. Normally, this didn't bother me, but for some reason, in that moment, I just wanted to make that smug grin disappear.

"Well, I received some interesting news today," I said, while I leaned back in my seat.

"Yeah?" Clarissa asked, happy that I was involved in the conversation. "About the promotion? I'm sure my parents would love to hear."

"Nope, not about that. I spoke to my father today."

Clarissa's smile quickly dissipated as she narrowed her eyes. "You did? But you never talk to your father."

For whatever reason, the subject of my father always troubled Clarissa, even though she had never met him. She certainly had heard me complain about him from time to time, but I gathered the real reason she found him to be poisonous was because he was once an authority figure in my life and, technically, though highly unlikely, could one day become that again. Clarissa saw my life as a jet plane: If you were to give the controls to someone unqualified, even for a second, the whole thing would hurtle towards the ground until it exploded in a million pieces. Unfortunately, this included myself. To her, I was just a passenger in my own body.

"Yeah, he invited me on a trip with him. To Sweden."

Clarissa reacted like I had just suggested we all take turns sodomizing her father with the sharp ends of the silverware.

"*What?* When?"

"Tomorrow."

"Tomorrow? Like HELL you are going."

This reaction actually surprised me. And offended me. "I never said I was going. I said I was invited. I—"

I cut myself off as I noticed Mt. Clarissa was about to erupt.

"ARE YOU CRAZY! You can't just pick up and go off on some ski trip with your father. We're a team and we have a wedding to prepare for. Not to mention your job, your promotion!"

"Sweden is as flat as the Midwest; you're confusing it with Switzerland. No one is skiing. Don't you ever watch the Discovery Channel? Plus, it's summer."

"No! I don't ever watch the Discovery Channel!" Clarissa answered in a voice not meant for public. Clarissa always answered rhetorical questions when she was angry.

Mr. and Mrs. Chang clearly seemed surprised by their daughter's reaction, but it was clear they had no clue of the issue.

"Well, you should, because the HD signal seems to work best on the Discovery Channel, don't you agree, Mr. Chang?" I asked, trying not to laugh at the absurdity of the current scene. Mr. Chang was unable to find the words to correctly express himself in English. I guess he didn't know how to translate the Mandarin versions of "fucking" and "asshole."

"Are you trying to get smart with me? Because we have an appointment with Mitzy on Thursday and she was really pissed off when you missed our last appointment!"

Actually, the idea of missing an appointment with our overzealous wedding planner was reason enough to go. Directly after this thought, I noticed that the Andrea Bocelli wanna-be entered the dining room in search of victims to annoy with his baritone voice. I attempted to make eye contact with him and subtly nodded like he was a parking attendant I was planning to bribe for a good spot.

"Well, I guess I won't go then. No one likes Mitzy when she's mad."

Andrea finally noticed my look and confidently headed over to our table.

Clarissa's eyes were wild with anger. I could hear her grit her teeth. "This is not the time for sarcasm, Brandon George."

She actually used my middle name when she was angry with me. Like a mother would. Clarissa shook her head with disappointment; she was ready to drop a bomb.

"I forbid you to go," she said, directly.

Forbid. Wow. Forbid. Suddenly, I wasn't so amused. And that was when Andrea decided to flex the golden pipes.

"Wheeeeenn theeeee moooooon hits your eye…"

"You forbid me? I'm a grown man, Clarissa. You cannot forbid me from doing anything," I shouted over the singing. I had no intentions of actually going.

"Like a biiiig pizzzzza pieeeee, that's *amoreeeee*…"

"But why does he want you to go to Europe with him?" Clarissa said, slightly annoyed by the performance. "You know he's—"

I was just happy Clarissa knew Sweden was in Europe.

Clarissa's sentence was cut off by faux-Andrea's escalation in volume. Mr. And Mrs. Chang, clearly not aware of tradition, stared at the singer like he had forty-seven heads.

"When the worlds seeeems to shiiiine like you've had too much wine…"

Clarissa shot a glance at him that I swore could have made his heart explode. She did not like being cut off. Ever.

But this guy was a performer and would not stop until the fat lady sang…or the petite Asian screamed: "WOULD YOU SHUT THE FUCK UP!"

Clarissa yelled loud enough to cause a waiter in the adjacent restaurant to drop his tray.

Suddenly, Andrea's performance stopped and the ambient noise of the restaurant grinded to a halt, as all eyes focused on us. Clarissa didn't seem the least bit embarrassed, which was more than I could say for the singer, who was only well intentioned. He was visibly hurt, and I motioned to him that it was OK by circling my finger toward my head to signify Clarissa was crazy. She did not notice this, but turned her attention back to me and searched for the perfect thing to say.

"And you HATE your father!" she screamed as she threw down her napkin in defiance and stormed off to the bathroom. Clarissa always had to have the last word, even when the last word was already hers. This spawned an even more urgent conversation between her parents. I turned my attention back to the menu, ignoring the multiple stares from other patrons and pretended that nothing had happened.

"Hmmm, so what do you think looks good?"

I smiled to myself and allowed her parents' chatter to become white noise. Clarissa had a functional relationship with her parents and normally heeded their advice, more like their commands, except for when it came to one thing: me. For whatever reason, Clarissa picked her love life as the subject of her rebellion. And I liked that. It made me feel dangerous and forbidden, like I was covered in metaphorical tattoos, offensive tattoos that would suggest I rode a motorcycle and kicked ass for fun. And when Clarissa got something in her mind, she saw it through. So no matter how much my presence pissed her parents off, no matter how much they urged her to rediscover The Fong (even if she secretly wanted to), she'd protect me like a cornered animal would its young. In fact, their anger toward me only seemed to embolden her. I knew part of my appeal was the fact I was an "other," but for some reason this didn't bother me. In fact, it made me feel unique, which is next to impossible for a white kid living, well, anywhere. This attractive tenacity manifested itself in other parts of her life too. Even though I thought her job was completely worthless, I did admire how she so easily climbed the rung-less ladder that is the entertainment business.

But I realized Clarissa's best trait actually helped me to become the person I did not want to be. When we first started dating, and I was attempting to get my journalism career off the ground, Clarissa was supportive during every bump in the road and did all she could to aid my career along. She gave me long speeches about sacrifice and hard work and would often convince me to keep honing my craft, even when I was tired and just wanted to take a walk to the Coffee Bean and do nothing. But unfortunately, I'd only earned just enough success to keep the delusion of achieving a career in the field alive. And because of this, I really had done nothing with my life over the past few years other than waste my time with work, especially now with a job I could not stand. While I should have been appreciative of her care, I suddenly felt resentful, even if that was unfair.

Clarissa came back to the table and wiped away her smeared mascara to make herself look presentable. She tapped me on my knee.

"I'm sorry I freaked out, but we *will* talk about this later."

Not much was said for the rest of the meal, other than casual conversation with the waitress and something about the amount of money designated for floral arrangements at the wedding. The remainder of the discussion was in Mandarin and, though in the past I was curious as to the subjects of their banter, I just wished I had a breadbasket I could hoard from the rest of the table.

Regardless, it was worth the price of admission, alone, to watch Mrs. Chang eat with a fork.

Decisions

As I stood over the toilet, I released a piss so vicious I thought it might break the porcelain. During our fantastic dinner, I convinced Clarissa to drink wine, fully aware she had that weird Asian alcohol allergy and that the after-effects would quickly put her to sleep. I was not exactly proud of poisoning my fiancée (well, the word "poisoning" is slightly dramatic), but I really didn't feel like having the conversation (lecture) I knew she was planning.

I walked back to bed to find Clarissa sprawled out, dead to the world, as the red digital clock beside her blinked 4:22 a.m. I rubbed my hands over my face, considered physically moving Clarissa to create room on the bed, but clearly realized there was no way in hell I'd go back to sleep.

All my life I had a digital red clock; in fact, I'd go nuts without one. One of the small treasures in my life was waking up naturally at, let's say, 3:00 a.m, quickly noticing the time, then falling immediately back to sleep knowing full well I had a solid few hours left before I had to wake up for work or school. In fact, as I grew older, I would actually set the alarm for two hours before I had to wake up, just to ensure the enjoyment of the knowledge that I had more time to sleep. But as I sat at the edge of the bed next to a now snoring Clarissa, all I could do was stare at those numbers slowly changing in what felt like the longest few minutes of my life. If I only had an hour to live, I would have spent it in this moment, because it would have lasted fucking forever.

I don't know why I suddenly felt the urge to be defiant. Clarissa was right; we had a ton to do. We were getting married in a few weeks and there was still a plethora of planning, but then I remembered she never really seriously consulted me on anything. When deciding on what food to serve, she asked for my input, but when I suggested simple California type cuisine, she scrunched her nose, made some "hmmm" type sound, and overruled me with something she'd prefer, while shamelessly suggesting that I was part of the decision. This was her M.O. for each of our conclusions, so I honestly didn't need to be there, and I couldn't give half a shit if Mitzy was offended or not.

I had no clue where the time went. I swore it felt like just the other day I was perusing Match.com, pretty much emailing every chick that looked somewhat presentable, including the cute Asian girl with the hot rack that three years later would become my fiancée. There was not a day that went by when I thought how different my life would be if I executed the original plan for that evening which consisted of downing two Tylenol PM, jerking off, and going to bed early. Or what if I had decided to go out that night? What if I caught a movie on HBO? But instead, I decided to drink green tea and felt compelled to make an Internet-dating profile because I thought I was lonely. The next three years of my life, for better or worse, had been a result of that. After the next few weeks, it would be an entire lifetime.

Someone old once told me the idea of a perfect woman only existed in your head. The best you could do was find someone you didn't want to kill and spend the rest of your life with that person. I didn't want to kill Clarissa all the time and she was very supportive of me, even if she needed to be my sun. She got off on the fact that, without her, my life would conceivably be worse. And I thought about my father, my parents, and his callous words about my current lifestyle, including my upcoming nuptials to my soon-to-be blushing Asian bride. Then I thought about spending days with my father in a foreign country and listening to him bullshit about the past four years of his life and all the mistakes I was making with mine.

And suddenly, I felt compelled to go.

I looked back at Clarissa, with her mouth wide open as if she were trying to catch flies, and I knew the maelstrom that would come if I actually chose to go on this admittedly insane trip with my father. Really, what good could come out of it? I had no interest in salvaging a relationship with him; that was long past. Plus, Sweden did not sound like the most exciting vacation destination, even though I'd never been out of North America in my entire life.

But despite this, I found myself standing up, walking to my closet, and pulling out my small travel bag. Before I could stop myself, I was shoving socks, underwear, shirts, and pants into the bag, all the while spying Clarissa to make sure she did not stir. With my bag full, I slowly tiptoed to the drawer in the living room to grab my un-stamped passport.

Crazy wasn't exactly part of my mind's vocabulary. Most of my life involved the safe choice, the choice of least resistance, the choice that would lead to the least bit of drama. And this continued in my relationship with Clarissa, which progressed about as textbook as one could. Simply put, we never went or did anything exciting. Sometimes I would croon, "let's do something crazy, something absolutely wrong," in her ear like I was Leonard Cohen and then suggest some retarded activity such as skydiving or sex in the mall bathroom. Each request was returned with the same disappointed look and some line about being mature.

And I knew that, for the rest of my life, I'd be on the straight and narrow. I guessed I figured it was time to do something stupid before I'd never be able to again.

I popped my head in the bedroom doorway to find Clarissa still splayed in the same position; she wouldn't be up for hours. I approached her and removed the hair from her eyes to give her a soft kiss on the forehead. I thought maybe I wanted her to wake up to beg me not to go. But she remained motionless.

I gently walked to the window and gazed toward the street in front of my building. As promised, there was a black Lincoln town car waiting out front. I grabbed my keys and what was left of my dignity.

My Father

The one thing that was still recognizable about my father was his loud, choppy snore. As I approached the waiting area thirty minutes before our plane was scheduled to depart, I watched my sleeping father pound out a snoring symphony with his neck arched up and mouth wide open, as if he was a baby bird waiting for a worm. My father's greatest talent was sleeping, and he looked as comfortable sleeping at LAX as he would in his own home. I've watched him sleep through weddings, rock concerts, sporting events, no matter how loud the venue, it didn't matter; my father would eventually doze off. It's too bad sleeping wasn't an Olympic sport because that would have been his one chance to grace the cover of a Wheaties box.

As I stood over him, with my travel bag slung over my shoulder, I was momentarily disarmed, as he suddenly strongly resembled the father that I used to know. The father that took me for burgers and ice cream every Sunday night when I was young. The father that would stay up late helping me with science projects and studying for quizzes. The memories of me climbing on my sleeping father to shove random household objects in his wide-open, snoring mouth, flooded my mind. I remembered pretending I was Michael Jordan while shooting Milk Duds into his gaping maw. I could have killed the man when he once choked on one of the chocolate treats, but he responded with laughter, instead of anger, and punished me with a tickle torture that made me laugh until I cried. Suddenly, I felt sorry for the way I had treated him these past four years, but then quickly recalled the stunt he pulled shortly after his winning numbers were drawn and remembered why I could barely stand him in the first place.

It had been just over a year since I'd last seen my father and he more or less looked the same, save for ten or so extra pounds, a Burt Reynolds mustache, and cream-colored linen suit over a blood-red, parrot-themed Hawaiian shirt that was six times as obnoxious as the one he wore to Grandma Sylvia's funeral. Hawaiian shirts are the heroin for old men. Seriously. At some point, these male fifty-somethings wander into a Tommy Bahama, probably to kill time while their wives are trying to squeeze into something that will barely fit them at Banana Republic, and notice a seemingly innocuous, beige shirt with a palm tree on it.

Perhaps with the ocean in the background. For some reason, they are drawn to the shirt, maybe because it reminds them of an old vacation, perhaps of a relaxing moment in their lives, or maybe even freedom. They think, "hmm, that scene looks really peaceful. I think the gray chest hair that'll barrel out of the top of that fine shirt will really impress the Missus." Then, each time they purchase a new one, the color scheme and design get a little more daring. Two years later, these horrid excuses for clothing occupy 75 percent of their wardrobe and cause their closet to appear as if it threw up a Mango-a-go-go from Jamba Juice all over the hangers. I hoped he wouldn't wear that to dinner. Actually, I hoped he would.

The flight attendants announced the commencement of boarding and I considered waking my father, but something stopped me. I suddenly noticed the other passengers, most of whom looked native to Sweden, were dressed conservatively and gave off the appearance of being decent human beings. Every five seconds, a different passenger would steal a glance at my sleeping father and probably wondered either if an actual person had been creating that noise or if Jimmy Buffet had gained a hundred pounds. He looked about as out of place as someone could be and, in turn, made me feel excluded because I was actually with him. Then again, at that moment, he'd look silly in any crowd, unless he was waiting to put down a sawbuck on a poor greyhound at some God forsaken dog track in south Florida.

With each passing second, I regretted my decision a little more and suddenly became burdened by the current responsibilities of my life; not to mention I couldn't get Clarissa's disappointed voice out of my head, nor the thought of her mother's monster hands gripping my neck. I hadn't received a phone call or a text from her, but I assumed that, once she tried me at work and noticed I hadn't called back within twenty minutes, she would start to wonder. Then, at lunch, she would storm home and notice my passport was missing, after which she'd scream obscenities and probably call the National Guard. I expected a barrage of calls and texts as if the power of her words could magically turn the plane around. I shouldn't have come here. Plus, work had started to get busy, since we were preparing to launch our fall shows, so it really wasn't the best time to leave the country, even if it was just for a few days. And *Mad Men's* season premiere was rapidly approaching, I hadn't set the TiVo, and I knew Clarissa wouldn't record it for me 1) out of spite and 2) because she hated the show since she "didn't understand it" and didn't like "shows that take place in the past," as if the program was a lecture on rocket science attended only by Civil War re-enactors. And if I didn't know what happened between Don and Betty Draper during the upcoming episode, well, I just couldn't live with myself. Fuck it. It was just not the right time.

Fueled with an urge to return to my normal routine, I quickly turned around with haste to make my way to the exit where I'd grab a cab, a coffee, and pretend I'd never come here. But after two steps, I heard my father's snore pattern change and the inevitable choke that briskly freed him from his slumber. When his eyes shot open, I knew there was no turning back.

"You made it. Good," he said with about as much enthusiasm as someone ordering egg whites for breakfast. "I knew you'd come."

"I almost didn't."

"I knew you'd come."

He always thought he could predict my behavior. Like I was a leaf and he was the wind.

"Well, yes I did, but I just realized it was a mistake, so I'm leaving now."

"Nah, you're not."

"Watch me."

"Nah, you won't," he said through a lion-like yawn.

Though I knew the smart decision involved me running in the other direction; my feet felt like they were in concrete. My father and I shared a long glance that told each other nothing, but which proved the unpredictability of the upcoming days. There were definitely questions to be asked, but not now. My father broke my gaze and grabbed an orange from his jacket while a second came tumbling out. He picked it up from the floor and replaced it in his pocket.

"What's with the oranges?" I asked.

"Huh?"

"The oranges. What do you have a vitamin C deficiency or something?"

"What? No. It's my thing."

"Your thing?"

"Yeah, you know, everyone's got a thing."

"Eating oranges is your thing."

"Yeah that's my thing."

"How long are we going on this trip for?" I asked, without skipping a beat.

"Three days."

"And we're staying in the same room?"

"Yeah, you think I'm made of money or something?"

"Yes."

"Well, I only got one room. Are you done with the stupid questions?"

I shrugged and relented. We approached the airline gate and handed our tickets to the friendly employee who gave us a complementary pair of headphones that I hoped were not used.

"How long is the flight?" I asked my father.

"Fifteen hours, I think. You don't still get sick on flights do you? I remember the one trip to Disneyworld you begged us to ask the stewardess for Donald Duck orange juice, and you threw it all up forty-five seconds after you drank it. Remember?"

My father laughed at the memory; I did not. When I was younger, he constantly brought this up, which was only slightly more annoying than the condescending smile that graced his fat face every time he told the story. I didn't bother to respond.

"Then I had to take you to the bathroom to change, but you ran out bare-assed before I could help you put on new pants. And the stewardess had to chase you down because you were disturbing all the other passengers, remember that? I still don't know what was going through your mind that day, not everyday you see someone run down an airplane aisle with their dingy danglin' for everyone to see."

I couldn't believe he still loved that fucking story. And more so, embarrassing me with it.

"They are called flight attendants, Dad." I sure showed him.

"What?"

"You called them stewardesses. They're flight attendants."

"What the fuck are you talking about?"

I sighed. I didn't even know.

"Never mind," I said, as if I had just given up every fight I was about to encounter over these next few days. I was exhausted. Not only because I had not gotten much sleep the night before, nor because I was slightly hung over, but I was just ...exhausted.

As we walked toward the plane and became overwhelmed by the whir of the engine of the 777, I suddenly missed Clarissa and would have done just about anything to be in Mitzy's office discussing tablecloth patterns and whether or not we'd serve lattes with dessert. I suddenly missed my apartment and the stupid black placard on the bookshelf. I just missed my routine.

Once the plane entrance was in sight, the next few steps made my exit from Clarissa's Mexican dinner party seem like a stroll lined with primrose.

Flight 1

On my way to the airport, I'd dreaded the various top-ics my father and I might discuss on the flight. I fig-ured I'd be treated to a plethora of stories, whether true or not, about his adventures around the world as if he was a modern-day Indiana Jones. But if there was one thing trans global travel had taught my father, it was that Ambien was his preferred flight companion. As soon as we sat in our seats, he popped two pink pills and after a brief comment regarding the wonderment of the mountains on his Coors Light bottle turning blue from the cold ("how dooooo they do that!"), he resumed his snoring concert much to the delight of the passengers in close proximity. But those snores were music to my ears.

Also, much to my own pleasure, the television embed-ded in the headrest in front of me was broken, which meant I was without any significant form of entertainment for the entire trip. I'd left my iPhone headphones at home, and reading something as simple as a magazine was just an invitation for nausea. After getting bored with daydreaming about Clarissa's various reactions, my mind went places it often did in extreme boredom: Random top ten lists!

Top ten list of perfect, congratulatory songs for a potty to play after successful use (in no particular order):

1. Whoomp, There It Is (Tag Team)
2. I'm So Excited (Pointer Sisters)
3. Simply The Best (Whitney Houston)
4. Feels Good (Tony Toni Tone)
5. Hey Man, Nice Shot (Filter)
6. Down In A Hole (Alice In Chains)
7. Dirty Little Secret (All American Rejects)
8. Champion (Kanye West)
9. End Of The Innocence (Don Henley)
10. Hallelujah (Leonard Cohen version)

I checked my watch and noticed that had taken only took thirty-seven minutes. OK...another list:

Top ten list of songs to listen to in the silent dark (in no particular order):

1. Cumulus (Imogen Heap)
2. Silent Flight, Sleeping Dawn (MONO)

3.   String Quartet #3 "Mishima" (Philip Glass/ Kronos Quartet)
4.   Let Down (Radiohead)
5.   Comfortably Numb (Pink Floyd)
6.   Sailing (Christopher Cross) (yeah, I know... yeah)
7.   Transatlanticism (Death Cab For Cutie)
8.   When It's Cold I'd Like To Die (Moby)
9.   The Dangling Conversation (Simon and Garfunkel) (yeah, sure Sounds Of Silence too)
10. Hallelujah (Jeff Buckley version)

That one had taken a little longer. Forty-two minutes. Christ. Still well over nine hours to go. Ok, one more list, but this time I decided to escape from music:

If I needed to create a starting football defense just using characters from *Mike Tyson's Punch-Out*, which positions would best suit the characters:

Left Defensive End: Mr. Sandman (He'd be a terror)
Left Defensive Tackle: King Hippo (Really, who would push him around? Unless someone hit him in the stomach, of course.)
Right Defensive Tackle: Bald Bull (Bull rush baby!)

Right Defensive End: Piston Honda (the tougher one you fight later on in the World Circuit, of course.)

Strong Side Outside Linebacker: Soda Popinski (Good thing he's off the vodka from the arcade version.)

Middle Linebacker: Super Macho Man (Was there any doubt?)

Weak Side Outside Linebacker: Mike Tyson (I'm running out of guys.)

Left Cornerback: Great Tiger (He'd use teleportation to trick opposing QBs)

Free Safety: Don Flamenco (He'd be fine just as long as someone didn't alternate left and right jabs to his face.)

Strong Safety: Von Kaiser (Germans suck at football, but he's our wily vet back there.)

Right Cornerback: Glass Joe (See Mike Tyson).

This, too, took a short period of time and only succeeded in questioning both my sanity and, more importantly, my geek quotient. To even things out, I considered making a list of top ten girls I'd love to bang in an airplane bathroom, but then realized I was just trying to impress myself with masculinity, not to mention having sex in an airplane bathroom seemed both difficult and a little disgusting (not that I would turn down the opportunity).

I looked toward my father's pocket and noticed his Ambien within sight, taunting me, but I decided against it as he might beat me with the empty bottle if he knew I took some. It appeared the only option I had was to try to sleep or stare at the back of the seat in front of me. Neither sounded all that appealing. I curled my head against the side of the plane and closed my eyes, knowing full well it would take a miracle for me to actually reach slumber.

I couldn't imagine a flight worse than this.

Intermission
July 24, 2006

I removed the gold-plated invitation from its equally shiny envelope and immediately became curious. My father had never really been the social type, but since he won the lottery only a few weeks before, he'd suddenly become what could best be described as gregarious; though perhaps this was the natural personality progression of someone who went from unemployed to millionaire in the blink of an eye. My father had lost his job, as a high school science teacher, only a year before due to an incident that involved a Bunsen burner, hydrochloric acid, and a D+ student that he referred to as a "bullshit misunderstanding." But because of the nature of the indiscretion, locating another job became equally as difficult as paying the bills. But just when it seemed like all hope was lost, he won the Powerball jackpot and could spend his mornings telling the world to go fuck itself rather than contemplating a membership renewal at Monster.com.

The night of the party began with limousines, Dom Perignon, and sheer decadence. My father had rented an entire four-star restaurant, which was set to hold over 200 guests. Growing up, my parents had a few sets of close friends, but like many adults, they lost more over the years than they gained. So, when I entered the restaurant for the party, I wasn't sure how they would fill the place to capacity. But as I looked around at the guests, I saw faces I hadn't since my childhood along with some I'd never seen at all. My mother's old carpool partners from when she used to teach twenty years ago. There was that friend of hers who looked like a horse, but I couldn't remember her name. My father's old golfing partner who was forced to quit playing because he got too fat and couldn't swing the club over his stomach. Derek Jeter (?!). My babysitter from when I was three years old. My grandmother's old friend, Luba, with her portable oxygen tank and coffee hard candy. My mother's friend Marty with the great laugh. My second grade teacher, Mrs. Nelson, who incidentally finally got her braces off and, now, had a nice smile somehow made the guest list. Even the woman who delivered our mail with the obvious blond wig and caked on makeup was in attendance. It was like a spin-off of the show *This Is Your Life*, but instead, it was called *This Is Everyone You've Ever Fucking Met* (and Derek Jeter).

At the front of the restaurant, adjacent to my family's table, stood an easel with a red velvet cloth draped over it. I asked my father what was under the cloth, but he just patted me on the shoulder and said, "You'll see." Then I asked how he got Derek Jeter to show up, to which he responded: "He must be a fan!" followed by the laugh of someone who had just fallen ass backwards into a ton of money. I swore that each one of his sentences was punctuated by this wide-mouthed guffaw, a subsequent shoulder grab, and the words "who cares, I'm rich," since he played those winning numbers.

My father approached every guest and briefly chatted with him or her. I never would have described him as classy, but that night he was the ultimate gentleman. He looked fantastic in his suit; it had to have been custom tailored, and though I hadn't seen him in a couple of months, it appeared he'd been working out. When I inquired about his diet, he waved off the compliment and told me it was the result of drying his face with one hundred dollar bills. I didn't doubt that he tried.

As post-meal coffee and dessert were served, my father strolled confidently to the front of the room and tapped the top of a microphone to get everyone's attention. He demanded that all the cooks and wait staff exit the kitchen to join the crowd. He even had the maître d' pull random people off the street to participate in the celebration. I had a feeling that if my father could have simulcast the event on the Times Square Jumbotron, he would have done it.

"I just wanted to thank everyone for coming out tonight to help celebrate this once-in-a-lifetime experience. Is everyone having a good time?"

The crowd hooted and hollered as they continued to guzzle the champagne that flowed like water.

"It makes it all that much more special that it could be shared with all of you. But I wanted to thank one person in particular. And I think you all know who I mean."

My father turned to my mother who brightly smiled as three hundred sets of eyes rested on her.

"Laura. You are the love of my life. And there is something special that I wanted to personally give you, in front of all our family and friends. Something I wish I could give you in front of the entire world."

The crowd collectively "aww'd." They must have thought he was so sweet.

"So why don't you come on down!" my father said, like he was Rod Roddy and this was *The Price Is Right*.

The crowd applauded. My mother sprung up, curtsied to her fans, and joined my father at the microphone. He gripped his hand against the red velvet cloth that guarded whatever was underneath.

My mother glowed. I never thought of her as particularly pretty. I mean she was not ugly, but she was my mother, and I chose never to judge her looks one way or another. But, in that moment, with her diamond necklace shining and her black dress hugging her body perfectly, she really looked beautiful. Maybe she dried her face with money too.

"Laura, throughout my life, you have been my best friend and my partner in crime. And it really has been a special ride."

My mother smiled so widely I thought it might stick forever.

"You have supported me emotionally, intellectually... *physically,*" he said with a wink and a nod to the crowd. All the men responded in laughter; even Derek Jeter gave his date a knowing elbow and a wink. My father waited till they quieted. In fact, the pause was so long it became awkward.

"But this past year, I have appreciated you most. Because, more than any other time in our relationship, you supported me in a different way...financially."

Huh.

My father pulled the cloth off the easel to reveal a large check that resembled one Tiger Woods might win in a golf tournament. It was made out to my mother for $20 million dollars. The crowd gave a smattering of applause, but as I searched the faces around the room, I saw more confusion than appreciation or understanding. I wasn't sure what to do, but when I noticed Derek Jeter uncomfortably clapping, I joined. After all, the man was a champion and knew a thing or two about accepting $20 million dollar checks.

My father had never been so confident of anything in his entire life, but I'd never seen so much conflict in a human's face as I saw in my mother's. My father's smile contrasted any negative thoughts she might have had, but something was not registering. She fidgeted. The only time I'd seen her nervous like that was while waiting in the emergency room after I'd shoved a Lincoln Log up my nose and couldn't get it out. And before you assume she was a bad mother for leaving her toddler unattended while playing, I was actually fourteen when it happened.

"So, Laura, in front of all our friends and family, I want to present this gift to you."

I could have sworn I heard her ask my father what he was doing through her gritted teeth. But maybe that was just me.

"Take this check, Laura. And, please...get the fuck out of my life. For good. Forever."

The crowd gasped as the champagne glass dropped from my mother's hand and crashed to the floor, breaking into what seemed like fourteen million shiny pieces. But my father's smile never wavered. He grabbed the check from the easel and placed half of it in my mother's hands, while he draped his free arm around her shoulder. He faced the crowd as if his guests were a team of press cameras eager to snap their picture. My father kept saying, "Eh? How ya like that? Eh?"

My mother shook violently, merely a second away from either fainting or outright dying. But instead, she held the check as my father released his half. It looked like she wanted to say something to the crowd, but words couldn't come out. She, like the entire group of people before her, was paralyzed. Even Jeter stood frozen, mouth agape—everyone except my father, who just offered his shit-eating grin.

Reality finally hit my mother and she quickly ran across the hardwood floor toward the exit, fighting back a Niagara Falls-esque cry. Her stiletto heels, pounding against the floor, echoed through the absolute silence. The only thing to break the noise was the subtle sound of six hundred eye-balls simultaneously turning to follow her. She ran out the door.

And I never saw her again.

Not even a murmur followed the incident. The guests, one by one, simply got up and left without a word for my father or anyone else. They couldn't leave fast enough. I sat still in my seat as if I'd just watched someone get murdered in front of me, and then watched the murderer show zero remorse. It's a feeling I couldn't understand.

And four years later, I still couldn't.

PART TWO

Stockholm

It's not often a person can stare at human behavior for five minutes and still not be able to make any sense of it.

Traffic was bumper to bumper at a roundabout in the city centre, which resembled a haphazard parking lot more than a major avenue in a country's capital. A five story phallic sculpture, surrounded by an enormous fountain, sat in the middle of the roundabout and probably gave drivers something boring to concentrate on during their exhaustive wait; perhaps the designers should have programmed the fountain to dance to Lionel Richie as well, or at least Ace of Base if they needed something more patriotic.

Regardless, there was finally a dick that would properly fit Mrs. Chang's hands.

But that wasn't what was strange about this moment.

In the middle of the vehicular chaos sat a long flatbed truck with strobe lights and seven speakers blasting an elongated version of "Wipeout." A rotund, graying man, no less than seventy years old, stood in the middle of the speakers and danced his ass off, nonstop, in the center of traffic. But, again, this wasn't the strange part. From a nearby overpass overlooking the traffic jam, I watched this man dance for five straight minutes without showing any signs of tiring. When I looked closer at the actual truck, I noticed that the back window of the cab was completely open with the steering wheel unmanned. So, not only was this man dancing in the traffic, he was also a *cause* of the jam.

But, still, that wasn't the strange part.

This was:

No one seemed to give a shit. During the entire five-minute show, I did not hear one car honk, and in the throngs of tall, blond people who strolled the sidewalks, I did not see one pedestrian even bother to look in his direction. Not even a word was uttered. It was as if this man stood on this flatbed truck twenty-four hours a day, in that very spot, and danced. The surrounding people just seemed used to it.

A Stockholm weed. And despite the lack of attention, the man kept dancing.

I quickly thought about what would happen if this man pulled a stunt like that in the middle of Los Angeles traffic. My most educated guess involved, at best, an argument with at least twenty angry commuters, at worst a bullet, and most probably a trip to the city jail for disturbing the peace and for being a douche. Either way, someone would have caught it on a phone video camera and, had he only picked a current top-40 song, he'd have been an instant YouTube sensation.

Regardless, I'd never felt farther from home.

The buzz from the phone distracted my attention back to reality. In the past few hours, I'd felt that sensation twenty-five times, wearing on me a little more with each vibration.

Clarissa's latest text:

—I'M SORRY...PLEASE COME HOME ☹—

I hated when she used emoticons.

In the course of these hours, Clarissa partook in a one-sided text conversation that spanned the human condition:

It began with disbelief (Texts 1-5): Versions of "Where Are You?" and "Did you do what I think you did?"

Continued to denial (Texts 6-10): "There's no way you could have done this!" "No Way." "I know you will be home soon."

Then to self-pity (Texts 11-15): "How could you do this to me?" "What did I do to deserve this?" "You know I can't handle this now."

Which evolved to anger (Texts 16-20): "I can't believe you. I hate you, you jerk." "Only an asshole would do something like this, asshole" "You are a fucking coward, you fucking coward."

Then finally to acceptance and rationality (Texts 21-25): "I shouldn't have said those things." "I love you," and of course the latest installment involving her desire to see me come home, punctuated with the small yellow face to accentuate just how sad she was.

I rationalized my lack of response by mentally recalling the steep international roaming charges my phone would incur, but I really just didn't know what to say. I wanted to tell her something, something about needing to do something, but I did not even know what that something was, so I chose to say nothing. I put the phone back in my pocket and wished this whole ordeal had taken place fifteen years ago, before the advent of the cellular telephone, when I'd truly be off the grid. How the fuck did people even communicate then?

My father and I walked toward the restaurant, which apparently was just over a mile away, to meet the Swedish Alec Baldwin. He gripped a bottle of wine he'd brought from his personal collection and continuously repeated that the taste would "knock the lederhosen off this jackass," despite the fact that I insisted only German people wore lederhosen. I didn't even know if that was true, but I felt like being an asshole.

My father was fairly certain we were headed the right way, but kept staring at the directions as if they were written in a code he hadn't quite cracked.

"Damn, if these street names weren't all so damn long, I think we'd have an easier damn time finding it," he said, the first of many times. He did have a point though. Street names like *Drottninggatan, Klarra Norra Kyrkogata,* and *Malmskillnadsgatan* not only drove my dyslexic mind crazy, but also led me to ponder how difficult Swedish hangman would be.

My father's constant fidgeting led me to believe he was actually nervous, but I was too distracted by the view from the sidewalk along the river to care. The area was immaculate, as was most of the city that was a healthy blend of antiquity and modernity. Not a piece of litter anywhere. And good luck finding a homeless person; they didn't seem to exist. No wonder the city smelled so nice.

The river moved swiftly from the cool breeze, driving the round orange buoys alongside the bridges berserk, though the quiet water taxis didn't seem to mind. The architecture across the river, which featured colorful row-like houses that appeared to tell stories, were easily older than anything in America that wasn't dirt, a tree, or Clint Eastwood. I gripped my jacket tighter to fight off the wind and slight drizzle that attempted to trick me into thinking it wasn't summer. For some reason, the weather combined with the ominous twilight sky and haunting buildings across the way reminded me of Halloween nights in the New York suburbs, where I was raised as a child. It was the thin, gray streak in Mother Nature's hair.

As we hit an intersection, my father studied yet another ungodly long street name that might have made Rumpelstiltskin jealous, while I listened to the ticking of the crosswalk signal intensify when it was our turn to go. But we remained still as my father crinkled his nose and glanced back toward the directions.

"Damn, if these street names weren't all so damn long, I think we'd have an easier damn time finding it."

Since we landed, my father hadn't actually said much to me. During the train ride from the airport to the city, he only insinuated that he seemed surprised the land was so flat and joked that he hadn't seen girls in pigtails mixing hot chocolate in the fields. I informed him that the Swiss Miss was probably from Switzerland and not Sweden, to which he shrugged and said "whatever." He spent the rest of the ride checking his watch, while I stared out the window looking for an Ikea as if we were in the North Pole and it was Santa's workshop.

When not looking at the directions, my father's eyes were fixated on the ground while he walked. And though he was probably in thought, this was the practiced look of someone used to walking alone. And it kind of made me feel for him, as he grabbed an orange from his pocket that he bought at one of the million 7-11's that graced the Stockholm streets. Personally, even though I did not have much to say to him, the quiet, along with his visible anxiety, was only leading me to feelings of guilt. I felt like I should break the silence.

"So, ummm...how many Swedish women have you slept with? More than the Chinese ones?" I asked.

My father laughed slightly.

"I've never been to Sweden before."

"Oh."

"But they do seem pretty cute," he said with a soft, innocent smile. Perhaps it was his tone, the tender way he re-adjusted his glasses, or maybe the protruding nose hair that made the comment seem innocuous, but it did not cause me to vomit like our conversations about women usually did. There really was something different about him tonight.

"Are we close? What's the address?"

"There is no address. Apparently it's the only door in a long corridor in the Old Town area thingee thing."

"How the hell are we supposed to find that?"

He looked down at the directions again.

"Well, damn, if these street names weren't all so damn long, I think we'd have an easier damn time finding it."

We crossed a walking bridge to the section of Stockholm known as Gamla Stan (Old Town Thingee Thing), which was its own small island in the Stockholm archipelago that probably earned its name because it was, well, old. A medieval looking church towered near the bridge, as the streets thinned to corridors, some of which were only a couple of meters wide. Loads of pedestrians jammed the cobblestone streets with footsteps and noise. To my naked and untrained tourist eye, it actually kind of resembled that town with all the magic stores near Hogwarts in all the Harry Potter movies.

My father checked the directions, yet again, as we navigated the small streets past various antique stores that appeared to have gray beards and newer souvenir shops that boasted strange claims like "probably the best souvenir shop in Old Town Stockholm." Outdoor cafes littered the area, and a mixture of foreign language, which I assumed to be Swedish, could be heard emanating from them. I had always figured it was harsh, like German, but the natives spoke sentences that always ended with an upward lilt, as if they were constantly asking questions. It was actually rather pleasant to overhear, clean really, a welcome change from the Mandarin vomited by Clarissa and her parents the night prior, which sounded more like a live cat screaming while getting blended on high.

As we walked through a thin corridor bordered by a small, empty park, my father stopped outside a low, open window that provided a view into someone's empty apartment. A flowerbed rested on the windowsill.

"You know what's funny? This actually reminds me of my honeymoon with your mother. We were in Vienna and they had corridors like this, lots of European cities do. But all of the windows had little flowerbeds right outside them just like this one. And I picked her a bunch, even though she'd yell at me like I was stealing them." He smiled at the memory as he picked a pink flower and handed it to me. "Man, I knew I loved that woman in the first twenty-four hours I knew her," he said, as if he was only talking to himself.

I looked at the flower and rolled my eyes as if to suggest, "What the fuck am I supposed to do with this now?" Not to mention, the act of my father handing me a pink flower was flat weird and incestuously gay. So I just tossed it back through the open window and hoped the homeowner wouldn't perceive their dead flower as some sort of horsehead-like threat.

"What'cha do that for!" he asked. "I was re-living a nice moment there."

This entire exchange touched a nerve and, suddenly, all the differences I'd just seen in my father began to annoy me. Naturally, suspicion replaced sympathy.

"Are you fucking dying or something? Is that what this is all about?" I asked in my best accusatory voice.

My father slapped me upside the head.

"What the fuck is wrong with you? Why would you say that?"

"Well, why are you suddenly getting so nostalgic?" I said, rubbing the back of my head. "And saying all this bullshit!"

My father continued walking. I sped up to walk alongside him.

"What? So now you suddenly have regret?" I asked, with a hint of anger.

My father broke my gaze.

"I don't regret anything I've done," he said sincerely.

Sadly, I actually believed him.

My father stopped again to look at the directions as if to signify our conversation was now over and the search for the restaurant would continue. He scanned for the street signs that were attached to building walls and double-checked them against his list.

""Damn, if these street names weren't all so damn long, I think we'd have an easier damn time finding it," my father said with a little more urgency.

"You still never told me why you told this guy I worked for NASA."

"For your sake, I hope you can fake it; otherwise, you'll sound like an idiot," he said clearly.

"I've seen *Apollo 13*."

"Brandon, this is serious. What if he asks something you don't know?"

"Then I'll tell him it's classified. Why won't you answer my question?"

He responded by checking the directions again while he continued in silence.

"Well?" I demanded.

He hesitated and searched for an answer, too preoccupied with his surroundings and probably his lie.

"I guess we got to speaking about our kids. It sounded impressive to tell him that."

"It makes no sense. And I still don't even know why we're here."

"Because I lost a bet."

"And since when are you a man of your word? I figured you'd just tell the guy to fuck off and that would be that."

"Then why did you agree to come?" he responded.

I didn't have an answer for him. I shook my head and continued walking. My father seemed satisfied that he finally shut me up. He knew why I'd come, even if I fully didn't.

"I think it's just around the bend over there."

"So what do his kids do?"

"Whose kids?"

"The guy we're seeing tonight."

"I don't think he had any."

Unreal.

We reached the bend and hung a left into a thin, dimly-lit cobblestone corridor bordered by long, yellow and red buildings; a doorway with a small sign hung from chains and created a shadow in the distance. Though the streets of Old Town were buzzing with pedestrian noise, the further my father and I walked down the long corridor, the quieter it became, to the point where it felt we had actually traveled somewhere remote.

My father stopped in front of a door where the symbol of a hammer hung from an iron sign. The door looked rundown, as did the borders of it. The chipped paint betrayed the aesthetic, or perhaps gave it character; I couldn't decide which. He crinkled his large nose, did a quick visual search of the surrounding area, and shrugged his shoulders.

"Well, I guess we found it," he said.

"Even with the damn street names being so damn long!" I responded.

He didn't pick up on my joke.

I felt the phone buzz in my pocket again. This time, I chose to ignore it completely.

Dinner

"What the fuck is half this shit?" my father not so quietly exclaimed, while he surveyed the menu. "How'm I spos'd to order when I don't know what half the shit is?" he continued, as he peeled a fresh orange in protest.

"You know too much vitamin C can make you sick," I said.

"Really?"

Again, I just felt like being an asshole.

"I dunno," I shrugged and looked at the menu with indifference. I realized I didn't have the energy.

I genuinely couldn't answer his menu concerns since the entire thing was in Swedish, save for some French wine names and Pepsi Max. We had been seated at a corner table on the second story of the restaurant that provided a sensation one might have after stepping out of a time machine. Dimly lit, the large wooden chairs that resembled thrones sat tall on the stone floor. Frilly curtains that matched the immaculate white tablecloths shaped the arched windows and contributed to the restaurant's old-world feel. There were even silver goblets that sat in the center of the table, which I assumed were for decoration, considering elaborately designed wine glasses completed the place setting. At least the sterling silver forks and knives eased my concerns that we'd be dining Medieval Times style. Large paintings that I imagined to be from the Viking period hung from the walls, even though the rudimentary art, which honestly resembled work I'd seen in elementary school art class, contrasted the opulent motif of the restaurant.

My father's golfing partner still hadn't arrived, but we were informed by the maître d' that he would be along shortly. I pawed at my pocket while I resisted checking my phone. Despite the current surroundings, all I could think about was what I'd have to go back to. And if this whole thing was a mistake, which I was actually sure it was. I suddenly had a mental image of Clarissa crying to her parents about my trip and then remembered the time she took me to her uncle's barbecue in the Valley, where I witnessed Mr. Chang sneak up on a random hawk and slam it upside the head with a tiki torch because he was afraid it would steal food. Seriously, hardcore. I shuddered at the thought of my head meeting the same fate and desperately tried to think of what I could text Clarissa so she (and her parents) wouldn't be too angry upon my return.

"How're the pits?" my father asked, while lifting his arms like a child waiting for his mother to help him remove his shirt.

"Fine," I said through a sigh. I couldn't believe I actually checked.

"Good, I was feelin' a little misty under there during our walk."

I looked away as he not so subtly sniffed the not so damp area. I wondered how much paternity tests cost.

"What's on your mind?" my father asked. "You've been biting your lip all night."

"Nothing."

"Nothing, my ass."

"I'm just hungry."

"So you've resorted to self-cannibalism?"

"Yes."

"Well, hopefully this place has some shit you can eat."

"It's a restaurant."

My father looked at the menu again and squinted, as if the action would magically turn the Swedish to English.

"So they say," he said.

He put down the menu.

"Where is this guy anyway? You sure he's showing?" I asked.

"He better. We came all this way."

"Can you please explain this to me now?" I figured I'd try asking one last time.

"Explain what?"

"Why we are in Sweden eating dinner with a complete stranger?"

"Are you a fucking broken record? How many times do I have to fucking tell you? I lost a fucking bet."

"I'm asking because I don't believe you."

My phone buzzed again. I ignored it, but this time with a groan. I really wanted to smash it against my father's face, but then figured he would point out, with pride, that the streams of blood from his ever-growing forehead matched his beautiful shirt. I hadn't lied to my father; I was really hungry and would have killed half the Swedes in this place for a breadbasket. My father cleared his throat and played nervously with the orange peels.

"So...you read up on being an astronaut, huh?" he said, while staring at the broken peels.

I noticed my father's face and tone were completely serious. Normally, he loved embarrassing me, and this was the type of moment he'd claim would make a fantastic story. And because of his eccentric humor, I actually could see why dragging me to a foreign country just to watch me bumble through a speech about jet propulsion, while some clueless foreign man listened, would be humorous to him. In fact, I could easily picture my father skipping the Ambien to laugh about it during the entire fifteen-hour plane ride home. Except, this time, there was no sly smile. There was no short laugh. He was serious. Apparently, I really needed to know something about being an astronaut.

I grabbed the napkin and threw it on my empty plate. "I knew it," I said, as I gritted my teeth.

"Whaaaat?" my father said, like he'd just been caught with his hand in the cookie jar. Which was probably a familiar place for him. "I just asked a simple question."

"Will you just cut the shit and tell me what this is all about?"

"It's nothing!"

"Bullshit. Tell me or I'm gonna leave right now."

"Oh stop being a little shitheel, ya shitheel."

I called his bluff and rose from my seat. I quickly put on my jacket and paused to give him one last opportunity to explain. When he didn't take it, I turned to leave.

My father sighed. "I just need you to play along for something. It's important."

Any pity or understanding I had felt in the past two hours went straight to my fists in rage. All I wanted to do was grab him by the neck and repeatedly slam his face into his plate while I punctuated each thud by calling him an asshole. But instead I just walked toward the stairs.

The moment I stepped outside to the pin-drop-quiet corridor, I ripped the phone from my pocket and immediately called the airline. I didn't care how much the call would cost. I just needed to get out of there as soon as possible.

The call went through.

"Welcome to Delta. Are you a sky miles member?" the friendly automated female voice said. She sounded as if she was in a good mood.

"Representative," I said calmly.

"Alright, from here you can say…"

"Representative," I said, a little less calmly.

"OK. Which would you like to do, shop for a flight…"

My patience was wearing thin.

"Representative!" I said, definitely not calmly.

"To get you to the right represent—"

"FOR THE LOVE OF PETE JUST GET ME TO A FUCKING REPRESENTATIVE!" I yelled.

I sure showed them. But then, of course, my cell phone exhibited its usual modus operandi during an important call: it dropped. Perhaps it didn't appreciate my yelling, perhaps it was sensitive, or maybe it was just a piece of shit, but, regardless, it was the last thing I needed. Well, maybe second to last:

A smug clearing of the throat from a random stranger was the last. A clear, unquestionable sound in my direction that suggested I shut the fuck up and have the decency to realize my vocalized drama might be annoying to others in the vicinity.

You know that charming human reaction where you instantly fabricate an entire personality for a complete stranger based on one usually harmless action? Like how you'll quickly categorize someone who cut you off on the highway in the same group as you might place Hitler? And if he or she actually provoked you just once more, you might rip his or her head off without even a brief thought of the consequences? That was the thought running through my head as my body turned to face whoever it was that had made that horrible sound, that sound that offended me so. It didn't matter that he or she might have had a point or that I was dead wrong; it was just not the time.

"WHAT!" I said, as I faced a lit cigarette being smoked by the vague outline of a female standing in the shadows of the street. Without seeing her face, I immediately assumed this was some old hag, the Swedish version of Clarissa's mother sent by some evil manifestation that got a kick out of making me cry. I half expected this woman to emerge from the shadows with clown shoes big enough to cover abnormally large feet after I'd mutter "cunt" or "bitch" or some other English word she might not have understood.

"Du forstor detta for mig," she responded. That voice did not sound old. In fact, it was rather direct and calming, sexy maybe.

Within seconds, my eyes adjusted and she slowly came into focus. White blond hair that was too light. Crystal, piercing-blue eyes that were too blue. High, pronounced cheekbones that were too pronounced. A small freckle below her right eye on skin that was silky smooth—too smooth. At first glance, her striking looks were almost off-putting, but as my eyes adjusted like a camera's autofocus, I quickly realized this was the most beautiful girl I'd ever seen. Normally, this type of image would shake my brain until it became dumbly blank, kind of like clearing an etch-a-sketch, but this wasn't a normal situation. And my mind was ambivalent between feelings of anger and feeling disarmed. I just wanted to rage, to kick and scream, and suddenly I couldn't.

"Do I look like someone who can understand what you're saying?" I asked with a dash of frustration, but a heap of exasperation.

"Vänligen...håll...käften," she said slowly, as if that would help. Like I was mentally retarded and her speaking

slower might help me understand. She didn't smile; she wouldn't provide much reaction at all, but I knew she wasn't simply giving me a hard time; she really wanted the quiet.

"I hate this fucking country," I said softly while shaking my head, my personal sign of unwanted surrender. Kind of like the last word in an argument I wasn't winning. The "I know you are, but what am I" to this girl in front of me, to Sweden, to my father, to just...everything.

But she still stared at me. Then she took a long drag off her cigarette and carefully blew the smoke into the night sky, as if to consider something I hadn't a clue about. I quickly averted my eyes in the strange silence, but when they returned, hers were still transfixed on me. She was still lost in some kind of thought, which made me serve myself a mental cocktail of self-consciousness and worry. But though the look was intense, it wasn't frightening; it was more like a jigsaw puzzle without a finished picture to guide me.

"Is something wrong?" I asked. I didn't know what else to say, I just wanted to break the awkward silence. She didn't respond; of course, she probably had no clue what I was saying and just took another long drag off her cigarette. I normally found a girl smoking to be wholly unattractive, but as I watched her, I quickly recalled a study that suggested a person found another more desirable in the moment they puffed a cigarette. I'm not sure how they could establish such a conclusion, but in that moment, I agreed whole-heartedly with the study. Perhaps it was because I was in Europe, when in Rome and all. Regardless, there we were, standing there, watching each other, but saying nothing. So, I figured, in all my infinite wisdom, I'd provide her some health advice:

"You know, that stuff will kill you."

I always said the most retarded shit to women; it's a miracle I'd ever been laid at all.

As if she understood me, she pulled the cigarette from her mouth and flicked it harmlessly in my direction.

"Tack," she deadpanned.

I watched her walk inside and I stood still for a good thirty seconds, as I processed all that had just happened. After all, it was a seemingly harmless conversation between two people who didn't speak the same language, but it felt like something was communicated. It's always easier to review life in hindsight and I quickly tried to formulate why I suddenly felt numb. Just moments ago, my father had confirmed every dirty thing I believed him to be. I stepped outside to implore Delta to place me on the first flight back to LA, so I could get reamed by my fiancée, but now I stood on the dark street, staring at the phone as if I had just been transported from the eighteenth century and was handed a completely foreign piece of technology.

And as my consciousness finally gathered itself, I felt strangely at ease, yet nervous at the same time.

I didn't know what else to do but walk back inside. I nonchalantly searched but could not find the girl who had been there only a moment ago. As I ascended the stairs and re-approached my father's table, I noticed the "Hitler-loving cocksucker" had arrived and that my father had been right: He did look like a blond Alec Baldwin ... if Alec Baldwin was forty pounds heavier, eight inches taller, had a pronounced cleft chin, a sharp scar above his right eye, and looked completely different. I shouldn't have been surprised; my father also thought my seventh-grade math teacher looked like Patrick Stewart. Except my seventh-grade math teacher was female and had a full head of hair. And was black. Don't get me wrong, Mrs. Kupsher wasn't going to win any beauty pageants, but she looked nothing like Patrick Stewart. Maybe Patrick Ewing.

Faux-Blond Baldwin's Swedish accent boomed throughout the room while his laugh suggested strength and power. I slowly approached my seat until the two men noticed my presence.

"There he is!" my father stated happily, probably relieved that I actually came back.

I quickly searched the area for the girl, but it was as if she had never entered the small restaurant at all. Perhaps it was all a hallucination; I did feel like I was approaching the brink of insanity anyway.

"Well, sit down! Join us," Swede Baldwin stated. "It is a pleasure to meet you. I am Gustav. You must feel lucky that your father is a shitty golfer, eh?" He extended his bear-like claw that enveloped my hand, though he shook with a gentleman's touch and a comforting chuckle that betrayed his large stature.

"We both know you'd be havin' steaks in the States now if that little chapass didn't cough durin' my backswing," my father said, as he patted Swede Goliath on the back.

"Nice to meet you, Sir. This restaurant looks quite unique."

"It will be the best Swedish meal of your entire life."

That wouldn't be hard; it would also be the first.

"This restaurant is as old as Stockholm, and the inside has remained unchanged since the seventeenth century," he continued.

"Well, I hope the food has changed a little since the seventeenth century. I once saw a special on the Vikings on the History Channel. I hope we don't have to eat boiled horse."

I regretted that as soon as I said it, but Gustav's laugh boomed. He turned to my father.

"He is funny, your son," he said, while squeezing my father on the shoulder, as if he had done a good job raising me. I wasn't, but that was nice of him to say.

The conversation was interrupted by the sound of a chair scratching against the stone floor. I turned my head left to notice that someone was joining us.

Her.

Without expression, she sat down and tussled her hair while straightening her dress. She gave me a glance that provided no insight into her thoughts or even that she recognized me as the one who had insulted her smoking habit. My heart immediately started pounding, which actually surprised me, considering I recently wondered if it beat at all. I touched it, as if feeling I could somehow slow it. At first, no one acknowledged her and I felt like I was imagining the entire thing, and then I suddenly sat up straight, as if on guard from being completely exposed. Then, just as I thought she might have joined the wrong table, Big Gustav smiled at her presence.

"Ah, there she is. I thought she ran away. This is my daughter, Saga. Saga, this is Brandon and Richard."

She nodded at both of us, but not a word was uttered. I glanced at my father who raised his eyebrows in approval. I knew that eyebrow raise; I just responded with my extended middle finger. I stole a quick glance at Saga who was neatly folding a napkin on her lap.

My father took out the bottle of wine he'd brought to compare with Gustav's and, while they were distracted with each other, I turned to the silent Saga and searched my mind for something to say.

"So, you understand English, huh," I said. Always great at icebreakers. "I'm sorry...for all that," I continued, as I waved my hand dismissively toward the street.

She said nothing back, didn't even acknowledge my statement. Normally, if I'm ignored or asked someone a question they did not hear, I crawled into my turtle shell and pretended the whole thing never happened. But, again, nothing about this was normal, so I vacantly stared at her much like a small child watching television. I was probably being creepy, but if she noticed, she didn't let on. I wasn't done.

"Saga is a very interesting name. Especially consider-ing what it means in English," I said softly, careful not to disturb my father's conversation.

"What does it mean in English?" she responded.

"Like...a story."

"Ah, it means the same in Swedish."

"Oh really? I guess you must have stolen it from us," I said with a stupid laugh to punctuate the even stupider joke.

"It's actually a Nordic word. You stole it from us."

"Oh."

"I guess the History Channel didn't teach you everything."

That one sent a sharp pain to the tip of my dick. I probably should have hid in the aforementioned, metaphorical turtle shell in the first place.

But then she did something curious, and it occurred in no less than two seconds. It was a sharp glare, a look that expressed a deep, troubling thought. But it was not directed at me; it was for Gustav. It was a look that would have instantly turned him blue had he been one of my father's Coors Light bottles. I couldn't for the life of me place the sense of urgency and despair in that brief look. I had no clue if it was my stupid conversation that was the offense, but I could only imagine it cut much deeper. But in those two seconds, I instantly viewed her differently, and barely noticed her escape toward the bathroom because I was concentrating on Gustav who didn't acknowledge his daughter's emotion at all. He was too engrossed in a bullshit conversation with my father about wine.

"Trust me, this wine goes perfect with the meal we are about to have," Gustav said convincingly.

"Well, trust me when I tell you that *this* wine could make dog shit taste good. I guarantee after one sip, you'll be beggin' me to let you drink my piss later!"

Words cannot describe.

I wasn't sure how much time had passed, but it felt like hours, even though it had to have only been minutes because the appetizers had only just arrived. It was as if Saga's empty chair slowed time. Gustav was explaining the courses he had ordered, and though I heard words like "lutefisk" and "herring," I really wasn't paying much attention, though I'm sure my nodding led him to believe I was truly interested. I had perfected this practiced look of fake interest over the course of my relationship with Clarissa, which is why I had to quickly re-gather my thoughts when Gustav clasped his hands and leaned toward me: apparently a universal gesture signifying when one is ready to get down to business.

"So, Brandon, your father tells me you work for NASA. That is a very important job," Gustav said.

My eyes averted from his and toward my father, who nodded to me like Mr. Miyagi did to Daniel-san before the Crane Kick in the original Karate Kid.

"Yes, well, it can be," I said confidently.

Prior to the dinner, I had a fantasy of completely blowing up my father's scene in this moment. I would call him a liar and tell Gustav I was a clown in the circus that got off on scaring young children. I even considered juggling the dinner rolls. It would have been beautiful, poetic justice of sorts, but now it was the furthest thing from my mind.

"In which department do you work?"

Meeting his intense gaze, I gave his words thought, though his question never quite registered.

"Would you excuse me for a moment?" I asked.

I didn't wait for an answer or reaction, but sprung from my seat and headed toward the back of the restaurant, where I planned to duck into the men's room and maybe sit on the toilet for a while to gather my thoughts. I didn't even have to go, I just really wasn't in the mood to bullshit my way through a conversation that required more knowledge than I had acquired from repeat viewings of *Contact*.

But when I entered the small foyer-type area that housed the men and women's restrooms, I was greeted with a line of frustrated women, each one complaining louder to the next about something in Swedish. In fact, as my eyes scanned the line, the level of complaint seemed to rise the closer they were to the door. And just as the woman in the front banged on that door of the restroom for, what I could only guess was the millionth time, I heard a familiar voice bark back in Swedish. Saga's voice. And I'd spent enough time on this Earth to know what someone sounded like when they were speaking through tears.

I'm not sure what the plot was, but I could feel it thicken. And for some reason, I needed to know what was happening.

Suddenly, the men's room no longer appeared as a desirable destination, though I admittedly had no clue what I was doing. When in another country, there's some strange feeling of invincibility; like if you engage in a cultural faux pas, you could chalk it up to a misunderstanding and laugh it off like it was cute. So I had no qualms tapping the woman in front of the line on the shoulder.

"Excuse me, ma'am, how long have you been waiting?"

Her confused look suggested she didn't understand my English or was horrified that a male was asking a question regarding the wait time of the ladies' room. And, honestly, I didn't care about the answer and had no intentions of waiting for one.

I may not have worked for NASA, but I was now on a mission.

"Do you mind?" I asked, while I pushed passed her confidently, as if men cutting the line for the women's restroom and barging on in was as American as apple pie. I quickly slid my body through the small crack I created and closed the door immediately, like I was trying not to let a dog out.

To say Saga was surprised to see me in the bathroom was an understatement. To watch her expression change from mild shock to realization to anger was a bit scarier than I thought.

"I just wanted to see if you were OK," I said genuinely, hoping to quickly calm her.

I knew I was looking at her, I thought my mind was registering reality, but somehow I never saw her grab the nearby toilet brush and definitely never noticed her club me in the face with it until the dirty bristles stung my skin and actually knocked me off balance. I did, however, feel the numerous subsequent swings hit my back, arms, and shoulders.

WHACK WHACK WHACK!

She screamed loudly through her swings, though I was too distracted to understand what she was saying. It really didn't matter.

I quickly regrouped and, perhaps using the skills I had learned from those karate lessons I took when I was eleven, managed to grab her wrist mid-swing, holding it still, and suddenly displayed untaught ninja instincts to grab her other wrist, which was hurtling in my direction in the form of a smack. Her trembling, tear-streaked face was only inches from mine. She clenched her teeth in frustration, though the violent streak subsided as I felt her resistance softly wane. I half expected her to bite my face off, but she just quickly wrestled her wrists away and turned as if to no longer be exposed.

"Get out," she said calmly, yet sternly.

Feeling safe for a moment, I touched my face, not even wondering what nasty shit (literally) that toilet brush may have recently touched. Though she told me to get out, I actually felt like I finally had my in.

"I just wanted to see if you were alright," I said calmly. "That's all."

Saga still had her back toward me. By the movement of her shoulders, I could tell she was still breathing heavily. I wished I could see her expression.

"I'm fine," she said matter of factly, still doing a good job of keeping up her guard.

"Are you sure? Because I—"

"Why do you care!" she screamed.

Her words stung. They actually caused me to step back, as if their power formed a threatening fist. It wasn't a question as much as it was a warning. Regardless, I wished I had an interesting response to the exclamation. I didn't know why I agreed to accompany my father on this trip, I didn't know why I got up from the table, I didn't know why I barged into the ladies' room, and I didn't know why I cared.

"I just do."

"Please leave," she said, while placing her hands on the side of the sink, much like I did the night of Clarissa's promotion party in the dingy Mexican restaurant bathroom. The quick moment of silence was broken by the impatient ladies in line, slamming the door as if they were only moments from storming in and kicking both our asses out. I ignored them the best I could.

I tried my hardest to look to Saga with sympathy, but she never bothered to meet my gaze.

"Why are you crying?" I finally asked.

"Why were you yelling outside," she quickly responded.

It was kind of a checkmate. No, more like a stalemate. But I also knew her rhetorical question was not a simple one. She asked because she knew I couldn't answer it while standing with her in a ladies' restroom on the verge of being taken over by a bunch of angry women with near-exploding bladders. She knew I had a problem. I knew she had one. We clearly didn't know what the other's was, but there was commonality.

I held my hands out as if to signify I meant no harm by my next statement.

"I don't think either of us want to be here right now; let's just get out of here. We don't have to talk about any of this," I said with purpose. That's right, real directed purpose. I entered a zone, which was bad news for the lady who decided to bang on the door one more time. I slammed my fist back as hard as I could and yelled, "Shut the fuck up!" equally as loudly. At least it produced a moment of peace.

Saga bit her lower lip.

"I can't."

"What...them?" I asked while motioning to the dining room. To our fathers. To whatever the purpose for both of us being there was. "Fuck them."

I never took my eyes off her. It might have been the most sincere thing I'd ever said. And, finally, she relented.

"C'mon."

Saga and I slowly walked back in the direction of the commotion in Old Town. Much of the bustle from earlier had dissipated, but, as we approached the end of the corridor, ambient noise from the outdoor pub areas outshined our deafening silence. I snuck a quick glance as she puffed a drag from her newly lit cigarette. Saga appeared as if she had been trained to walk. Her head high. Posture perfect. I noticed a slight bump on the bridge of her nose and wondered if that was genetic or the result of injury. But even that was beautiful.

We didn't tell either of our fathers we were leaving, and I'm not sure they would have cared. As we snuck out, I half expected to hear either my father or Gustav rhetorically ask where the two of us were, but the only thing I heard bellowed from my father was "you guys make a hell of an orange here in Sweden," as we escaped down the stairs and out the door. I didn't know where we would go or what we were doing, but my body felt as if it was driving in cruise control anyway. I just hoped it wouldn't lead me directly off a cliff.

We continued to walk without saying a word and entered an open area in the middle of a town square. Cafés and a closed museum lined the boundaries of the square, while artists and locals playing string instruments sat in random chairs sprinkled around the uneven cobblestone. If not for graffiti that said TITS on the side of a small concrete slab, it would have looked like a festive oil painting. Then again, I figured if there was anything in the world worthy of written celebration, why not tits?

It began to feel like a game of chicken over who would talk first, though I thought I was probably the only one playing and figured she would have been satisfied saying nothing at all. The girl seemed icy cold and I figured she'd be hard to handle, kind of like an Otter Pop on a cool summer night. I knew I needed to break the silence or this would go on forever.

"It really is a beautiful area, a beautiful city," I said, while listening to the string instruments and watching the faces of the musicians lit by candlelight.

"I haven't heard someone refer to Stockholm as that in a long time," Saga said.

I really did appreciate everything I saw, though I wasn't sure how much I meant it. But after years where my eyes consistently stared at pollution, ugly buildings, transvestite bums' ass cracks, and the sad excuse for a Los Angeles skyline, this was a deep breath of fresh air.

"In the seventeenth century, this entire area would be dark at night except for people who would wander around with torches. And the streets were never named, making it nearly impossible for anyone not from the area to navigate," Saga said, while keeping her eyes forward. I thought this to be an odd fact to tell considering the many associated with the area, but I was just glad to hear words and was pleased that it was anything other than "go fuck yourself."

That fact inspired only one possible comment: "You have really pretty eyes."

A natural response to an anecdote about Swedish history, right? When someone tells you about what citizens of Stockholm did a few hundred years ago, the only possible retort is a comment about a pretty facial feature.

Saga's shoulders slumped and she shook her head a bit. Apparently she didn't share my theory.

"I don't have time for bullshit."

"Excuse me?"

"This was a mistake, I should go back."

"What? Wait, hold on," I barked back in defense. "Ten minutes ago you were crying in a public restroom and now this is a mistake?"

Saga didn't know how to answer and just looked away, as if that would cause me to quit. Many times in my life that may have worked, but it wouldn't tonight. All the frustration and whatever else I'd been feeling over the course of the last few days, in that moment, escaped my mouth in one pointed thought. "Jesus fucking Christ, this is all just so...you know what's crazy? When I was like fifteen years old, I always thought I'd come to a place like Sweden, sit in some kind of rowboat in some lake and find the meaning of life. But you know what, I don't even know what the fuck I'm doing here."

It was all so dramatic, so petty. But it was true. And as if the now-released words had been holding me upright, I slumped against the nearest wall and slid until my ass hit the street. I ran my hands over my face, no longer caring about keeping the appearance of confidence. I really didn't know what the fuck to feel anyway.

Though I expected her to already be halfway down the street, back in the direction of the restaurant, I could hear her footsteps cautiously approach me.

"Why are you so desperate to go home?" she asked.

"Actually, I'm not. At all," I said, while looking up at her. Straight in the eye, 100 percent truth. There was zero chance she could take that as insincere.

"So if you don't want to be there, and you don't want to be here, why not go somewhere else?"

Her question was a good one, and I gave it careful consideration as we continued to walk out of the square and down another quiet corridor, lit by a few free-standing street lamps that muted the color of the building walls while slightly illuminating antique items in closed shop windows. Through the indistinct light, I could see the outskirts of Old Town and the lights of some spacious, palace-like buildings across yet another waterway. A refreshing breeze blew down the corridor that caused Saga's hair to flutter like a lazy flag.

Though we were in the middle of a major international city, we were alone.

"I wish it were that simple," I said.

"Why isn't it?"

"Where could I even go?" I asked, as if she could actually provide an answer to my unanswerable question.

"At the end of this corridor there's a subway that goes directly to Arlanda airport. You could go anywhere."

I could see the faint light of the station entrance at the end of the corridor. I swore I could hear my breathing echo.

"Oh yeah, anywhere?"

"Sure. China, Brazil, Australia. Anywhere. What's stopping us?"

There was one word in that statement that gave me pause.

"Us?"

Saga shrugged. I searched her expression, but it hid no hyperbole.

"Are you being serious?" I added.

She did not answer, but it was obvious she was. I didn't know what to do. It seemed like one of those half-baked ideas I would one day claim I wish I put into action while sipping coffee with a friend, years later, during a conversation about how life sucks and the only antidote is chance. It would have been an adventure. The ultimate adventure. But in the actual moment, it seemed completely absurd, probably because it was.

"We can't just pick up and go to China," I said in a tone that suggested she was crazy.

"Is there a warrant for your arrest there?"

I didn't quite understand any of this. I breathed out a short half-laugh and half-sigh, while looking at her suspiciously out of the corner of my eye.

"Just like half an hour ago you wouldn't talk to me in English, then you assaulted me with a toilet brush and now…" I drifted off, unable to complete the thought. "Why?"

Saga provided no answer; she only looked away.

"What happened back there?" I asked, indicating the direction of the restaurant, truly wanting to hear her entire story.

Saga looked down the corridor for what seemed like a moment too long. I didn't know what she was looking at exactly, I didn't know what she was thinking, but I could imagine she was as lost as I was. She turned back toward me as if she took that moment to think of a question, "If I gave you the opportunity to meet that fifteen-year-old version of yourself, the one that wanted to sit in the rowboat, for one minute, and one minute only, what would you say to him?" Saga asked.

I wasn't sure what she was getting at, but I looked down at the cobblestone and gave the question some serious thought. I thought about my current life in Los Angeles. I thought of my job. My friends. And for the first time in a while, I thought of Clarissa. I couldn't remember the last time so much time had passed (sleeping aside) when she did not cross my mind once. I suddenly stiffened.

"To change everything," I said quickly, in an honest tone that even surprised myself.

The answer caused Saga to sigh softly, just through her nose.

"It's not worth it, you know," she said dismissively.

I didn't know what she meant.

"You can go back to yelling at your phone now."

The next moment felt like a thousand as Saga smiled softly and turned away. I waited for her to say something else, anything, but she just walked toward the subway entrance and disappeared down the steps. It all happened so quickly, I wasn't sure what had caused her to leave, what it was that I had said that seemed to offend her. If I could relive the moment, I'd have said anything else, even if there weren't a right answer. Was she really going to go to the airport? Was she going to go to China? What had just happened?

I briskly approached the subway entrance until it was only a few yards ahead of me and stared at it like it was some portal to another universe. I knew the wind was blowing hard against my face, but I honestly couldn't feel it. I considered chasing her, but I wasn't sure what that would accomplish or what I truly wanted. And then, in some ways, I actually felt relieved. After all, all this was unnecessary and probably wrong. Definitely wrong. I needed to text my fiancée.

But instead, I stood frozen like a statue and suddenly realized I had no clue where I was. To my left was the corridor leading back to the center of Old Town. To my right was a large dark building without even one illuminated lamp to give it life. To my front was a steep downward slope leading to the river, and to my rear was pitch-black silence and the rest of Stockholm.

Oh Shit

Though the world is an overcrowded and hectic place, there is always one area where a man can find his solitude: the can. One can easily assume the pose of Rodin's "Thinker" and ponder the complexities of life while trying to make sense of its twists, turns, and the not-so-subtle wrenches that cause you to overanalyze and compartmentalize the muddlement that is living. God bless the can.

And boy, did I have a lot to think about. And thanks to the time change, the tiny bite of appetizer, and general stress, my body sure kept me there long enough to not only figure out my own issues, but also probably world peace. I wasn't sure if Montezuma had a cousin in Leif Erickson, but their curse seemed mighty similar. Mighty being the key word in that sentence. Unfortunately, I was never all that bright, so, instead of solving world hunger, I just became more confused as the night moved forward.

The bathroom of the hotel room was sleek and modern, yet really small. I'd never felt so lucky to be relatively thin, as someone carrying a spare tire might have had problems maneuvering in such a tiny space. The shower had a window that provided a fantastic view of the river and a city island beyond it and, even though I was in a major metropolis, the buildings below felt distant and quiet. Isolated. It was a good feeling and provided a sense of safety and security (even if false) that gave me solace.

After I had read every possible piece of literature I could, and by literature I mean all the shampoo, conditioner, and lotion bottles, I still had no clue how to face reality. From the minute I re-entered the hotel room, I could only think of one thing: Why hadn't I chased her down? I pictured her looking out the small circular window, forlorn, and ignoring the flight attendant offering her peanuts while 30,000 feet in the air on the way to Timbuktu or India or wherever she decided to go. I wondered what it would have been like to be sitting next to her. What I would see. What I would learn. I wasn't sure if the pains in my stomach were due to intestinal issues or if it was my gut screaming for me to trust it. I knew there was some kind of common ground, but fuck if I knew what it was. I was always shitty at taking chances.

But similar to my earlier thoughts, I knew no good could come from the daydreaming and fantasizing. I was to be married in just a few short weeks and figured I just wanted something I couldn't have. Perhaps it was the result of being an only child, another thing to blame on my father.

I knew the sooner I sent tonight out on an ice floe, the better.

As I pulled out my phone to review Clarissa's messages, to which there had been a few more "Call Me Pleases" added to the original bunch, they suddenly did not seem so dire. I still had zero clue of how to respond, and I full well knew any response would lead to a much longer conversation than I was willing to have while sitting on a foreign toilet at three a.m. local time. But though this absence of sense and thought had bothered me to the point of almost altering my travel plans only a few hours before, they now felt trivial, as if I was playing a game. I placed the phone back in my pants and ran my fingers through my hair. I figured once I arrived home, this situation would work itself out, or it wouldn't. I wasn't sure how much I even cared at the moment.

After flushing for what might have been the six-hundredth time, I sauntered back to bed to find that my father still had not returned. Perhaps he originally had other plans, or maybe he and Gustav decided to extend the evening getting hammered at a bar. Maybe he was spanking the ass of a Swedish hooker, or perhaps he got a good look at the size of our bathroom and wanted to skip out on the embarrassment of Swedish firemen prying him off the toilet using the Jaws of Life. Frankly, I didn't care and was thankful for the silence. I hoped he wouldn't come back for a few reasons, but mostly because I did not want to deal with his snoring.

The red digital clock informed me it was 3:30 a.m. I was not tired enough to sleep, so I felt ripe for a good J-session figuring it would help ease some nerves. I skipped the usual mental catalogue of choices as my thoughts immediately went to Saga. But for some reason, I just couldn't do it. I tried not to think of her and quickly recalled the time Clarissa let me blow a load all over her face. She looked like a Chinese glazed donut. Always did the trick.

I had no clue what I was going to do the next day and, for once, that was perfectly fine.

The Next Morning

I barely noticed the covers being ripped from my tired body as I lay motionless, sunken in the form fitting bed. As soon as my consciousness registered, my eyes slowly opened, breaking the crust from the corners, until my vision was greeted by the red digital numbers: 10:30. My first hazy thought was to kill my father. Just because he had been out all night, he didn't have to ruin my sleep. I felt a hand grab my calf and a subsequent shake that was neither gentle, nor rough. My head refused to move and all I could muster was an unpleasant groan.

"You need to get up," a female voice said, clearly not my father's.

What strange turn-down service they had in Sweden, I thought. Plus, I could have sworn I put out the "Do Not Disturb" sign the night before. I knew my father should have picked an American hotel; apparently, these people would get fired if they did not clean the room on time. I closed my eyes again.

"C'mon. We have a lot to do today," the voice said again.

"Can't you just clean the room later? I'll be up soon," I said in a sleepy tone.

I heard a frustrated sigh.

"If you don't get up right now, I'm going to kick you out of bed."

OK, now this was not traditional. I thought maybe my father found some bondage hotel where the cleaning staff berated you until you obeyed. I figured once I turned over, there would be some busty, enormous Swedish woman pouring out of a French maid costume ready to punish me with a whip and sodomize me with a high heel.

"Now," the voice demanded urgently.

Feisty.

I opened my eyes halfway and pushed myself up to look at the perpetrator. But when my eyes finally came into focus, I lost my balance and tumbled off the side of the bed. I looked in her direction again, but there was no French maid outfit, not even fresh towels. Just that sunlight-blonde hair that caused me to wonder if my pupils would damage if I stared at it too long. Somehow Saga had broken into my hotel room.

I guessed she never went to the airport.

I immediately gathered myself and tried to sweep away the open packet of shit medicine that was scattered across the nightstand in a way that suggested a long and painful night. I hoped she hadn't seen.

She moved her hair out from her eyes and tucked it behind her ear. Men get turned on by all sorts of different things. Some guys will go from soft to hard from a hot pair of tits in a tight shirt (well, all guys do). Some guys like long legs, some enjoy a big ass popping out of tight jeans, some like the sight of an innocent girl working on a popsicle while mentally picturing the cherry treat to be their wiener. But for me, what drove me crazy more than any other action was a beautiful girl absent-mindedly moving excess hair from over her face and tucking it behind her ear. When Clarissa found out about this weird fetish (is it a fetish? Probably not.), she constantly did it on purpose while winking at me and posing like a sex kitten. But all this did was annoy the shit out of me.

"So, are you going to sit there or are you going shower and get ready?" she asked.

I was much more curious as to why she was standing before me, suddenly demanding to take me somewhere after last night when she had seemingly dismissed me. But I could tell this was not the time to ask; I knew she was a bank safe that locked down if you entered the wrong code even once.

But, because I loved getting in my own way, I needed to make some sense of this. I figured I'd start simple: "How... how did you get in here?"

Saga stood up straight, her face turned serious. "Fine, I will leave."

She started toward the door. I knew it.

"No. no."

She didn't even turn back around while she grabbed the door knob. "Good, get ready, let's go."

"OK, but how did you find me?"

"The knob for the hot water is on the left," she responded.

Thanks.

While I gathered myself, I realized that my father had never actually made it back last night. I checked my phone, but there were no missed calls, only a few new texts from Clarissa, the grand total now over fifty. I really should have cared more, at least one of us did.

"Today," Saga ordered.

I sighed in half-hearted defiance, but she just put her hands on her hips and shot me a look that suggested she was in no mood for my bullshit. I turned the shower on and looked out the window to the city. The sun was shining on the colorful buildings below, not a raindrop or even mist to be found. Though all of this was completely bizarre, and I had no clue what I was doing, I was excited to do it anyway.

Blind Leading The Blind

A bsence was an activity that visited my childhood, but was long lost as memory categorized as normal, therefore unimportant. When you're young, the view of the world is so narrow that inconsistency and outliers easily mask themselves as commonplace. While I welcomed my father's most recent disappearing act, it certainly wasn't abnormal since my childhood was dotted with similar occurrences. This is not to suggest any sort of real frequency, but it happened enough times that it seemed as notable as annual doctor physicals.

His extended family breaks usually commenced the same way: He'd enter my room at some ungodly early hour, sit on my bed, and rub my head while informing me he'd be going away for a few days. He wouldn't even propose it under the guise of a business trip or visiting a friend; he left it simple and nebulous, and I just accepted it for what it was. But of the few times this did occur, one clearly sticks out in my mind.

My mother's fortieth birthday was supposed to be a special one. Prior to the day, my father dragged me to multiple jewelry stores around New York City in a desperate search for a blue topaz ring that my mother had commented on long ago. And when he finally found it, he gripped it in his hand like he was Frodo and informed me that the gift would be from both of us. And even though I obviously did not contribute a dime, I offered whatever was in my piggy bank and honestly felt as if I was part of it, perhaps because I made the trek all over the city along with him. And though I can't remember how the argument escalated or what it was even about, my father stormed out of the house only moments after presenting her with the ring. I remember the way the coat rack crashed to the floor from the force of him ripping his jacket from it; it was the only thing he took aside from his car keys. And he didn't return for three days. The next time I saw him I was raiding the refrigerator for Kool-Aid at three a.m., during a sleepless night, as he walked through the door with a heavy sigh. He made eye contact with me and harmlessly shrugged his shoulders, as if I could commiserate. I had no clue what it signified.

None of this seemed strange until I relayed that story during a random post-coital moment with Clarissa a year or so ago. After I finished telling her about that instance and the others concerning my father's habit, she calmly said, "Dude, that's fuckin' weird." Clarissa only cursed when she was really angry or really close to orgasm, so I knew that I probably needed to reassess the way I remembered those occurrences.

The irony of my recent escape from Los Angeles had not eluded me. In fact, it scared me a little more than I cared to admit.

Saga and I stood at the counter of an old coffee shop that bordered a bike path along the river. Unlike the night before, it was perfectly clear and the temperature registered a brisk 72 degrees (22+ Celsius) with a crisp breeze that made it feel like early fall.

While Saga ordered in Swedish to a bitter, ancient, fat woman that appeared as if she stored golf balls in her wrinkled cheeks like an enormous, confused chipmunk, I noticed the large glass containers that held herbs and teas behind the counter, which gave the small wooden café the feel of an old apothecary shop. Perhaps it was a modern design made to look aged, but judging by the woman behind the counter, who appeared no younger than one hundred, sixty (and along with her hefty build), I thought she might have constructed it with her own two hands back in the 1800s.

Once the food and drinks had been procured, Saga led me along the bike path toward a number of large sailboats docked along the side of the river. For some reason, half the boats had English names and I chuckled to myself as we passed one called "Bjorn's Childrens." When Saga noticed my laugh, she nodded and placed the food and lattes on the boat's edge as she prepared to board it.

"Is this your boat?" I asked.

"No."

She made her way to the bow, which was out of my sight.

"Are you sure this is a good idea?" I called after her, while searching the area to make sure no one saw her.

But there was no response.

"Shit."

I gave one last look before I commandeered the boat along with her. When I made my way to the bow, she had already set up the muffins and drinks on a little table that looked like a captain's wheel. The boat featured about six Swedish flags, but I assumed that covering a vessel with Swedish flags did not make you a hick like wallpapering your boat with confederate ones might. The Swedish flag, with its light blue and yellow, looked too innocuous and didn't quite pack the same racist punch as the stars and bars anyway.

I sipped my drink and dug my fingers into a moist blueberry muffin like a savage, while I watched Saga carefully peel the wrapper from hers and mix sugar in her latte with a gentle touch. I briefly considered how the food would react to my already sensitive stomach, but since I had eaten the Pepto like it was a pack of Spree, my intestines felt like a barren wasteland anyway. In fact, I thought I might shit out tumbleweed in a week or two.

"So...you like to sail?" I took a sip of my drink, which was equally as tasty.

"I don't know, I've never been," she said.

"Oh...so you just like sailboats?" I asked, while I looked around the vessel as if it would help my confusion.

"Maybe I just like stealing things."

"We're going to steal the boat?"

"Of course not. I don't sail," Saga said through a sly smile.

She liked fucking with me.

"So, you just normally use other people's boats for breakfast?"

"First time."

"You're used to getting what you want, aren't you?"

She paused for a second and quickly averted her eyes. "No."

She punctuated the banter with a serious tone, but quickly readjusted herself as if to re-invite levity. But I noticed.

"I just thought having breakfast on the boat would be prettier than a park bench," Saga said. "Plus, how often do adults get the chance to be rocked like a baby?"

Any conversation, at least to me, just danced around the elephant in the room (or on the boat). By all accounts, Saga was cheerier than she had been the night before; in fact, it now appeared as if she hadn't a care in the world, as if she had figured out the secret to life in the past twelve hours. *Rocked like a baby?* That was too comforting an analogy for someone who had wielded a toilet-cleaning device like a mace only one day ago. I wanted to ask her what happened, where she went in the subway, why she was on the verge of escaping her life, why she suggested I do the same, and what wasn't "worth it"...but I didn't want to upset her and the possible promise of an interesting day.

A cool breeze that smelled fresh enveloped our table. It rustled the leaves in the overhanging trees, which sounded like music. I forgot that the wind never blew like that in Southern California. Plus, I couldn't remember what unpolluted, smog free air tasted like. I could feel my lungs thank me. I turned my head toward the shore area, but I only saw some bikers and a few runners.

"Why are you looking at the path? You think the owner will suddenly come on board and kill us?"

"Maybe."

"Take the stick out of your ass and enjoy how much better this is than eating on a bench."

"The stick helps my posture."

She didn't seem amused by my joke, even though I thought it was clever. I just wanted to change the subject and not look like a pussy. Plus, even though I spent time with her, was assaulted by her, and was asked to go halfway around the world with her, I didn't know a God damn thing about her. And I really wanted to.

"I've been meaning to ask. I know everyone here seems to speak English, but how is yours so good?" I asked.

Saga searched me, as if sizing me up to see if I was worthy of just a modicum of personal information. She lit a cigarette and took a drag.

"I lived in Japan for three years," she responded as she exhaled smoke.

"Ah, 'cause that explains it."

"There's not exactly many areas in Japan that speak Swedish, let alone schools that teach it, so I was placed in an English school since I had a somewhat decent grasp of the language then."

"Why'd you live in Japan?" I asked.

"I moved with my parents and one of my sisters a few years ago. My father's job. But I moved back two years ago."

"So, I guess you fit in pretty well there, huh?" I circled my hand around her to encompass her appearance.

She took another drag of her cigarette, raised her eyebrows, and nodded along with my sarcasm.

"People in the subway used to come up to me to ask if they could touch my eyeballs."

"Why?" I asked, as a choked a little on the dense muffin.

"You would have to ask them."

"So, you moved back with your father?"

"No. I moved because of my father."

I took another sip of my latte, trying to evaluate the distinction, but only foam entered my mouth. Drinking from cups that were long empty had always been a nervous habit of mine. I guessed I was pretty nervous because that was the fourth time I had done that. I'm sure she noticed and would make a short bus comment soon, if they had those in Sweden.

"So where are your mother and sister now?"

"There."

"Oh," I wanted to pry, but her expression told me to refrain. Instead, I figured I'd go with plan B and say something retarded: "Think they're suffering from Saga withdrawal?"

"I don't know. What do you suppose the symptoms are of such a thing?"

"My guess would be a big headache."

Saga sneered and brushed some errant muffin crumbs in my direction. I did the same with mine. She opened another sugar packet, placed some in the palm of her hand, and blew it on me like it was pixie dust. The sugar covered my sunglasses, which probably made me appear like I had borrowed them from Pablo Escobar. I made sure not to move my face and just nodded. She smiled and covered her mouth as she laughed.

"You know, I could throw you in the water right now to get you back," I said.

"You wouldn't."

"Maybe, but I have a feeling if you could lift me, you might try," I said.

"Absolutely."

She put out her cigarette and pushed her chair from the table.

"You ready?"

I actually wanted to stay on the boat a little longer and enjoy the moment, but Saga had already walked to the stern and I knew she would not wait for me.

Baby's Way Cruel

Most Saturdays, Clarissa and I would have brunch simply because she refused to have breakfast or lunch. Those meals were for weekdays; brunch was made for weekends, she'd say as if that made any sense. After our late breakfast, we'd proceed to some afternoon activity that usually held little interest for me like making pottery or heading to some street fair because Jessica Biel would be there to show her some ugly jewelry. It became sad when I actually started to notice the differences between women's clothing designs and home knick-knacks at places like Crate And Barrel, though I suppose this made it easier when we decided to tag team the wedding registry. (On a side note, I fought like hell against a wedding registry. I thought a registry was arguably the most obnoxious idea a privileged human has ever created. Think about it: You interrupt the lives of over two hundred family members and friends, causing many of them to travel against their will, and then, once they accept the invite to your wedding (party) and already plunk down at least a grand for flight and hotel expenses— Clarissa *demanded* people stay at the Four Seasons—you then decide, in all your infinite wisdom, to provide them a *guide* on what *gift* to get you as if they haven't done enough. Like we really needed fucking two-hundred-dollar Passover Seder plates when I hadn't celebrated Passover in ten years and, last time I checked, beef and broccoli were not the chosen foods of Moses and his people. Yes, I completely understood this was commonplace in society and wedding culture, but it's beyond absurd. Upon hearing this, Clarissa was appalled and ranted on and on about how people felt honored to give these gifts. Honored, you say? I often wondered what planet she was from.)

I didn't know what Saga had planned; I had no idea what her idea of fun might have been, though it wouldn't have surprised me if violence were somehow involved. However, judging by the historical facts she spewed on our walk from the restaurant the night before, I could tell she was, at least, somewhat educated in the history of her country. Also, from my thirty years of living, I found people interested in history also to be sentimentalists, so perhaps she was going to show me something important from her childhood. So imagine my surprise when she said, "We're here," while we stood outside the entrance of a shopping mall in the city centre.

Someone wise once told me that if you are ever far away from home and suddenly feel homesick, go ahead and find the nearest mall because they all look, more or less, the same. This was definitely true in America as every mall has a GAP, Banana Republic, cheesy décor, and a food court that features small Japanese people (who are probably Chinese) offering a sample of their chicken teriyaki that tastes fantastic in small doses, but uninspiring as an entire meal. The mall in Sweden was no exception, well, save for the small Japanese people, who were replaced by blond women with heavy eyeliner to give the appearance of being Asian (I kid, but that would have been funny.) Some of the stores were different and twice as expensive, but the architecture and fluorescent lighting were basically the same. Instead of best sellers greeting customers to the bookstore, there was a table of "Swedish History" that consisted of about ten books on ABBA, a smattering of hard covers with Vikings on the book jackets, and a few paperbacks that featured Lindsay Lohan. Though when I thought about it for five seconds, I realized "Lindsay" was actually Pippi Longstocking. Unfortunately, Hot Dog On A Stick was nowhere to be found.

But even though the wise man made a good point about the similarities between shopping malls, I didn't feel homesick and actually would have preferred not being reminded of them at all.

One of my first dates with Clarissa took place at the Beverly Center, a typical mall smack in the center of Beverly Hills. While we shopped, she ran into one of her friends and, upon introducing me, flat out lied to her about what I did for a living: she said I was a successful journalist that was published in many journals and off-beat publications. She claimed to have said that because she had just read the two hundred pages of bullshit, otherwise known as *The Secret,* and suggested that I had to start acting successful if I was to be successful. Lies. In actuality, she just didn't want to tell her friend I spent my days behind the counter at a Jiffy Lube (it was just for two weeks, before I got my current job), because, to a type-A like Clarissa, that would have been more embarrassing than squeezing out a wet fart while fucking. Plus, the only thing Clarissa ever read was *US Weekly*, so maybe she just learned about *The Secret* from an episode of Oprah, though more likely from one of her douchetard clients who probably claimed it to be the next big thing after they tired of Kabbalah and Scientology. Regardless, I was annoyed by her comment and demanded we eat at Sbarro after I originally promised her a meal at the "fancier" Cheesecake Factory knock-off downstairs, which I knew she craved because she liked their chocolate soufflé dessert that she'd often joke about having sex with. The unoriginal joke wasn't funny the first eight times she said it, and I kind of enjoyed watching her pout and pick at her end-of-the night schwag veggie pizza while I obnoxiously slurped up the gooey cheese that hung from my fresh slice of regular. That showed her, though perhaps that incident was why she was so insistent on taking me to Cilantro'R'Us every chance she got.

I really should have known then. Loneliness is a vicious bitch.

But I really didn't want to be thinking of these counterproductive memories.

Saga led me past the numerous make-up counters and, as I looked at various older Swedish women as they ordered around the cosmetologists, I began to worry that I'd be treated to a boring, Clarissa-like afternoon full of window shopping, meaningless bullshit, and flushed hopes. I had an image of not so patiently sitting outside a dressing room, as Saga showed me fifteen different versions of a dress she was interested in buying, but never intended to wear. I almost searched for Jessica Biel.

But, just as my mind went to its usual cynical state, Saga led me to a large store that wasn't a store at all. It was spartanly decorated, but featured various game tables and a decently sized, figure-8 racing track along the side, though I could not tell what kind of vehicles it serviced. Saga continued inside until she stopped in front of an air-hockey table and patiently waited until I joined her on the opposite end. For some reason, I hesitated. Like I'd recently been allergic to fun and was afraid of what might happen if I tried to have some. Perhaps I really was spending too much time with the Changs.

"What? Afraid?" she asked, while knocking her paddle against the table.

Just really surprised. I walked toward my end of the table and grabbed the paddle.

"I wasn't expecting this," I said, pleased. And I was. Very pleased, actually. Even though I'd spent only a few hours with her, I'd have never guessed air hockey would be on the agenda. I realized I hadn't played in years, which fucking sucked, because I used to love air hockey and would often play for money at the local arcade when I was a kid. I couldn't tell you how many packages of Dipsy Doodles I purchased from air hockey winnings, but probably enough to fill a bathtub, and certainly enough to make Billy Frack, the town shithead I beat most often, insanely jealous.

"Not expecting what? The ass kicking I'm about to give you?" Saga taunted.

I raised my eyebrows. Trash talking. She was competitive.

"I'll have you know I actually won back-to-back town air hockey titles when I was in fifth and sixth grade," I said in a proud nostalgic moment.

"Well, you never played a Swede before. Not to mention I'm actually half Czech, which means I was born hockey tough. But I'm sure you find plenty of time to play in between surfing and rollerblading."

I'd never done either. Surfing seemed dangerous and rollerblading seemed gay.

"Haven't you ever heard of the 1980 American Olympic Hockey Team? Miracle On Ice?"

"I'm not Russian," she said, while lightly banging her paddle on the table again.

"We beat Finland for the Gold Medal that year."

"I'm not Finnish, either."

"Close enough."

She rolled her eyes.

"How would you like it if I called you Canadian?"

"I'd be honored. I love Canadians."

"Fine, how would you like it if I called you Mexican?"

"Let's rock."

I figured this was a cute idea for an afternoon activity and felt like it was something producers would have chosen for the old TV show, *Blind Date*. I pictured a half serious round of air hockey, complete with some laughs, and maybe it would end with a hug and the promise of a round in a Jacuzzi. That's how it worked on the show anyway.

Saga allowed me to go first and I half-heartedly hit a few shots toward her goal and attempted flirty commentary, which was as effective as my shitty flirting normally is. When she finally successfully possessed the puck, she paused for a moment and looked intently at my goal. For a while.

"You gonna sit there all day or are you gonna shoot?" I taunted.

Saga's demeanor immediately changed. She wound up in an awkward motion, completely alien to air hockey, and nailed the puck so hard against the left side of the wall that the carom was sent airborne and slammed me directly in the right cheek. And it fucking hurt. I stuck a finger in my mouth to show Saga the crimson evidence of her attack, but when I looked at her, her face offered zero remorse. None. She really wanted to win this game. And suddenly, as I tasted my own blood, a feeling came over me: I had to beat her. No question. In fact, it wouldn't have shocked me if she just bolted if I lost. It seemed well within her odd personality, like this was some sort of test. I felt like the emotionally drained Rocky the moment Adrian woke up from the coma and told him to "win" in *Rocky II*. I spit blood to the floor like a badass and felt inspired.

When Saga regained the puck, she wound up awkwardly again and I flinched as she sent the speeding puck straight into my goal. She confidently held up one finger to denote the score.

"Fuck," I said to myself in a whisper. I didn't even want to look at her.

My competitive juices hit overdrive as I studied her defense and prepared my next shot. Hollywood had beaten this emotion out of me after so many years, but I channeled that sixth-grade champion and knew it was on. I deftly blocked her next few shots, while I gained accuracy on mine. I fired a shot off the right side for my first goal. That unmistakable rattle of an air hockey puck shooting through the thin slit brought relief. Tie score. She gritted her teeth. Perhaps she beat the crap out of some of her past dates, but it wasn't going to happen this time. When I regained possession again, I scanned for an open area in her defense and blew a straight shot right past the one spot of the goal left unguarded. I was a sniper.

"That's two," I said. "You can quit any time you like."

She did not appreciate the comment. She tried firing her shots harder, but like Jim Craig in the 1980 Olympics, I was defending an upset in the making (or so she thought.)

The score quickly became 5-2, in my favor, with the puck in my possession and only one score needed to win. For some reason, I actually got nervous. I was never very good under pressure, but I knew I had to block all negative thoughts and just concentrate on one last goal. I didn't just want to win; I wanted a blowout.

My mind was officially put at ease after a few volleys, my last goal a result of her over-aggressiveness: she fired a hard, aimless shot that ricocheted with similar speed back toward her goal. 6–2. I arrogantly spun my paddle and let it settle like I knew the outcome before we had even started.

"Nice one, Gretzky. Wanna go again?" I said confidently. I could feel my testicles descend again. Sadly enough, it was the first time in too long that I actually felt like a man. I hoped she'd say no.

She sneered and walked farther into the store toward what appeared to be a wrestling ring. When I caught up, Saga was already stepping into one of those Sumo fatsuits, complete with the black nipples, which I supposed were there for accuracy. She successfully zipped hers, as I was still trying to figure out mine, all the while thinking that I, at least, sort of got to see her topless. Once I finally donned the enormous suit and turned toward her, she charged and flung her entire body at me, knocking me completely off balance and on my ass. She managed to pick herself up, but I had more trouble. Like a floundering fish, I tried to contort my body in a way that would best allow me to rise, but it was to no avail. Saga reached for my hand, which I gladly accepted, but after helping me up only halfway, she dropped me so that I fell like a ton of bricks...or like a fat sumo wrestler tipped over. She laughed at how pathetic I looked.

And as I briefly lay on the back of the fat suit, I actually felt alive.

"Oh, you're dead," I exclaimed. "Once I figure out how to get up."

"Bring it on, fatty."

At the sound of her insult, I sprang up, and like the incredible Hulk, charged her with wild eyes. Saga, feigning fear, turned and ran (waddled quickly) away from the ring and toward the racetrack, which I could then see were populated with Segways, otherwise known as one of the most useless inventions of the twenty-first century. The Segways might have cost money to rent, but Saga quickly commandeered one and motored away. I swiftly followed suit, grabbed one of my own, and chased her around the store.

As we weaved in and out of the tables and other players, she looked back and taunted me with crude hand gestures that suddenly made our little display rated R. Neither of us really cared that a nebbish nerd with a pancake for a face and a huge zit in the middle of his forehead that caused him to resemble the Mahatma was yelling, imploring both of us to return the machines that were specifically to be rented for the enclosed track. As I pressed my Segway closer to her and got within a fat arm's length, she took a sharp turn to the left and sped out of the store. I straightened my body, rubbed my fake black nipples to show I was serious, and went after her. The apoplectic attendant chased us while he quickly waved his hands and screamed bloody murder in Swedish.

Saga and I cruised the Segways through the large corridor of the mall, past a multitude of curious patrons who acted like they never saw two people in beige sumo suits speeding through a mall on motorized people movers. No one yelled, but everyone we passed stopped in their tracks to follow our movement.

"C'mon!" Saga screamed after me as she ducked into a rather large, two-story H&M.

Using my weight, I increased the speed of the vehicle to its maximum potential, zooming past blond heads, almost hitting a few. These select few screamed something at me, either rooting me on or calling me an asshole; I could safely assume the latter. I guessed they didn't care that I used the little horn attached to the handle to warn them. I wondered if the Segway beeped like a tractor-trailer if I went in reverse.

I entered the H&M to find her dodging clothing racks as shoppers screamed in terror, as if Saga were wielding a Samurai sword. I tried to take a short cut through the tables of cheap sweaters to reach her on the other side of the store, but my attempt was horribly unsuccessful as I knocked over three mannequins, popping a bikini top off one, much to the delight of a ten-year-old boy obviously desperately in need of porno mag if the sight of a naked mannequin excited him.

As I exited the store in hot pursuit, I heard an urgent yell from behind me and noticed we had earned the attention of five security guards who were sprinting in our direction. But these guys weren't the fat pathetic ones who eat donuts all day like we had in the United States. From the looks of it, these five were five Ivan Dragos who had no problem living by the creed "if he dies, he dies." I gulped and imagined possible headlines in tomorrow's paper.

Saga took a sharp right turn into another corridor, but as I tried to do the same, I had to jerk the Segway sharply to avoid hitting a pedestrian, which caused me to lose my balance ever so slightly and the innocent bystander to lose her lemonade, which splashed all over my face and stung my eyes. Disoriented, I attempted to straighten the machine, but completely lost control of the steering and, doing my best imitation of George W. Bush (I think the only known person to ever fall off a Segway), the vehicle fell forward, propelling me off and down a small flight of stairs, bouncing like a superball due to the puffiness of the fat suit. With each bump, I groaned until I fell flat on the plateau next to the second set of steps that led to the first floor.

Security immediately surrounded me like the suit was filled with dynamite, pestering me with orders in the language I did not understand, while threatening me with their nightsticks. I managed to flip my fat body over and ran my hand across my forehead, where I noticed some blood dripping from my hair line. While glaring up at the barking officers, I saw hordes of people lining the railings, looking on with a mixture of interest, concern, but most of all amusement. Though I knew there was a high possibility that one of these men would slam me in the head with his club, I couldn't help but laugh.

And just then…

A fat, beige blur with black nipples rumbled down the stairs unbeknownst to the angered guards. When she was within striking distance, Saga screamed her Viking war cry, leaped between the guards, spread eagle, and belly flopped on my fat, padded body. The crowd *roared* like we were gladiators in the Roman Coliseum as the security guards flashed to frenzy and barked into their walkie-talkies, as if they needed backup to stop us. The poor Segway attendant entered the scene and looked completely crestfallen upon seeing the wreck that was my Segway lying a few feet from me. So much so that I thought he might have been in love with it. He joined in the frenetic yelling as if I had just killed his first-born. Well, now I felt bad, though I hoped I wouldn't have to pay for that.

Saga placed her face close to mine, about an inch away.

"That's two take downs," she said.

"I guess we're even now?" I responded with a smile.

She brushed some of the blood away from my forehead, as I looked straight into her big blue eyes. Without thinking, I arched my neck up to plant a kiss on her lips, but she pulled back and pushed my head back down to the ground with a thud.

"Ouch..," I genuinely exclaimed in a happy, yet exhausted tone.

Saga rolled off of me and pointed to my pathetic body on the ground.

"You can arrest him now," she told them.

I hoped she wasn't serious, but in the moment, I actually didn't care. I couldn't stop smiling. My eyes met hers and I noticed that she could not stop either. And while the security guards struggled to get both hands behind my back to cuff me, all I could think of was how I hadn't had this much fun in a long time. And by the way the on-looking crowd cheered, I could tell they probably hadn't either.

The Aftermath

As I was finishing my dinner, I gently felt the small bandage on my forehead that covered my wound and winced slightly from the soreness. After the guards had cuffed me, Saga spoke to them briefly until they agreed to let me go. She refused to tell me what she said to them but, regardless, the guards looked mighty disappointed when they were cheated out of the chance to beat the shit out of me before taking me to jail.

Anti-Semites.

I ate the last of my sushi rolls and Saga made quick notice of my clear plate.

"I don't know how it works in America, but there's not a time limit for you to eat."

I always ate my meals like they were going to be taken away from me. This probably started when my father picked at my food as a child after he gorged his. It actually turned into a bit of a childhood game; he'd challenge me to eat my dinner in under a certain time and, if I didn't, he'd make these Godzilla type sounds while pilfering my french fries. At the time, I enjoyed it, but it became another one of those things that I did not recognize as tremendously odd until later on in life.

We sat in a stylish restaurant that stood about twenty stories above the ground and provided a panoramic view of the city at dusk. It was easy to see the various islands and meandering waterways that cut themselves through the city landscape. Boats and buoys were still on the dark water, as I noticed drizzle droplets appear on the window next to me.

I looked at Saga who sat directly across from me and felt a moment of surreality. Just a few short days ago, I had sat in a drab Mexican restaurant on Beverly Boulevard entertaining Clarissa's loud and obnoxious co-workers while dodging heaps of cilantro-based gunk, and not so seriously pondering suicide while listening to bad music in the restroom that smelled like old taco meat. Now, I was dining on top of an international city, with what could best be described as an international beauty, in an atmospheric eatery that featured perhaps too much veg-etation, a creek with a small bridge that led to the dining room, and the sounds of live crickets that completed the ambiance.

And even though I never once brought up the odd occurrences of the day before, I suddenly felt comfortable. In fact, Saga's complete change in behavior signaled that maybe I was over-blowing or even misremembering the memory. Or maybe she was schizophrenic. I hoped for the former, but I also knew I was fooling myself if I honestly thought the other shoe would never drop. There was something still amiss, some secret, but I was in no rush to find out what it was.

"Do you mind if I order dessert for us?" she asked, completely changing the subject.

I held out my hands to signify that I did not mind at all. When the waitress came, Saga pointed to the menu, ordered in Swedish, and took a quick sip of her water while she stared over my head. I noticed she'd looked above me throughout the meal and, finally, I turned around to see a Japanese painting that featured bare trees under a large moon with flying birds passing through the mountainous background of muted color.

"I wonder where that is," Saga said. "It looks peaceful."

I didn't quite understand why. It looked like a rather boring scene. She noticed my questioning face.

"It looks like it would be a perfect place to live, don't you think?" she followed.

"Not particularly."

"Why not? Because there's no TV?"

"Why do foreigners assume Americans just watch TV all day?"

"Do you not?"

"I have my shows," I said defensively.

"So, what's wrong with that painting?"

"I don't know."

"So, you're just saying it to be negative."

That's what I normally did. Never understood why either. I had to think of something. Some kind of artistic bullshit, like how I'd make up a load of crap while critiquing poetry in college only for my professor to view me with pity, wondering how many times my mother had dropped me on my head as a child. And maybe as an adult.

"See those black clouds?" I pointed to the top of the painting. "It's going to rain soon."

"What's wrong with rain?"

"I dunno, it's stupid."

"Lovely reason. But in this picture, there are no raindrops."

"So, you just expect time to stop? I'm not sure what world you live in, but I haven't figured out how to freeze time."

Saga leaned back to consider my statement. She narrowed her eyes.

"Life is just a series of moments," she said.

"I just don't see your point, I guess."

"Why are you angry?"

"Who says I'm angry?"

"You're transparent."

I did not like being exposed, especially when I didn't even think it was accurate.

"Well, what about you? Tell me something, since I'm obviously an open book."

"What can you tell from me?" Saga shrugged as she asked.

"Nothing," I said, straightforward, albeit a bit too whiny.

"So?"

"So..." I didn't really know how to express myself, so I just leaned back and tossed my hands to suggest articulating my thoughts would be overwhelming.

Saga didn't take her eyes off me.

"Really, all you see is dark clouds?" she asked.

I shrugged and held the awkward moment of silence. Saga did not look disappointed, but confused. I just wanted to change the subject. I looked at my phone as if I was checking a message.

"I still haven't heard from my father. Yours didn't say anything about what they might be up to?" I asked, trying to lighten the mood.

"Why are you so interested in your father's business?" Saga asked. It was actually a really good question.

"Did you know he invited me here to talk to your father about being an astronaut?"

"Yes. He had told me you worked for NASA. But the second I saw you, I figured it wasn't true."

I didn't even take that as an insult.

"Would you like to know what I really do?"

"There are millions of things that make up a person, and what they do for a living usually isn't in the top 500,000 interesting ones to me. Unless you were a circus clown or something."

"I can juggle."

"So, are you a circus clown?"

"Feels like it sometimes."

"Why? Do you and your father share shirts?"

"No, we actually barely talk."

"So, who cares if he brought you here under false pretenses."

"Don't I have the right to be curious?"

Saga shook her head. I was taken aback by her casual dismissal of my issues.

"If you were back home in Los Angeles right now, what would you be doing?" she asked.

"You have an answer for everything, don't you?"

"That was a question."

"See, you do."

"Life would be much different if I did."

There was something pointed about that last comment that made me believe she wasn't grilling me to be difficult. I checked my watch and quickly did the math for the time difference.

"If I were in LA right now, I'd probably be figuring out ways to kill half an hour till lunch."

Sadly true.

"Yet here you are, sitting at a beautiful restaurant, in a foreign country, all because your father was selfish and whisked you away on a free vacation. But all you see are dark rain clouds and all you are doing is complaining about his motives."

I felt challenged by her point.

"You do realize we've only known each other for about twenty-four hours," I said with an accusatory tone.

"That's long enough."

"Long enough for what? And wait, why is this all about my anger toward my father? You actually left a country to get away from yours."

"I didn't leave because I was angry. I left because I had to."

"Why?"

"It's not important why."

Saga was building frustration inside me, and I quickly tried to gather my thoughts on the subject, but didn't quite know how to articulate how I felt or if I actually wanted to.

"Can we just drop this?" I asked.

"No."

I shook my head and bit my cheek while I broke eye contact, but noticed her lean forward, placing her chin in the palm of her hand. She wanted an answer.

"Fine, it would just be nice if something made sense, for once."

"Good, now how did that taste?" Saga said through a laugh.

'What?" I asked.

"Your bitter words."

"Pretty fucking bitter."

She smiled.

The waitress interrupted the conversation when she placed the plate of dessert between us. They appeared to be brown, glazed marshmallow pastries pierced by a skewer. Four for each of us. Saga calmly picked one up in her hand and watched it intently as she twirled it.

"You really want to know something about me?"

I did. She sized me up much as she had on the boat. Last time I tried to look sincere, like a puppy behind glass in a pet store; this time I remained serious.

"Three years ago I visited a friend of mine. She was in Panama for a couple of months on some sort of student exchange program. Actually, no, she was an au pair for the summer," Saga said. "I was there for about two weeks and, on my last day, it was a Sunday, we walked to the local bakery to get some pastries that she'd been raving about the entire time."

Saga placed the dessert back on the plate, but didn't look me in the eye.

"While we waited to cross the street alongside a few other people, a car came full speed toward us and screeched on the brakes only a few meters away. Some guy came rushing out of the back, and the next thing I know, he shot a bullet through the head of the man standing three feet to my right. Just like that. No questions, no warning."

My eyebrows rose in surprise and I probably mouthed the word "Christ," though I cannot be sure. But it seemed like the only appropriate reaction and response.

"He waved his gun toward the rest of us, screaming something I can only imagine to be threats in Spanish. I closed my eyes and grabbed my friend's hand. The next thing I can remember hearing was the longest five seconds of my life. The sound of his jacket arm rustling as he swayed the gun left to right. The person next to me whimpering and my own heartbeat. I finally breathed when

I heard the car screech away. I went back home to Sweden the next day, immediately crawled in bed and held on to my favorite stuffed panda for what seemed like an eternity. My mother had given me that panda ten years before, but until that day, I hadn't noticed that the panda had a white spec of fur under its tail and a tiny stitched-in smile right under its nose. But I noticed it then and suddenly felt the bear had personality. It was more complete, not to mention more adorable."

I couldn't get the vision out of my head: Saga covered in blood and brains like she starred in some Tarantino movie.

"Wow..."

Always the wordsmith, I was.

Saga nodded and picked up the dessert once again and held it in front of her like she was displaying it for me.

"Do you know what this is?"

"It looks like toasted marshmallows."

"It's called Dango...it's like a sweet dumpling," Saga said. "Japanese people eat them during a period in the spring called Hanami. Have you heard of that?"

"I haven't," I responded.

"It's a Japanese custom that simply involves watching the cherry blossoms bloom. People eat Dango under the blossoms to celebrate their appearance in the spring."

Saga looked straight at me again.

"And that's all."

Saga ripped one of the dumplings off with her teeth and chewed in delight.

"And they taste really fucking good," she said with her mouth completely full.

She held her skewer to my mouth and I bit one off. She was right. They were delicious.

"Moments," she stated.

I ate another Dango.

After Midnight

After dinner, Saga insisted we partake in one of Stockholm's greatest traditions, though it had nothing to do with folk dancing or yodeling (if Swedes yodeled). It actually involved one of my favorite things in the world: boobies. Much to my delight, she took me to the city's oldest strip club and, much to my surprise, proceeded to buy me a lap dance from their most renowned stripper: a fifty-five year old who went by the name of Helga and possessed lethal weapons, otherwise known as tits the size of Cleveland. Saga sat me in a throne while Helga shimmied in front of me for a minute before swinging her body to and fro, whacking me in the cheeks with her large breasts that felt like uppercuts from a heavyweight boxer. But this wasn't once or twice, this show went on for a full five minutes until I was punch-drunk. How many people can say they got their ass beat by a set of tits? I tried to ask Helga if Saga could sit across from me while she spun in place, slamming us both with her gifts like a paddywhack, but I quickly realized my request was lost in translation.

After I became "Helga-ized" (I even got my Polaroid hung on the back wall, similar to finishing a 72-ounce porterhouse at a Texas steak joint), we walked back in the general direction of city centre through a large, pristine park that was, as Saga told me, a royal fruit garden for a king in the sixteenth century, though I sincerely doubted the skate half pipe was a part of the original blueprint. Tall oak trees lined the thin path that weaved its way past a few massive, old, white buildings with small clock towers and statues dedicated to men she never heard of. If this were Los Angeles, I would be counting the seconds until someone lurking in the shadows attacked us, or until we heard two covert businessmen having sex in the bushes. But in this park, the only sound to interrupt the silence came from two men arguing over a game of late night bocce. I stopped to watch them actually pull out a tape measure to resolve a disputed call and wondered what circumstances led to a match so late in the evening. Judging by their passion and histrionics, combined with the air hockey game from earlier, I figured a simple Swedish game night probably started with Monopoly or Jenga and ended with a hospital visit. But as we walked through the park, I couldn't believe how peaceful a place in the middle of a major city could actually be. I started to understand what Saga meant by capturing moments.

The streets of city centre were desolate, save for a few areas that housed bars (a TGI Fridays? Really?) which would be open all night. But once beyond them, nary a soul could be found, providing us the false sensation that the city was asleep and under our control.

I had felt my phone buzz a few times throughout the evening, but neglected to view the messages and actually had forgotten that they were sent moments after their arrival. Perhaps it was the isolated feeling of Sweden, but Los Angeles felt like a world away, and I was in a place that transcended time. I thought that, once I returned to America, I would come home to find Clarissa sleeping in the same position I had left her, only for her to wake up and never realize I had been gone. *Back To The Future* style. And then I would be forced to question whether the entire trip had actually happened at all. I wasn't sure it was really happening and I had been experiencing it.

Saga and I made small talk as we walked to nowhere in particular. She told me a little about her sisters. One was sixteen and desired to study English in America; the other was twenty-two and was dating a tri-athlete that she would probably marry. I told her about the time a herd of goats trampled me on my first day of summer camp and also the incident in which Sam the Mule almost tossed me off the side of the Grand Canyon simply because he was hungry and decided to eat some vegetation growing off the edge of the walking path. Saga said she liked short, harsh English words like "chunk" and "fork." She liked pizza and thought bananas tasted like "the seventh lair of hell." But most of the information she gave me barely scratched her surface and, each time I attempted to dig deeper, she changed the subject or simply refused to discuss it.

We strolled past closed restaurants, coffee shops, record stores, and movie theaters that advertised ridiculous-looking Swedish movies that featured extremely random groups of people on their posters, as if the combination of a race car driver, a priest, a black guy, and a bride holding a Pomeranian brought the promise of hilarity (They really had nothing on *Honey Buns*). I knew my hotel was somewhere in the area, but I was not about to mention it even though it was late and I was rather tired. Perhaps it was because I was enjoying my time with her, or perhaps I wanted to avoid my harsh reality, but, regardless, I wished the night could go on forever.

After a few more blocks, I found myself in a familiar area. Before us was the fountain in the middle of the round-about with the tall phallic structure in the center, but the man dancing to "Wipeout" was nowhere to be found.

Saga led me toward the fountain. Multiple jets shot water high into the air, even though it was after one a.m. and not a soul was in the area to enjoy the show. As we approached the fountain, I could see rope hanging over the edge of the base.

Saga started to remove her shoes.

"What are you doing?" I asked.

"It's not exactly a lake, but how about in a fountain in the middle of Stockholm?" Saga stated in the half-mocking/half-genuine tone I had gotten so used to in the past thirty or so hours.

I thought she might be crazy. And maybe she was, but with her shoes off, she pulled on the rope to reveal a small yellow inflatable raft from the darkness. With a few more pulls, the raft was fountain side.

"Are you ready?" she asked.

I searched the area to see if we were being watched, not because I was afraid of being caught, but because I wanted to see if anyone else was around to witness the absurdity of what we were about to do.

"Are you serious? How did you even get this in here?"

Saga gently lowered herself into the raft just big enough for two. Before I could let another moment pass, I found myself kicking off my shoes and socks and rolling up my pants to prevent them from getting wet. I not so gracefully pushed myself into the raft as Saga untied the rope from the side of the boat, allowing us to float freely through the maze of shooting water. There were lights below that illuminated the area, which caused it to feel like an unguided "Pirates Of The Caribbean" ride. Water sprinkled over our heads, though we managed to paddle clear of the direct stream. We found a quiet, shadowed spot near the edge of the John Holmes penis sculpture and remained in silence. Saga sat with her back to the opposite side of the raft and her legs at a 45-degree angle between mine. The only sound between us came from the friction caused by the slightest movement between our bodies and the rubber of the raft.

"This is really amazing…" I whispered. I wasn't sure if she could hear, but I really just said it to myself while I surveyed the area. My attention quickly returned to Saga, whose eyes had never left mine. Her stare was stunning, intimidating, and often unreadable. *Fuck it*, I thought. I couldn't think of a place in the world I would rather have been, even if it *was* cold and wet.

It was time.

I awkwardly sat up and placed my fingers under her delicate chin. I leaned forward, afraid that she might pull away, but she held still. I gently placed my lips against hers and kissed her softly, almost afraid. I slowly, nervously pulled away to meet her gaze, and as soon as I created only a few inches of distance between us, she lunged at me with her lips, knocking my head against the cushy edge of the boat. Our tongues forcefully met each other's, as I quickly raked my hands through her hair and down her back, until both were gripping her tight ass that was even better to the touch than it was to the eye. She quickly unbuttoned my shirt as I fumbled with hers in an effort to get each other's tops off as fast as possible. I dug my head in her sweetly perfumed neck and ripped open her bra. She arched herself up to put her tits in my face and I sucked on her hard nipples, which caused her to moan and for me to pull her waist tighter against mine. We deftly removed each other's pants as she pressed her waist back against mine to rub herself along my hard dick. The force of our movements freed the raft from the quiet, dry area and sent it toward the launching water jets that made up the better part of the middle of the fountain.

Saga placed her mouth centimeters from mine as she lowered herself onto me. She released a short sigh as I gripped her waist firmly and slowly pushed up into her. She wrapped her arms around my neck and rotated her hips, breathing heavily against my mouth before I met her lips again. The raft moved closer to the firing water that pounded us with streams of cold liquid, which only quickened our motions. The boat jackknifed and rebounded with every thrust. The harder she moved against me, the harder I pushed back. The raft was on the verge of completely tipping over, completely filling with water, but neither of us could feel the cold, or the danger of falling in. I gripped her hips tighter and jammed my tongue against hers, almost violently, as we both completely lost our collective breath. Our joint climax was epic. After letting out a loud moan, she fell on me, as if the demon possessing her had been exorcised. We held still. As our bodies gathered oxygen, we looked at each other while the water continued to cascade both around and on top of us. We kissed gently again and lay, soaked, in each other's arms. She placed her head against my chest to catch her breath. My eyes wandered through the shooting water toward the night sky. Stars. We didn't have those in L.A. either. There was a long, quiet moment.

"They should do that under the cherry blossoms," I said, relaxed.

I felt Saga's cheeks rise against my chest. She was smiling.

After exiting the raft and placing our soaking-wet clothes back on, we wordlessly, yet hand in hand, walked back to my hotel which was only a few blocks away. As we approached the entrance, we said nothing, but shared a long hug; our wet clothes clung together and provided warmth during the cool evening. We did not kiss, and even though tomorrow was my last day in Sweden, as my flight was scheduled to depart the next evening, I knew I would see her again.

She walked toward a cab without looking back. I dragged my wet body through the revolving door, past the front desk, where the attendant eyed me curiously, and into the elevator. While riding up to my floor, I felt my phone faintly buzz; I had forgotten that it was in my sopping wet pants. I pulled out the phone and saw a completely water logged piece of technology that was fighting to stay alive. The colors of the screen bled into one another, creating a mess that was hard to decipher. But I did notice I had ten more text messages from Clarissa and, actually, one from Bryan. I checked Bryan's quick enough to read…

"MY BABY SHIT IN THE POTTY!"

…before the phone completely died. I tucked it back into my wet pocket as the elevator doors opened to my floor.

I pumped my fist for the kid.

The day was bookended by beauty.

Capsizing

Nothing convinced me that the notion of a "soul" was completely bullshit like staring at the remains of a skeleton. It's inconceivable to suggest that a skeleton is just a vessel for an ethereal conscious when they are the physical manifestation of withered personality. In fact, not one thing in the entire universe could make a person seem so delicately human as being faced with the skeletal remains of another.

Saga spared me an additional embarrassing morning and interrupted my slumber with a simple phone call that informed me she was waiting in the lobby. I was still jet lagged from the flight only days before and spent my nights in Sweden mostly tossing and turning. I did not rule out that this might also have been caused by the fifteen million thoughts stomping through my mind as if they were an elephant stampede. I was set to leave for the United States in just under ten hours and still had not heard from my father since the dinner. I wondered whether he was caught in some sort of trouble and, after I judged his history, I just assumed he was safely up to something I was better off not knowing about. I was also fully aware this meant I only had ten remaining hours with Saga and hadn't thought of what the future held. In fact, my actions still had not hit me, which was strange for someone who normally pored over the mundane minutiae of the everyday. I did feel sort of guilty, but probably not as guilty as I should have.

Since I had showered at five a.m. in an attempt to help me sleep, I quickly brushed my teeth, threw on clothes, and met Saga in the lobby where she greeted me with coffee in hand and told me she needed to show me one of her favorite places in the city before I left. Even if it was, in fact, a tourist attraction.

The Vasa was a warship built in the early 1600s that was supposed to be the most impressive of the Swedish navy during the Thirty Years War. Though the ship was beautifully designed, it suffered from structural flaws, as it was built too top heavy with improper ballast, and was sunk by a gust of wind just minutes into its maiden voyage from the shipyard. It didn't even die with the dignity of a cannonball explosion; I had never felt embarrassment for an inanimate object until that moment. Because the ship had settled deep into the mud at the bottom of the brackish river, the original wood was extraordinarily preserved, which resulted in the ability to raise the entire ship, intact, in the 1960s. They housed this old embarrassment to the fleet in a modern museum, along with many of the objects they had found inside it, including a handful of skeletons of shipmen that did not make it out alive.

Saga and I silently stared at these skeletons in their transparent coffins. I noticed different jaw lines, foreheads, and bone structure. I studied the unique eye sockets, rib cages, and hand bones. After reading the short descriptions above the display cases (caskets), in which they provided the skeletons arbitrary names as if they were pets, they pointed out flaws in the bones that suggested earlier trauma or birth defects. Judging simply by the skeletons, they even ventured a guess as to their occupations and backgrounds. These skeletons told stories and were decidedly *human.* Their perpetually open mouths almost appeared as if they had something more to say. I tried to think about the day that old "Filip" excitedly told his old ass wife Inga that he was off to man the maiden voyage of this beautiful ship. And how just hours later, a simple gust of wind flooded the interior and drowned him nearly instantly. That was it. That was his life. No more old ass Inga. No more children. No more dinners of boiled horse. Gone.

We looked through the old cannon holes and climbed to the highest story of the museum to peer at the top deck of the ship. Saga leaned her forearms against the rail and silently watched people as they took photographs of the ship below her. I noticed her expression that I first assumed was indifference or momentary apathy, but it appeared to have a touch of melancholy with each passing millisecond. I tried to track the path of her stare and figured the only thing she could be looking at was either a left behind sweater that lay harmlessly on the floor or a young couple, arm in arm, reading some information on the wall. She suddenly looked different. Perhaps paler, I wasn't sure, but something was just slightly obscure. I wondered if she knew the couple reading the wall and wanted to avoid them. I wondered if she saw us in that couple, though they really appeared to look nothing like us. Or maybe she was slightly chilly and just yearned for the forgotten sweater. I didn't rule out the possibility that her eyes might have just turned vacant for a moment, that unexplainable lapse in consciousness where a person simply just stares. Either way, if she had any idea that I'd been studying her, she did not let on, but I felt like something serious had just crossed her mind. It was a Saga I had seen in brief moments but hadn't understood. I wanted to, but perhaps I was afraid of what I might have found.

We found a bench, sat for what felt like an eternity, and were soon joined by a tired mother and her young son, who was probably around six. She sat with an exhausted sigh while her son, still full of energy, stood in front of the bench, tucked his thumbs in the belt loops of his jeans that were too short for his legs, and danced around, stiff legged, as if he was a short Frankenstein, to a song that he softly mumbled to himself.

"Alec, please stop," the mother said in an exhausted British accent. "Just sit down." It was easy to tell that she was wiped out from chasing her son all morning.

But Alec ignored her and carried on. My attention was quickly diverted from the ship to this little, strange kid, absent of embarrassment, spinning in circles. I tried to remember if I ever did such things when I was his age and quickly recalled an incident when I stood up in front of a movie theater, halfway through some typical '80s film my parents dragged me to, and started dancing a few feet from the front row simply because I was happy. Earlier in the day, my parents had bribed me with a He-Man toy and I could not wait to get home and play with it. Perhaps Alec just had A.D.D. and was in desperate need of Ritalin; maybe he was just bored and wanted to entertain himself; or maybe, he, like me as a child, was just in a good mood and felt like dancing.

I wondered at what age this ended. At what point did I have enough understanding of the world where jaded energy dominated my condition? At what point did I find it silly to dance when I was happy?

Alec noticed my staring and, instead of accusing me of being a pedophile, simply stuck his tongue out in jest, smiled, and resumed his awkward motion while his tired mother watched, as if she was moments away from slipping him some Vicodin, slapping him upside the head, or falling asleep.

Saga inched closer to me, placed her arm through mine while grabbing my hand, and rested her light bulb blond head on my shoulder. I felt the entire side of her warm body pressed up against mine. I could feel her breathing. And in this moment, all I wanted to do was tell Alec that I understood exactly how he felt.

See Ya

When I was fourteen years old, I took my first solo vacation. And I did it completely, till this day, unbeknownst to my parents, well, to the best of my knowledge. That summer, my parents decided to take a two-week vacation to Europe and, because I had exhibited enough maturity (or fooled them), they left me behind with a fourteen-day supply of Stouffer's French bread pizzas, six hundred dollars, and my own devices.

I was not exactly the most popular freshman in high school (maybe I would have been if I actually had my roaming baby polar bear) and, due to this fact, my name was never written on the inside of a heart drawn on a girl's notebook or whispered in the depths of the girls' locker room. So, like any normal ninth grader with thick glasses and cystic pimples, I resorted to delusion. It was around then that I developed an unhealthy celebrity crush on *Baywatch* star, Nicole Eggert. For those who do not remember, Nicole was the "other hot girl" during the Pam Anderson years, which made her seem more attainable to a thirteen-year-old with silver braces that yearned to fix an overbite only a walrus would have been proud of. Nicole represented everything I wanted at the time: a beautiful face, big tits, a beautiful face, and big tits.

Throughout the spring, watching episodes of *Baywatch* were handled as if I were attending church. I would stash recorded episodes of the show deep in my desk drawers as if they were pornography contraband. I'd even sit on the deck during quiet, cool nights like I was fucking Fivel, staring at the sky and wondering if Nicole was looking at the exact same stars. I kept my crush on Nicole secret from everyone, but the minute I discovered my parents were traveling without me, I circled the date as the one where I would finally take action. I would meet Nicole, fall in love, and marry her. Simple.

Three days before they left, I secured a roundtrip ticket on Amtrak for Los Angeles. The trip would take five days each way, which left me only a couple of days to find Nicole in the city of Angels. But since I believed in silly things like fate at that point in my life, I figured she'd feel my presence and make herself available. After all, I did try to communicate my travel plans to her telepathically while lying on my Superman sheets in bed. She had to have heard.

Without much of a plan, I embarked on the journey while I thought of all the amazing possibilities in store for me. At no point did I consider what I'd say to her. I figured the language of love was universal.

After I arrived in Los Angeles, I sat on a Beverly Hills bench for two hours, my head on a swivel, but I did not see Nicole. After I finally walked away from the bench, I was hit with a sudden sense of accomplishment. I had made the effort. There I was in LA, taking a chance. And for some reason, that had become enough. Perhaps I realized the absurdity of my actions in that moment, but I recalled just being happy to have shown up. I spent the next two days checking out the sights and staring at palm trees. I looked around for Nicole, but never more than a cursory glance at a blond head. For a long time, I held this trip high on the pedestal of daring moments in my life. But a few years ago, I fully realized that I had really just pussied out and didn't even come close to following through with my original intentions. Maybe this sounded retarded, but even though there was zero chance of it working out, I, at least, could have tried.

Saga accompanied me to the ticketing area of Stockholm-Arlanda airport. We did not say much to each other, beyond her asking for the time and gum, and me verbally wondering about my father. It was just chatter to avoid the awkwardness of the situation. I wasn't sure if my father would even be on the plane; perhaps he just left Sweden after the dinner. It seemed completely plausible.

As we reached the security area, it hit us both that our moment was officially coming to an end. She walked me to the back of the line. I really had no clue what to say to her, but she did.

"How do I know that when we both look at the sky, we see the same shade of blue?" she asked.

"Excuse me?"

"Like how can anyone be sure that everyone sees color the same way. It's impossible to describe. We would have no way of knowing if each human on Earth saw color a little differently. Sure we all see blue, but how do I know if we look at the sky, it's the same shade of blue?"

She searched my eyes for an answer. I did not blink.

"I guess it's just blind trust."

Saga nodded and looked to her toes.

"Do you believe in that?" she asked.

"I hope so."

It was so cheesy, but My Lord, I fucking loved it.

She looked at me again, but this time it appeared she tried to stare through me. Like if she concentrated hard enough, she would see some sort of truth.. She opened her mouth slightly, as if to say something, something that she'd been waiting to say, but just as quickly as her lips parted, they closed, and whatever moment she might have been hoping for had clearly passed.

Up until this point, we had not exchanged phone numbers, email addresses, or anything of the sort. I didn't even have a picture of her. In fact, I didn't even know her last name though I assumed my father did, if he was still alive. But I was certain, in my heart of hearts that asking for this information would be the biggest mistake of my life. I had a life. I had a fiancée. Fuck, I was to be married really soon. And this, this just was what it was, a great vacation story and last hurrah before marriage. Saga grabbed my hands and planted one last soft kiss on my lips. And, without words, we parted.

I turned toward the security line and felt a deep rush of sadness and emptiness. I had not expected that at all, it was like being punched in the gut by Mike Tyson (or Helga's tits) forty straight times. I didn't want to leave, I had to, but I needed to see her one last time. I turned around and noticed Saga still hadn't moved. And that's when I saw a tear streaming from her beautiful blue eye down her soft cheek. Saga had been many things over the past couple of days, but I never saw her as tender. And I didn't know if it was true, but in that moment, I felt like I was breaking her heart. I couldn't do that. I knew this was not the end. But what could I do? And then it just came out:

"Saga..."

Her eyes flashed to me, expressionless.

"...Marry me."

What the fuck did I say?

She gently smiled and nodded, as I released a high-pitched sound best described as a nervous giggle. Almost paralyzed, my body eased into cruise control and turned back to security. I did not bother looking back again. I placed my bag on the conveyor, took off my shoes, quickly passed through the metal detector, and walked briskly to my gate as if I was covertly trying to avoid something following me. I wouldn't turn around, even though I knew she was long out of sight.

Oh fuck. What the fuck.

Once at the gate, I sat by the window, ran my hands over my face, and stared at the open landscape beyond the empty runways as if answers grew alongside the long grass dancing lightly in the breeze.

I wondered what she tried to say to me.

Flight 2

I walked down the aisle of the plane and noticed the faces of the passengers blended in color much like a Monet. My spinning subconscious reacted to the stupidity of my clearer self, as I now was the possessor of some potential soap-opera-like drama. I located my seat and plopped down like a bag of garbage, completely unaware that my father was seated right next to me.

"You made it," he deadpanned as he peeled yet another orange.

His voice startled me. All morning I had wondered if he'd be on the plane, but after my proposal, I completely forgot about him. I shook some sense into myself.

"What happened to you?" I said in a tone that suggested curiosity rather than concern. I tried to act natural.

"I had to take care of some business. I figured you wouldn't be bored."

"I wasn't."

"What did you do?"

"Nothing."

"Nothing?"

"Yes. Nothing," I repeated.

"That sounds boring."

"It wasn't."

"You did nothing, but you weren't bored?" he asked suspiciously.

"No."

"I saw you left the dinner early," my father said with a sly smile.

"Yeah, I was bored."

I turned away from him and hoped he would stop prying. He shifted in his seat, a physical signal that meant he was about to completely change the subject.

"I want to show you something," my father said, while he leaned down toward his carry-on. He shuffled through a few papers until he pulled out a manila folder and threw it in my lap.

"What's this?"

"This is what I was doing."

I opened up the manila folder and found what appeared to be blood test results. I picked up the first sheet but, since I lacked a medical degree and had never read a Wikipedia page on blood, I had zero clue of what I was staring at.

"I thought you said you weren't dying."

"I'm not, you little shitfucker. Those tests are immaculate. Check it out."

My father pointed out a few other results on the page for his heart, his lungs, muscles, joints, brain—pretty much every body part other than his spleen and anus.

"Look at that urine. Have you ever seen such beautiful piss? One hundred percent normal," he continued.

I was confused.

"So...you thought you were dying?"

"No, I never thought I was dying. What the fuck is wrong with you?" my father said impatiently.

He quickly grabbed the medical test results, which revealed another set of papers underneath. These included a photocopied check for twenty-five million dollars to some agency that had a strange Russian name. I picked up the sheet and furrowed my brow, inspecting all the zeros. My father tapped the piece of paper proudly with his finger.

"It's all gone now."

"What is?"

"My money," he said with a nod and a smile.

How the heck did someone spend over one hundred, thirty million dollars in four short years? And why was he paying anyone twenty-five million dollars?

"You fuck with the wrong Russian mobster or something?"

My father sat back in his chair and interlocked his fingers just over a neon yellow palm tree print that covered his fat belly.

"Do you have any clue what it's like feeding a lion in its natural habitat? Or standing next to a frozen river in Siberia? How about walking through the streets of Baghdad only to have a pipe bomb explode just one hundred yards away from you?"

"No, no I don't," I responded, while I turned away to look at anything else, the universal sign of not being interested. I really just wanted him to shut up so I could concentrate on my own issues.

"Did you know I helped deliver kangaroos in the Australian outback? Seriously, can you picture your old man doin' something like that? I was ass deep in kanga-placenta, but I tell you, it was just as exciting as the fucking day your ass was born."

Nice, your only child...a kangaroo...makes sense.

"Is the plural of kangaroo, kangaroos or is it just kangaroo?" I asked.

My father looked annoyed and moved on.

"What I'm trying to say was that winning the lottery has allowed me to do everything I've ever wanted to. And every moment has just challenged me more. I mean, the things I've seen and had the chance to experience. It's been the best four years of my life."

"That's really nice," I said sarcastically.

"But there's one place I haven't been," he said. "And the guy we had dinner with was the guy that'll help me get there."

This factoid actually did snag my interest. I did not really engage Saga about her father, since it seemed like a sore subject, but I sincerely doubted she would have provided me much information anyway. Suddenly, I felt like my father was the key to a safe that held unknown contents. Simultaneously, I figured out exactly where he was going. Things started to make sense.

"So, you're going into space," I said, unimpressed.

"Yeah! How did you know?"

"My years at NASA tipped me off."

A few years ago, Clarissa told me some wretchedly boring story about working on Lance Bass's publicity team when he attempted to join a Russian space mission. My father's doctor results, the cost, and his self-indulgent story about his trip around the world sealed my guess.

"I needed to pretend someone in my family worked for the space program. You know, to make it look genuine."

That made no sense.

"I leave for training outside of Moscow in a couple of weeks. Go up to the final frontier soon after," he continued.

"So you're gonna miss the wedding?"

"I wasn't invited to that shit show," he responded quickly. "Not that I'd go anyway."

"And miss the opportunity to have your date flash all the guests?"

"That would probably be the only entertaining thing about the evening," he stated.

I couldn't be mean to him because there was still some information I needed.

"So...who was that guy anyway? Gustav."

"Now, you're suddenly curious?"

"Where the fuck have you been? I've been curious the entire time."

My father absent-mindedly grabbed a *SkyMall* magazine and flipped through it.

"Some kind of Ambassador."

Saga was the daughter of an ambassador. How distinguished. I guessed that made sense. It was probably why I wasn't arrested for Segway murder in the first degree.

"Are you sure that's what he is?" I asked.

"No. What is this, the Spanish inquisitive?"

"*Inquisition.*"

My father brushed away the correction.

"Oh, check it out, I can buy sheepskin slippers," my father said, while pointing in the *SkyMall* magazine. "Ever walk with those? Like fuckin' pillows for the feet. Like walking on a fucking cloud."

I sighed. I'd had enough.

"Whatever, just go to space and shut up."

All I wanted was quiet. If my father wanted to go up to space for his last great adventure, I really did not care. He could even do it solely in those sheepskin slippers.

But he wasn't done.

"I know, for some reason, you don't approve of my life-style. But I hope one day you will get the opportunity to understand," my father said casually, as if his lifestyle was completely normal and I was the crazy one.

I thought about the night he presented the check to my mother and ignored him. I'd tried in vain to contact her since, called cousins I barely knew, aunts and uncles I'd only seen once, but to no avail. My mother always dreamed of vacationing in New Zealand; I wondered if she found some strapping young man to feed her strawberries while she lounged on the beach. Then I realized that I was thinking of my mother and that image was a little gross. Either way, I hoped, wherever she was, she had found some old Jewish women to gossip with.

I looked at my father with renewed disgust as he leaned his fleshy body closer to me.

"I let your mother walk out of that room with the only dignity she had left," he continued.

I looked at him, appalled.

"Really," I said, disgusted.

"Absolutely," he said with no irony.

"You know what, I've got a ton on my mind, so just shut the fuck up. But after we get off the plane, never talk to me again. You're an asshole."

My father threw his hands in the air to signify he gave up. He pulled his sleeping mask over his eyes and, within minutes, his Ambien took control and he was snoring.

The plane engines whirred to life and the house lights grew dim. I requested a sleeping mask that I pulled over my tired eyes with little intention of taking it off for the duration of the long flight. I had fifteen hours to figure out exactly what to say to Clarissa. There were tons of emotions that should have been running through my mind, but the overwhelming two featured one I had expected and one I had not. The mixture of nerves and fear was the expected one. But the other one came as a bit of a surprise: extreme happiness. I couldn't get the events of the past few days out of my head and replayed them with frequency, as if it had become my favorite movie on cable. The whole situation was unrealistic, and since I had none of Saga's contact information, it was probably gone forever. An amazing story that couldn't be told. But as I touched the cut on my hairline to recall a memory, I realized both the physical and metaphorical wounds had not yet closed.

The one positive about a long flight was that time virtually stood still for the passenger. No one could contact you; there was nowhere to go. It was as if you ceased to exist while suspended in the air. All I had were my thoughts and, unfortunately, I had enough of them to last much longer than fifteen hours.

Well, my thoughts and my father's snoring.

I couldn't imagine a flight worse than this.

What I'd Do Upon Returning Home on a Friday in 1986

Fuck. Life was hard.

Racing up the front porch of my parents' house on a Friday afternoon, flanked by my best friend Clinton, was about as exciting as it got for a seven-year-old on the cusp of a weekend. All of the problems and concerns of the previous week slowly dissipated in the fizz of a Pepsi-Cola and completely vanished in between chews of a Famous Amos cookie, even though my mother only allowed me one per day, which was absolute bullshit. After all, I was an active, growing boy with a fast metabolism; I could have handled at least three cookies per day. But though my mother was lenient with some questionable foods (she sometimes fed me McDonalds when she was too lazy to cook, which was, well, always), when it came to cookies, she was a chocolate-chip-hoarding Nazi. I wasn't trying to be defiant; I wasn't on some secret mission to get fat and unhealthy; I was just hungry for fucking cookies. Complete bullshit.

The previous week of schoolwork prepared by Mrs. Nelson, my aforementioned second grade teacher with thick silver braces that we swore could transmit radio signals, had been unbearable. A spelling quiz with words like "then," "than," and even "through," a math test that covered addition with triple digit numbers, *and* a social studies homework assignment on the Iroquois tribe all in the same five-day period. In addition, Little League tryouts were the following week and hours were needed at the batting cage to prepare. Not to mention, I was pissed off that they moved the Transformers cartoon from 7:30 a.m. to 8:30 a.m. and replaced it with some crap called "Beverly Hills Teens," which had to have been intended for girls or perhaps guys who hadn't yet realized that they'd one day fuck other men. What the hell was I supposed to watch in the morning before school? The news? Please.

And just when I thought the week couldn't have been worse, there was an actual dentist appointment in which they found no cavities, but performed their fair share of plaque scraping. It hurt to eat the dinner my mother had prepared that night due to my sore gums. And she didn't even make something I enjoyed; it was this gross chicken that was actually half cold. After all the pressure I had experienced during the week, you know what would have been a more satisfying meal choice? Fuckin' cookies. Three of them.

But, at least, I had Friday afternoon. The entire weekend was ahead and the possibilities were endless. And on this particular Friday at four, Clinton and I stood in front of the mountain of Nintendo games and, though our earlier problems seemed like a distant memory, we were faced with more immediate concerns. At the time, at that moment, it was easily the biggest problem in our lives:

Which game to play first!

If we played Super Mario Brothers first, we might not have time to get to level seven before my father came home and took us out for dinner and ice cream. If we played 10-Yard-Fight first, we would probably have time for a couple of games before Dad's arrival, but in the event that we split those contests, there wouldn't be enough time for a rubber match. Man, the decisions. I had no clue how we ever figured out such predicaments on a weekly basis.

"I have an idea. Why don't we play Excitebike now!" Clinton excitedly exclaimed while he grabbed the cartridge and blew on it to ensure that it would load correctly. "We could probably finish a bunch of tracks before dinner."

"That's right," I said. "Then, after dinner, we could play Mario, Ten-Yard-Fight, *and* even R.C. Pro Am. You know why?" I asked with a smile.

"ALL NIGHT PARTY, YEAH!" Clinton and I said, simultaneously, as we exchanged a zealous high-five.

Smiles abound, tragedy averted.

What I'd Do
Upon Returning
Home on a
Friday In 1996

Fuck. Life was hard.

Pulling into the driveway of my parents' house on a Friday afternoon, with Clinton in the passenger seat, was about as exciting as it got for a seventeen-year-old on the cusp of a weekend. All of the problems and concerns of the previous week dissipated in the promise of a kegger and vanished in the hope that maybe, just maybe, Christina Hawkins might get drunk enough to, once again, show her beautiful D-cups to a cheering crowd. Though last time she wouldn't let me touch them, which was absolute bullshit. After all, I was an active, growing boy and completely worked on my body to conquer my awkward stages. But though Christina let some of the boys fondle her perky round cantaloupes, when it came to me, she crossed her arms and guarded them like I'd planned to tear those sweet treats from her body and pawn them. I wasn't going to be rough, I wasn't planning on pounding them like a speed bag. Fuck, I had muscles and a lot of hair on my dick, which was getting pretty big by the way, and I bet it was twice the size of Andrew Martinez's, who felt them for like five straight minutes. I didn't want to hog them, I didn't want to place my face between them while I screamed "BRITZKE," I just wanted to squeeze some fucking tits. Complete bullshit.

The previous week of homework combined with baseball practice had been unbearable. An English essay on Shakespeare (who the fuck liked that shit anyway?), a geometry test (on *proofs* no less), a history paper on Communism (fuck them), and a long science lab where I dissected an earthworm all in the same week. (What's exciting about the insides of an earthworm? Fucking nothing, that's what.) On top of that, our new baseball coach watched some masochistic coaching video on baseball calisthenics and had us running extra wind sprints all week. I swore that conditioning made me so tired that I'd even fall asleep before I completed jerking off. A rarity. And just when I thought the week couldn't have been worse, I had to get a cavity filled. My first one! I couldn't think of a worse pain than the Novocain needle piercing my sensitive flesh, followed by the awful sound of a drill burrowing into my sugar-beaten tooth (probably from all those cookies I had been eating).

Clinton and I made a couple of phone calls on that Friday afternoon, received the relevant information, and though earlier problems were a distant memory, we were faced with more immediate concerns. It was the biggest problem in our lives:

Which party to go to first!

If we started at Neil Freidman's party, it probably would have been pointless since the hot girls wouldn't arrive till later, and we'd be forced to talk to a bunch of dudes about such exciting subjects as how much school sucked and how it felt to get your first blow job (though half of them probably performed it on themselves). But if we went to Marie Pollack's (a solid B-minus, would be a B+ if not for her hook nose and nasal voice) party first, we might get too drunk and then have to skip Neil's party altogether, missing out on the hot girls. After all, it was Neil's last party where Christina popped her top and also where Jennifer Malton passed out drunk with a twenty-dollar bill sticking out of her spread eagle hooha for the world to see; apparently, some dude from another high school had fucked her and that's how he returned the favor. Not to mention, Neil's neighbor, Jamie Greenfield, had a thing for me and always leaned in real close when she talked to me so I could feel her tits press against my chest. I fuckin' loved that, instant boner, and always tried to find ways to talk to her while pressing my hard-on against her leg. We hadn't hooked up, but I knew it was only a matter of time.

"I have an idea," Clinton said. "What if we go to Marie's first, force ourselves only to have *one* drink and maybe suggest we all go in the hot tub to see Marie and Callie Philborn (also a solid B-, would be a B+ if not for her slightly acne-scarred right cheek that looked like a topographical map of northern Nepal) in their bikinis, and then head to Neil's at around 11 p.m., which is when Christina and her crew normally show up?"

"That's right," I said. "Then we could have the best of both worlds and I bet Jamie Greenfield will be drunk by the time we get there, so my chances of finally seein' those beautiful titties will be twice as good. You know why?" I asked with a smile.

"ALL NIGHT PARTY, YEAH!" Clinton and I said, simultaneously, as we executed an ever-so-trendy fist bump.

Smiles abound, tragedy averted.

PART THREE

What I Did Upon Returning Home on a Friday in 2010

Fuck. I made life hard.

I tiredly shuffled into the elevator of my apartment building, dragging my light travel bag behind me, as I pressed the button for the fourth floor. The fifteen-hour flights, the sleepless nights, the days with Saga, the arguments with my father, sketchy Swedish food, and the diarrhea caused by said food had all caught up with me in a perfect storm of exhaustion. A pudgy mother and her small child with a pronounced cowlick, who I probably should have recognized but just didn't give a shit, stood alongside me on the slow ride up the building. The little boy stared at me with the subtlety that only small children have.

"Mommy, he poopie," the child said, while he reached to tug on his mother's jeans, but only came up with air.

Hey kid, get fucked. You don't look so great yourself; try hair gel, plus I got laid yesterday. What did you do? Watch cartoons? Eat a pop tart? That's what I thought (though a pop tart did sound good.) *So, you know what, maybe you're poopie.* His mother quickly apologized, while rubbing her son's head like he was a bad dog, but honestly I was too tired to care.

During the entire flight, the flight in which I was supposed to figure out what to say to Clarissa, all I had come up with were a few more top ten lists (always fun), random fantasies about what else Saga and I could have done in that fountain (even more fun), and what tattoo I would pick if I ever decided to get one (couldn't come up with shit). I also caught a crappy movie starring Katharine Heigl in which she fell in love, then out of love, only to fall in love again with a man she never expected. (Not specific enough? Exactly.) I spent the remainder of the flight fidgeting while I looked forward to taking pisses because that, at least, was something distracting. In short, I still had no clue what I would tell my fiancée (my original one), the one I left against her blessing. The one who probably texted me another hundred times the past thirty hours, even though I couldn't check them because my phone broke while I was having sex with another woman in the center of the Swedish capital. I wasn't sure how I would explain all that to her, though I figured the fountain fornication was better left a secret.

As the elevator doors opened, I stopped and watched myself in the hallway mirror for a good thirty seconds. I looked ass tired; my eyes were sunken like forgotten treasures, and my posture resembled one of an old, dying gorilla. But the way I appeared didn't just look sad; it felt weird. I searched my face for signs of Saga, as if reading my expressions somehow told the story of the last three days. At this juncture, I realized my main concern was not figuring out the rest of my life, it was actually just not getting caught. I just wanted to go to sleep and dwell on it tomorrow with a clearer head.

And while I looked at my ghoulish self, a strange feeling overcame me. Yes, I knew I had to tell Clarissa something; sure, it probably would be difficult, but I actually thought everything would be OK. I felt invincible. Perhaps the fountain water was a baptism, but one enhanced by fucking. What if Jesus had fucked in the holy water instead of just being baptized in it? When Achilles was a child, what if he had fucked in the magical river Styx instead of simply being bathed in it? My guess is that Jesus would probably have stoned the masses and Achilles would laugh off a harmless arrow to the heel. All I needed was a story to tell Clarissa, and really, how hard could it be? After all, in this case, truth was stranger than fiction.

I tried to formulate a quick tale full of intrigue, pain, and self-indulgence. I would tell Clarissa a half-truth while I explained the reason that surrounded the dinner with my father, and then maybe embark on an epic diatribe regarding my Dad's selfishness and how all I wanted to do was return home and see my blushing bride. I'd rewrite history and tell her I actually had gotten through to the elusive Delta representative while standing outside the restaurant, only for them to inform me there were no earlier flights available. I'd explain how I ranted and raved, a tantrum a six-year-old could have been proud of, but how they then threatened to take away my original flight if I didn't calm down (like a phone terrorist!). I wished I could force tears out of thin air, like if I could only conjure the memory of my dog dying when I was three (if I had a dog when I was three). I'd look like such a fucking mess, my sunken eyes, my tear-streaked cheeks, she would be forced to forget her anger, wrap her bony arms around me, and forgive me on the spot. I would proclaim that I would never, ever, ever want to discuss the trip ever again. If she ever brought it up in the future, I planned to simply shake my head and stare at the ground, as if I was thinking about my time spent in the hot zones of Vietnam. Fuck, if I'd only bought a gift for her. That would have sealed it. Maybe I should have made a quick trip to Rite Aid to buy some Swedish Fish and tell her I caught them with my own two hands while I was there. *Ah, fuck it.*

As the apartment door appeared in my line of sight, I thought about another option that suddenly seemed feasible: The truth. I wondered how Clarissa would react if I sat her down on the couch, grabbed her hand, and told her I had a torrid love affair with another woman. I wondered how her face would contort if I explained how another girl kissed me, how her body felt against mine, and, most of all, how much I loved it. I wondered how many tears she might cry if I told her about holding hands (something Clarissa and I never did) and how we shared dessert while overlooking the city (but I'd assure her it wasn't a chocolate soufflé). I would tell her that it was unexpected, but that it questioned my love for her and made the entire three-year relationship seem like a waste of time. Did I actually believe that? I wasn't sure. But it felt closer to the truth than option A.

I also considered the consequences of option B. All night crying. Days of fighting. Hours of Clarissa and I attempting to work things out, even though I'd have no interest in such a conclusion (I could be such a pussy). Then, there was the fact that one of us, if not both of us, would move out, and the subsequent custody battle over the Ikea coffee table and Bed, Bath, and Beyond comforter. I could picture her parents visiting the apartment and eyeing me like I was a dog and they were hungry for dinner. I could actually see steam rise from her father's head like a ready teakettle, and it scared me to hell even though it was just a thought. I had once asked Clarissa, in jest, if her father had ever killed anyone, expecting her to laugh and smack me playfully on the shoulder. But instead, she shrugged and claimed it was actually the one question she would never ask him because she feared the possibility. Suddenly, the truth, or what I thought might be the truth, didn't seem like such a hot option either. Too much hassle. Plus, that would really ruin the goal of sliding into bed and sleeping straight through till morning.

But as I reached the door, I knew I would have to say something other than "Hi," "What's up?" or "Do we have any pop tarts?" Unfortunately, this time, Clinton was not there to give me advice that would have suggested I spend half my time in the US married to Clarissa and half my time in Sweden married to Saga, followed by a fist pump and the declaration of an all-night party. Problems really were simpler then. I would have paid twenty-five million dollars to be back there for only fifteen minutes, fully unaware of the stupidity and retardation of future Brandon. I was reminded of the question Saga asked me regarding the advice I'd give my younger self. The answer seemed so obvious.

I was so fucking tired.

I breathed deep, turned the knob, heard the locks tumble, and opened the door.

And This Is What I Said

Ever open your own front door like someone who expected a surprise party, even though the only surprise that could have been possible was one that involved violence? Not a fun thought. But that was my fear as I trudged beyond the threshold and immediately made eye contact with Clarissa, who sat in front of a dark TV with puffy eyes and random tissues strewn across the aforementioned Ikea coffee table. She had a glint of hope in her gaze, like I was just about to open one of the numbered briefcases on *Deal Or No Deal*. She didn't move, clearly waiting for me to say something. Anything.

I dropped my bag to the floor and sat on the love seat adjacent to the couch. She gradually turned her body toward me and straightened herself, as if to look presentable for some speech I was not prepared to give. I placed my elbows on my knees and clasped my hands together, cracking my knuckles to either relieve stress or stall time; I wasn't sure which. Probably both.

Methodically rocking back and forth, I felt the lump in my throat grow with each passing second. I quickly considered both options I had conjured in the hallway and, as I closed my eyes for the briefest moment to concentrate, I actually decided which of the two options I would choose.

So, I looked back toward Clarissa and slapped both my knees in an effort to psyche myself up for the forthcoming conversation. But as soon as I opened my mouth to speak, I noticed her doe-eyed stare that always disarmed me. And, suddenly, I felt guilty. Confused. Worst of all, I had completely forgotten what I'd planned to tell her.

So, instead, I did the next best thing.

I rose to my feet, took two confident steps toward her, leaned in, and kissed her more deeply and passionately than I ever had before. She quickly wrapped her arms around my neck and met my kiss with the same urgency. I bent my knees, lifted her from the ground like a groom would his bride, and carried her to the bedroom, lips locked during the entire journey.

I placed Clarissa on the bed, tossed the excess laundry still on the sheets (she actually didn't yell at me for this, she normally would have), and climbed on top of her. I kissed down her neck and removed her clothes, while she did the same for me. I looked in her eyes; she was still crying, but I wasn't sure if it was from sadness or happiness. Either way, I leaned back down and melted into her. She wrapped her legs around my body as I slowly pushed in and out of her, rotating between kissing her shoulders, neck, and lips. She gasped with each pump, which caused me to move harder and faster with every motion. It was, by far, the best sex we'd ever had and was punctuated with me exploding my load deep in her for the first time in our sexual history. Not on her tits, not all over her ass, but deep in her body. Romantic shit. She moaned loudly as she felt my cum penetrate her. I fell on her, kissed her lips, and rolled to the side to catch my breath.

It was actually really amazing...even though it was arguably the greatest diversion of all time.

We relaxed, motionless. We still had not said a word to each other. Clarissa turned her head toward me and I could feel her gaze.

"I'm glad you're back," Clarissa said sincerely.

I gulped and nodded, as I anticipated a barrage of questions that would have been completely appropriate. But strangely enough, they never came. She placed her head on my chest, wrapped her arms around me, and nuzzled into my body. I felt her entire naked body against mine and remembered that I actually missed the feeling of her pencil-eraser nipples piercing the side of my chest. In a moment of nostalgia or perhaps comfort, I wrapped my arms around her like I used to and closed my eyes to fall asleep in an embrace. And like sun burning morning fog, the strangeness of my return slowly dissipated, quickly replaced with the mundaneness of my everyday, for better or for worse, until I reached my normal, yet dangerous state of indifference.

Clarissa raised her head slightly.

"We have to meet Mitzy next week to look at the venue," Clarissa said. "We got lucky; we can use the area Fergie and Josh Duhamel used for their wedding. There was a cancellation. Isn't that great?"

And that's how you completely ruin an even slightly decent moment.

She didn't care to hear my answer. I didn't really have one, anyway, especially one that didn't involve the word "fuck."

Clarissa placed her head back on my chest, as my eyes shot open like the metaphorical light forced its way from my brain out toward the atmosphere like a spotlight. I breathed heavier and watched Clarissa's head bob up and down with my accelerated gasping. I hoped it would make her nauseous.

I closed my eyes, as if it would transport me somewhere, anywhere else, but when I did, all I could see was Saga. Like her visage was tattooed on the back of my eyelids. I actually shook, which caused Clarissa to nuzzle deeper into me like an Eskimo coming to the aide of her cold spouse.

Invincibility? Totally gone.

I just prayed that I could fall asleep. And quickly. I hoped this feeling, like bad gas, would be gone by morning.

But I figured it might be here to stay.

He's Back

With sunglasses on and arms crossed, Bryan and I stood on Fairfax Avenue in the heart of Little Ethiopia, while we watched a cleaning crew remove yet another desecrated *Honey Buns* billboard. But this time, the perpetrator presented a more artistic and creative side. He had drawn a rather detailed, sizable penis (veins, ball hair, and all) pointed directly between Honey's firm buns, as if to simulate the painful sodomy we all might experience if we failed to remove it. The graffiti was actually kind of impressive, complete with shadowing underneath the shaft and just over the balls to provide the artwork some definition, though the small Ethiopian man who gesticulated wildly to the cops, waving yet another threatening note in his hand like it was a winning lottery ticket, probably didn't care too much about the artistic integrity of the vandalism.

"I wonder what's gonna happen when we put up the billboards for *Kiss My Lips, Sugar Hips*?" Bryan said with a serious tone that restrained an ironic smile.

I hummed in sarcastic agreement.

But as we recognized a dangerous trend was on our hands, I knew it was time to get down to serious business:

"So, how should we handle this?" Bryan asked.

"Well, you can start by giving me twenty bucks," I said.

"Fuck no," Bryan responded, just as I finished the sentence.

"Fuck yes. You bet twenty bucks a Jew did this, and there's no way a Jew did this. Think about it: We're in Little Ethiopia and, judging by that funny hat on the building owner's head, he's a Muslim. That's now two Muslims that have been threatened. They are sending a message to their own. And remember, this area is hardly, what did you call it? Jewishery? We've started a holy war, dude. They should put us in the fuckin' paper," I said confidently.

Bryan shook his head in a manner that suggested he, too, had taken the facts under consideration. He reached into his back pocket.

"My poor, poor ignorant friend. Let me teach you something about the world," Bryan said, as he unfolded a piece of paper.

"I introduce to you...the Ethiopian Jew," he continued, as he showed me a Wikipedia article. "Check it out. There are about one hundred, twenty thousand Jews in Ethiopia. One hundred, twenty thousand! Ain't that a bitch, eh?"

He pointed to the statistic on the printed sheet.

"Big deal. There's gotta be more Muslims there. How many Muslims live in Ethiopia?"

Bryan folded up the paper and placed it back in his pocket.

"I'm sorry, it appears I don't have that information," Bryan stated with a shit-eating grin.

"What, so you printed that shit out as soon as you heard about this?"

"I'm just here to provide facts," Bryan responded. "You'll see."

We really needed to take our jobs more seriously.

While the first *Honey Buns* incident on La Brea went virtually unnoticed, media attention surround the latest infraction after word of the second threat was released. A few photographers snapped pictures of the dismantled billboard while newspaper reporters asked each other the proper spelling of "testicle" and interviewed the baffled police, the apoplectic Ethiopian man, who seemed to get angrier as the seconds passed, and they even grabbed a quote from a young television marketing coordinator, otherwise known as yours truly. After all, I was partially responsible for this. Either way, since they were our billboards, and we had vested interest in the case, the cops let us beyond the yellow tape so Bryan and I had the opportunity to play CSI for, at least, one more day. Which, of course, made this whole thing worth it.

But as I gazed up at the cleaning crew while they power washed the graffiti foreskin from the billboard, I thought of the man who actually felt strongly enough to make these threats. What could possibly make him so angry? Seriously, what upset him so much that he'd be willing to risk his life or severe jail time in the fight against plump black ass cheeks? What would push someone so over the edge that he would threaten to bomb a building? Twice. I mean, with each passing day I became more of a misanthrope, but I wasn't about to bomb anything or run into a burning building. It was one of those things I figured I would never understand as long as I lived. The human mind visited dark places when it feared it could never overcome the repercussions of the everyday.

"What do you think Ethiopian donuts are like?" Bryan asked.

"I don't know, thin?" I responded. "Why?"

Bryan pointed in the direction of a donut store that claimed they had the "best Ethiopian donuts in town." He walked toward the shop and I quickly joined him, as I figured standing around while I pretended to do something constructive was harder to accomplish alone.

We entered the small shop that smelled like a healthy mixture of lamb and donuts and noticed the man behind the counter obsessively cleaning his cash register as if he was removing evidence. I scrunched my nose at the odd odor while Bryan dramatically tapped his lips with his pointer finger, as if he was pondering an important ordering decision, even though the menu only claimed to have two items: DONUT: $1.00 and COFFEE: $1.00.

"I think I'm gonna go with the donut and the coffee," Bryan said, as if he had just made an important and difficult executive decision. "Hey, I know you're supposed to make the call on this *Honey Buns* billboard bullshit, so if you don't mind, can you fuck this one up? I really need the promotion," he continued.

"Thanks for your support," I deadpanned.

"I'm serious, Dude. Do you know how much it costs to raise a kid?"

"I dunno, those commercials for the starving children say the same amount as a cup of coffee per day."

"Dude, this is Los Angeles."

"OK, maybe the same as a Venti Latte then?"

Bryan was not amused. I was.

"Isn't he using the potty now? At least you don't have to buy diapers anymore."

"Dude, I thought so too, until two days ago, when I found him sitting in an ocean of his own piss on the kitchen floor."

"I hear that's good for the skin."

"Is trying to make snow angels in your own urine good for the skin too?"

I considered.

"He's gonna watch the weird kind of porn when he grows up."

We got our donuts and coffee (after the agonizing decision) and found a small table in the corner of the shop that stood next to a plastic ficus plant that appeared to have been watered. I bit into the doughy brown treat.

"Ever taste a cigarette butt?" I asked. I continued eating it, anyway.

"So you never told me, Dude. How was your trip?"

I had been so preoccupied with how to explain my three-day getaway to Clarissa that I never considered what kind of story to tell someone like Bryan. I didn't know where to begin or how much to offer. The whole thing still felt surreal to me, especially as I sat in a strange donut shop in Los Angeles while, from the window, I watched a palm tree shed a dying frond that crashed on top of an old, rusted

Chevy and triggered its annoying alarm. This town could be so brutal.

My face gave something away.

"What?" Bryan asked.

"It was good," I said succinctly with a nod.

"That's it? Good? No crazy shit with your Pops?"

"Not really."

I took another bite of my donut, completely oblivious to the shitty taste, but glad it was there to distract me. Bryan sipped his coffee and seemed satisfied by my vague answer. But his lack of a follow-up question caused me to realize that I actually did want to discuss it.

"I got engaged, though," I said, as if I had just told him I had bought a new pair of basketball shoes.

"Yeah, no shit. You invited everyone you knew to that obnoxious engagement party at Koi, but were too cheap to pay for valet."

I rolled my eyes. He brought up that stupid party, which was not my idea, of course, every chance he could. He was right, though, it was obnoxious.

"No, *Dude*, I got *engaged*."

"*Dude*, I *know*," Bryan said to me, complete with that fake sign language used exclusively when implying someone had just asked you a retarded question.

"*Dude,* think about what I just said."

Perhaps it was the consistent emphasis on the "Dude," but Bryan finally stopped chewing and gave my comment some consideration. I could actually see the wheels spinning like rusted sprockets in his thick head. He looked away and then back at me, quickly, like he was trying to catch my expression performing a slight of hand.

"What the fuck are you saying, exactly?" he asked.

I sat back and shrugged like it wasn't a big deal.

"I went there because of some bullshit dinner with my Dad, and the dude we ate with, this enormous motherfucker who looked nothing like Alec Baldwin, had this daughter and well…"

As I heard myself say the words, the absurdity of the situation attacked my nerves like antibodies would a virus. *Shit.*

"And…you got engaged?" Bryan said with a small grin.

"Well, not that night…but yeah, a couple days later."

Bryan placed his hands behind his head, leaned back, and laughed like he had a royal flush and was calling my bluff.

"You motherfucker," Bryan said through his incredulous laugh.

"Why is this so funny to you?" I asked.

"Me? No reason," Bryan said through a louder laugh. "I'm just taking it in."

Of course he was.

"So, what's she look like?" Bryan asked.

"I just told you I got engaged to some girl I just met when I'm supposed to get married to Clarissa in a few weeks and all you care about is what she looks like?" I asked in disbelief.

"Is it not an important question?"

"Fine, she's the hottest girl you've ever seen."

"The hottest girl I've ever seen?" Bryan said, as if I had issued a challenge. "I doubt that," he said, complete with this new laugh that I didn't like.

"Yes, the hottest girl you've ever seen."

"C'mon, I've seen some hot girls. Show me a pic."

"Can't. The only picture I had of her was on my phone. And that broke in the city fountain we had sex in."

Bryan violently shook his head and then held it with both hands to keep it from spinning off. He gave himself a moment to think of the perfect question to ask.

"What?" Bryan asked with a smile as bright as Christmas morning.

I proceeded to tell Bryan the entire story. All of it. Every detail. Why not? Our walk, the boat, the air hockey, the Sumo suits, the dinner, the strip club, the fountain, the warship...everything. After I was done, the memories flooded so vividly that I desperately needed a drink of water.

Instead, I drank my coffee too fast and burned the top of my mouth. I could feel the little shards of dead, burned skin hanging like stalactites against the top of my tongue. I fiddled with them to induce pain.

Bryan stared at me with his jaw half open as he tried to process all of the information, like he was a one-man jury that had just heard a closing argument.

Once considered, he shook his head and wagged his finger.

"This is complete bullshit. No way," Bryan said, without a doubt in his mind, like the verdict was in.

"Dude…"

"Well, you're either making it up or this bitch is in it for money or something."

"Money? She's not a mail-order bride, Retard. Plus, she probably has more than I do."

"So this is for real?"

"Yes. Why would I lie?"

Bryan paused.

"And what about your Dad?"

"What about him?"

"She was at a dinner with him. You don't think she knows he's a millionaire?"

Fuck, I hadn't thought about that. I leaned back to consider his statement, as he seemed pleased to fill me with doubt. What if it was all fake? What if Saga was using me for something? But money? Her father was an ambassador. She probably had money. But then, again, she had a poor relationship with her father like I did mine. My father made it clear to me that I'd never see his money; maybe Saga's father made a similar shitty deal with her. Still, I didn't believe it. He hadn't play air hockey with her. He hadn't been in the sumo suit when she pounced on me. He hadn't kissed her like she kissed me. I tried to shake some sense back into my head.

"I'm just sayin'…I've been around the world, Dude, foreign women are ruthless," Bryan stated.

"Yes, foreign woman, very bad," the attendant behind the counter chimed in. Bryan pointed at him like he was a point guard that just dished out an assist in an NBA game.

"See!" Bryan said excitedly.

"Listen David Lee Roth. Wish all California girl," the man added while he pointed to his head.

I wasn't enjoying any of this, but considered the possibility again.

"I dunno. It was too good," I said, while I contemplated.

"Please, I know a thing or two about assholes and, you, my friend, are an asshole," Bryan said while he pointed and flipped another piece of donut into his mouth. "Let me ask you a question."

Bryan leaned in close. "When you fucked her in the fountain, did you use a rubber?"

"No…" I said uncomfortably.

Bryan laughed through his teeth to signify that I was an amateur.

"Dude, she just totally trapped you. I bet she shows up here in like three weeks all pregnant and shit and then, *then*, you'll be really fucked. Dude, you're getting married in a few weeks!"

"C'mon," I said nervously. I suddenly felt like I was the subject of an entire scam. I was embarrassed. I just wanted this conversation to end.

"Think about it," Bryan added. "You just told me she's the most beautiful girl you've ever seen. Why would the most beautiful girl you've ever seen agree to marry your sorry ass in three days? A connection? Go fuck yourself. That doesn't strike you as a little suspicious?"

Fuck, it does.

Bryan laughed again as I looked at him with contempt. He could be such a Blomax. I felt sick to my stomach, though I supposed that could have been from the donut. But the feeling came with a rush of helplessness, hurt, and confusion. I didn't know what to believe anymore. I felt my pits rush with sweat, another fine genetic gift from my father.

"What'cha tell Clarissa, or should I say the O.G. Fiancée?"

"I didn't."

"So what did you say when you got back?"

"Nothing. We had sex."

"With a condom?"

My look clearly gave my answer.

"Is she on the pill?"

"I don't know …"

Bryan shook his head again and stole part of my donut since he had finished his.

"Baby, you're fucked," he continued with a laugh. "Sooo fucked."

Bryan took one last sip of coffee. I ran my hands over my face and refused to look him in the eye.

"You crazy bastard, engaged," I heard him say through my muddled thoughts.

As I searched my mind for answers, an exit plan, anything, I suddenly, for the first time, felt happy that Saga technically had no way of contacting me, even if she had a knack for locating me. In fact, I kept expecting to get a phone call or text, though my new phone had been silent since I returned from Sweden. Maybe I would never hear from her again, and I hoped, right then, more than anything in the world, that I wouldn't. I felt ashamed, not because of what I had done, but because of the uncertainty around it. All of the sweet feelings I'd had from my time with her suddenly turned sour.

I lost the rest of my appetite, tossed the remainder of the donut at Bryan's mouth in the hope he might choke on it, and left without so much as an announcement.

Wedding Planning With the Changs

When I was five years old, I was terrified that one day I would have to drive a car. Seriously, I'd been in an automobile with both my mother and father countless times, had never been in an accident, but the idea of being trapped in a steel box that moved at high speeds, while surrounded by similar vehicles, scared the living shit out of me. I even had a recurring dream around then that featured me behind the wheel of a car that possessed a blaring stereo with bright, disorienting lights, like Kit from *Night Rider*. I was out of control on the dark highway, screaming at the top of my lungs, and knew that at any moment I would crash and my life would be over (there was no baby polar bear in danger this time though.) This was actually a real worry even though I wouldn't be eligible for a license for another eleven years. And it was this thought, this fear, which introduced me to the concept of marriage.

I'd witnessed my parents kiss and hug. I'd seen plenty of movies that involved couples falling in love. I'd even seen films that depicted people having sex and the sheer thrill the act brought upon the human mind and body (though I didn't discover what sex actually was until I went to Jew sleepaway camp in the fifth grade. Thank you "Fuck You, Asswhores Part 35" for teaching me all the basics...Yes, there were apparently thirty-four versions before it, though I can't imagine any were quite as magical as Number 35.) And while all the emotion and physicality sounded fine in theory, it still felt light years away. At that time, I was still entrenched in the "girls are gross" stage, although I did have fantasies of playing house underneath my babysitter's sweater. Regardless, this was still seven or eight years before I'd even discover the wonders of jerking off. But I did know one simple thing: I was never going to get behind the wheel of a car. And I knew another thing: I'd need a wife to drive me around.

This absurd memory ran through my head while I sat in the backseat of Clarissa's cramped Prius, as she drove her parents and me to our wedding site on a vineyard along the coast of Malibu. Apparently, there was a wedding of similar size in progress and Mitzy wanted us to get an idea of how our party would look on our blessed day.

Moments before we collected her parents, Clarissa informed me that she had told them about my "unexcused Swedish excursion" (her words, just imagine a disgusted tone), so I shouldn't be surprised if they were cold toward me. Great, what an exciting change of pace. I asked her how many times they mentioned Ronald Fong during that discussion, but she just hit me in the arm in a non-playful manner, which probably meant several.

Mrs. Chang sat in the front passenger seat, with her left hand enveloping the entire center console like an elephant stepping on a mouse, and Mr. Chang was next to me, though his eyes never left the headrest in front of him like he was counting the fibers in the upholstery. I kept my head firmly in my hand while I looked out the window and wondered how the hell I would get through this day and, also, if I would be home in time for *The Amazing Race* (I'd watched an episode; now I was hooked). Regardless, it appeared, at least in the current moment, that the wish I had made when I was five years old had come true. After all, Clarissa was chauffeuring me and any thoughts of actual love were completely absent.

I reached into my pocket to grab my phone.

"Are you expecting a call or something?" Clarissa asked, while she viewed me through the rearview mirror.

"Me? No."

"Then why do you keep looking at your phone?"

"I'm not."

"Yeah, you are."

Ugh. Shut up, please.

"How we doing on gas, Clarissa?"

"Don't start, Brandon."

Then don't bother me about my phone.

I actually hadn't even realized I'd looked at it so often. But each time my phone vibrated with an incoming call or text, I fished it out of my pocket quicker than Jesse James would his gun during a duel. And each time I expected to see a European number sending a text message that I'd be terrified to open, but was greeted with a mixture of relief and disappointment when it wasn't. In fact, the only person, aside from Clarissa, to text or call me was my father, but I ignored each and every one of his attempts.

I looked for a distraction, anything to take my mind off its current line of thought, and settled my eyes on Mr. Chang. Most of the ride had been silent, save for a brief conversation in Mandarin between Clarissa and her mother about God knows what.

"Have you ever tried sheepskin shoes?" I asked Mr. Chang with sincerity. "I hear they're great."

He slowly turned his head as his eyes grew to the size of saucers. I immediately wondered if the words "sheep" and "skin" meant something like "fuck" and "you" in Mandarin.

"You know, bec…because of your feet," I tried to explain. Clarissa said…you know …*SkyMall* magazine…"

A vein suddenly sprouted from his neck, and he appeared only a second away from releasing an animalistic battle cry that would succeed in exploding my head, causing my neck to spurt blood like a cherry water fountain. Perhaps it was bad luck to discuss the foot in China, or maybe he just really wished I would die so his daughter had the opportunity to have a happy life. I supposed I couldn't blame him. Maybe I should have worn blue.

I quickly rotated back toward the window and noticed Clarissa searching me through the mirror, again, like I was a child on the verge of hiding chewed gum under the seat. I would have given my right testicle for the car to careen off the road and settle into the bottom of the ocean.

And, to think, the day was only beginning.

The wedding reception for the Baxter and his bride Jennifer was actually much nicer than I had expected, even though I pondered whether or not Jennifer was marrying a dog (Baxter?), and after seeing her face, it seemed entirely plausible. Numerous round tables littered the lush green grass and sat beneath wires holding a number of multi-colored paper lamps. A large buffet sat opposite the stage where a band that actually didn't suck performed. All the guests could enjoy a nice view of the grape vines below and the ocean in the distance. Clarissa had been right; it was a beautiful place to have a wedding.

Which is probably why both Mitzy and Clarissa gasped as if the reception stood behind the white pearly gates of Heaven. They simultaneously held their left hands to their chest as if the aura of the party literally took their breath away. But no such luck. Mr. and Mrs. Chang surprised no one and held their usual scowl.

When planning the wedding, Clarissa insisted on this vineyard in Malibu and claimed it had been her dream spot since she was a small child, even though the vineyard had only been opened for seven years. When I brought this inconsistency to her attention, she asked where I'd prefer to get married in her snottiest tone. When I responded, "Disneyland," she laughed heartily and assumed I was joking. But I wasn't. Aside from Friday afternoon video games,

Disneyland was the bright memory of my childhood. I didn't care how lame it sounded. I thought marrying at the castle in the middle of the theme park would be cool. Clarissa reminded me that *celebrities* would be at our wedding, that we weren't children, that she still hated small children, and that she was an adult that never planned on setting foot in that "tourist trap" *again*. As long as we lived, Clarissa would never stop bitching about our one trip there. She could be such a cunt sometimes.

As if I didn't exist, Mitzy took Clarissa by the arm to show her the various aspects of the wedding that would be similar to ours, as I silently wondered if maybe those two should get married. Mitzy might not have been the most horrid person I'd ever met, but she was up there. She had an exaggerated Queens accent, even though she had grown up in the suburbs of Detroit, but the oddest thing about her, without question, was her solitary yellow front tooth. It was as if she had smoked cigarettes for forty years, solely out of that tooth and, due to this, I never heard anything she said to me because all my concentration would focus on the history of that tooth. It looked like she had spent several hundred dollars on Botox, and I wondered why she hadn't thrown some money in for a tooth whitening. Maybe it was impossible to clean despite numerous attempts by the best and brightest, like it was the white whale of the dental industry (ironic). I knew she was divorced, and I constantly wondered if it was because her husband didn't want his tongue, or worse his dick, touching that mangled yellow mess. It was reasonable grounds.

As Clarissa and Mitzy disappeared, I noticed some tiki torches in the distance, and steered clear of Mr. Chang in case the reality of his perfect Chinese daughter marrying a poorer white dude suddenly struck him again. I figured no one would mind if I marched up to the bar for a free drink, so I did. I don't drink much, but well, yeah.

I stood on the outskirts of the tables and watched the bride and groom dance alone in the center of the parquet dance floor; I presumed this to be their first dance. But what struck me more than anything, more than the numerous eyes watching them, more than Clarissa and Mitzy across the way fawning over the china plates, was the song the lovely couple had chosen for their first dance: Stevie Wonder's "As." Sure, it was a love song, but the beat was way too quick for a slow dance, and I'm sure it was never meant to be a dance tune at all. But there Jennifer and Baxter (confirmed a human) were, foreheads touching, eyes locked, swaying to their own beat in the middle of the floor as if they were the only two people on the premises. They had no clue that two hundred sets of eyes were watching them; in fact, it might as well have been eighty thousand; they didn't care, just as long as they were together in that moment. That song, a great song that had no business being a wedding song, meant something to them. Maybe they had fucked for the first time to it, maybe their first date involved a joint karaoke attempt at it. Who knew, but it was theirs. Perhaps in twenty years they would hate each other and divorce, curse each other's names and tell their kids things like "your cum guzzler of a mother is a filthy whore," and "your father with a retarded name is a no good piece of shit who constantly tried to put it in my ass," but today at their wedding, they were in love. And that's all that mattered.

As I took another sip of my gin and tonic, which had *way* too much tonic and not nearly enough gin, I tried to picture myself with Clarissa on that dance floor. I, of course, had no say in our wedding song, and she decided on Bryan Adams's "Everything I Do (I Do It For You)," and no offense to Mr. Adams, a fine Canadian, but come the fuck on. First off, I hadn't even heard the song in ten years. Second, when I finally did hear it again, all I saw was Kevin Costner shooting fire-tipped arrows as the song was used in Robin Hood, and third, and this was a fact, Clarissa found it on some website that featured "the 100 best wedding songs of all-time." I knew this because it was the top song from a list bookmarked on her Internet browser (Thank God she didn't select number 2: "When A Man Loves A Woman," by Michael Bolton). Also, and this was the best part, she asked if Jared Leto could perform the tune because he was one of her clients and told her, and I quote, "I was born to sing that song." Fuckin' Prefontaine was going to sing Bryan Adams during our first dance and, somehow, I was supposed to take that seriously. I mean, really? Jared Leto? What, were Alvin and The Chipmunks not available? And who the fuck claimed to be born to sing that song? An asshole, that's who. I don't even think Bryan Adams would have claimed that. She said it would mean the world to Jared because he hadn't gotten any work lately and needed a "pick me up." Well buy him a fucking Red Bull because I failed to see why our wedding should have been a vehicle to boost the confidence of some has-been. To me, this whole thing sucked just as bad as the stupid wooden placard about love or whatever the fuck from Target.

And while I thought about the song, and watched Jennifer and Baxter dance, completely oblivious that others had joined them on the dance floor, I knew there was zero chance I would be able to duplicate their performance. No matter how doe-eyed Clarissa watched me, I just didn't feel that I could dance with her for four straight minutes and smile like I'd just lost my virginity...especially in front of Jared Leto. I'd notice all the people gawking, I'd feel embarrassed. Clarissa would constantly turn her head and do stupid shit like stick her tongue out for the camera as if that was both spontaneous and funny, even though it was neither. It was going to be a fucking disaster; maybe I could fake a knee injury the day before the wedding and get out of it. But then I pictured myself dancing with Saga, even though I felt ruined in regards to all things love. I don't know what song we would choose, but I didn't care. I *could* picture myself dancing with her, with all the eyes on me, and enjoying it all the way through, even if she had a baby bump. Fuck, I'd even do it naked in the freezing cold. Perhaps Bryan was right and she was a money-grubbing slut, but maybe she wasn't. Either way, I missed her.

Clarissa approached me with her arms wide open, twirling like she was Cinderella and had just been handed a kingdom (I don't care if I'm mixing fairy tales). Mitzy followed behind her, marking things on a notepad with one hand, and picking something out of her gross Frankentooth with the other.

"What do you think? Isn't this beautiful?" Clarissa asked, with a smile so bright it stood a shot at whitening Mitzy's tooth.

"This is just gorgeous, isn't it, Brandon? Oh, honey, you two are gonna be like Richard Gere and Julia Roberts up there," Mitzy added in her horribly fake accent. Mitzy's references were always dated; it's as if she was still stuck in the early 1990s. Regardless, I found it humorous that she compared us to *Pretty Woman* considering Richard Gere played a rich businessman and Julia Roberts a whore.

Clarissa placed her arm through mine and squeezed it.

"Can't you just picture it? It's even better than I thought it'd be. People are gonna be so jealous. It's gonna even be better than Josh and Fergie's."

I couldn't say anything. It just would have been too mean. Clarissa placed her mouth inches from my ear as I halfway expected her to say something dirty. After all, it appeared the wedding commotion had titillated her. The band started a rendition of Beck's "Where It's At," while Baxter and Jennifer commenced a synchronized robot dance to one of my all-time favorite songs. I suddenly felt the need to be friends with Jennifer and Baxter, and felt bad for thinking Jennifer was only pretty enough to attract a canine.

"Brandon, I want to talk to you about something," Clarissa said in a tone that suggested this would definitely have nothing to do with doing it doggy style.

"Do you want to change our song?" I asked, hopeful. "Because I'm all for that."

"What? No. That song is a symbol of our undying love," Clarissa said, offended, yet completely serious. Bryan Adams. Yeah.

Clarissa led me to an empty, nearby table that was beyond the noise from the party. We sat on opposite ends while Mitzy hung over Clarissa's shoulder like the dark lord of weddings that she was. I searched for Clarissa's parents, but it appeared that they hadn't moved from the spot they'd been in the entire time; I wondered what the hell those two did all day other than eat and stare at the wall. I half-hoped Mrs. Chang would join the female crowd for the bouquet toss; the other girls wouldn't have stood a chance.

Clarissa reached across the table for my hands.

"I know we never talked about this, but I spoke to Mitzy and she gave me some really good advice that I think will just strengthen us as a couple."

I guessed Mitzy's years as a wedding planner also made her believe she was a qualified therapist. She nodded in the background and smiled. I thought the tooth might have magical evil power.

"It's true. You're gonna love this," Mitzy said confidently. I could have sworn I heard a villainous cackle.

Clarissa pulled her hands away and took out a piece of paper from her handbag. As she flattened it on the table and cleared her throat, I tried to see what it was, but she covered it as if she wanted to present it to me like an award or maybe a subpoena.

"I even talked to my parents about it and they agreed that it was a good idea."

"Ok, would you tell me what it is already? I want to get home soon. I need to find out who wins the million-dollar race around the world."

"Well, when you suddenly left the other day, it really scared me. Not because I didn't think you were coming back, but because it worried me that our level of trust wasn't where it should have been."

Oh Christ. I tried my hardest not to roll my eyes. My mind wandered toward the dessert tray that had just been rolled out. It featured an ice cream cart where guests pulled out strawberry shortcake bars. Fuck, that sounded good. Another point for you, Jennifer and Baxter. Oh shit, was that a chocolate fountain behind it?

"Don't you think that we should do everything to earn each other's trust, Brandon?"

It *was* a chocolate fountain! I would have to sneak a strawberry under that falling stream of heaven before we left, I thought. Clarissa snapped her fingers to get my attention.

"Yes, trust, of course," I managed to say, not knowing or caring what she was implying.

Clarissa smiled and seemed relieved for some reason.

"I'm so glad you said that. That's why I wrote up this contract. It's a love contract."

My attention snapped to when I heard the word "contract."

"A what?"

"A contract of love," Mitzy said, as if it was the most romantic thing since fuzzy handcuffs. Clarissa nodded.

"It says, among other things, that you cannot leave for days at a time without talking to me first and making a decision as a couple."

Was she kidding?

"A single unit, Brandon. And that goes for me too! I totally promise never to just pick up and leave without first talking to you about it and getting your consent."

"She's such a doll," Mitzy added, as if Clarissa's thought needed punctuation. "Like a porcelain little doll."

Racist.

Clarissa's parents wandered their way to our table and watched over the proceedings. Clarissa's mother cracked her enormous knuckles, which sounded like five consecutive sonic booms, while her father just stared at me as if trying to fry me with invisible laser beams that emanated from his eyes. I suddenly became nervous and cursed myself for leaving my sunglasses in the car.

"So, will you sign it so we can move on as a happy loving couple, completely immersed in trust for each other? Just sign on the dotted line and we can put this all behind us."

I felt like I was being pressured into buying a used Camaro.

I tried not to scrunch my face at the retardation of the request. This felt like one of those bullshit coupons I gave my parents for their birthdays as a child, where they could redeem the pieces of paper for fifteen minutes of vacuuming or laundry. But sadly, I could understand her concerns. I knew the other shoe would drop and all that good lovin' I gave her the other night wasn't enough. I guessed I was stupid for thinking she'd forget and, despite this contract, I knew I would be hearing about this for the rest of my life. But this, this was just plain stupid. A contract of love? What the hell did this even mean? Where was this contract valid other than in the United States of Clarissa? I had questions.

"So, what happens if I break the contract?"

Mitzy gasped. If she'd been holding a champagne flute, it would have been on the ground in pieces. I figured I broke a cardinal rule of the contract: never question your wife. Clarissa closed her eyes and breathed deeply, digging to find what was left of her patience.

"Why would you ever want to break the love contract, Brandon?"

"I don't. I was just asking what happens if I did. I didn't even read this thing, do I have to give you my kidney if my car breaks down on a random night and I'm late for dinner?"

"Brandon, you are missing the point," Clarissa stated.

"Maybe I should have my lawyer read this first."

"Brandon! Why do you have to make everything so difficult?"

Good question.

Mr. Chang's expression changed after Clarissa lost her composure. Her mother mumbled something in Mandarin, but her voice suddenly rose when she mentioned "Mian Bao," followed by another word before she said "Ronald Fong." Clarissa groaned, but in that moment, I became galvanized. I had no doubt that the middle word was like the "less than" symbol (<) in Chinese. That name suddenly had the same effect as the word "chicken" had on Marty McFly in *Back To The Future.* The fact that Mrs. Chang looked away in disappointment sealed it for me. *Fuck them.*

I grabbed the pen from Clarissa's hand and signed the stupid contract. Mitzy clasped her hands, happier than a clam. What was the difference? I was signing my life away by getting married, anyway. What was a stupid "contract of love," after all? After I signed, I looked her parents directly in the eyes and smiled like I'd thrown down a gauntlet. I didn't know what the fuck was wrong with me, but I never liked to lose. Clarissa excitedly signed and planted a giant kiss on my lips. We were finally ready to go home. Which was completely fine with me, though it appeared I was shit out of luck with the chocolate strawberry.

The drive home, much like the ride there, was silent. I watched the ocean fly by and concentrated on the few surfers in the water. That was freedom, I thought. Then, again, homelessness covered in my own urine would have been freedom. Albeit, a smellier freedom.

Just then, my phone buzzed again, and I was struck with that same conflicted feeling I'd felt all day. But I needed something, anything, to distract me from the car ride. I slowly took the phone out of my pocket to build suspense, but was utterly disappointed to notice another text from my father:

—I really need to talk to you, Brandon. Pop—

I erased the text as I overheard Mrs. Chang man-handling a Snickers bar like a lion devouring a hyena. I resumed watching the speeding world pass out the window and remembered all the reasons I decided to get a driver's license in the first place.

Solace

A couple of weeks crawled by and the gym, of all places, became my fortress of solitude.

Normally I thought the idea of running in place for an hour was as pointless as pissing into the wind, but it afforded me a solid excuse to avoid my apartment for a couple more hours a day ("But honey, you want me to look good in my tux, right?") I loved to use Clarissa's vanity against her.

My gym peers were some gullible fucks. Fat ass members dished out over fifty dollars for an hour of bullshit training that clearly would do 75 percent of them no good and, for the other non-training imbeciles, there was always a long line for the elliptical machines simply because they lied best about how many calories were burned per workout. And I was no exception (a proud elliptiphile) and fell into the same trap, just in case the machine was actually correct and I miraculously burned five hundred calories in twenty minutes.

It's easy to people watch while gliding on an elliptical, and I constantly wondered what kind of lives my fellow members led. For instance, there was this old Asian man (who looked like an aged version of the Chinese firecracker thrower from *Boogie Nights*) who never seemed to work out, but always sat in one of the comfortable red chairs and stared at the exercisers, like he was the guardian angel of the gym. Or maybe just the resident pervert. And what about the dude that looked like he was auditioning to be the drummer for Metallica while on the exercise bike? That motherfucker put on a show, punishing those air drums, though I wondered if he realized how ridiculous he looked. His puffy mullet pulled back by an American flag bandana and Guinness beer-patterned pants suggested he didn't. Though, those same things also suggested that he probably didn't give a shit what I thought either.

But most of all, the bustle of the gym allowed my mind to wander to places it normally would not, like the constant motion brought my entire brain out of atrophy and into a hypnotic state that permitted my subconscious to question my life and how pathetic it had become. I often dreamed about how it could be different.

But the following memory constantly haunted me:

The story of how I got engaged never ceased to amaze me. Especially because it was completely my fault. Yes, *fault*. A week before the "proposal," my grandmother Sylvia died and had a pleasant funeral that was ruined by my father's bravado and his girlfriend's small dress. Grandma Sylvia didn't have much; she was born poor, raised poor, and although she and her husband (Grandpa Hymen, yeah, Hymen) did OK for themselves, Sylvia never had money for many luxuries and was cheap anyway. When her mind started to go during the last year of her life, she still knew the price of white rice at every neighborhood grocery store and would gladly travel the extra mile, cane and all, if it meant saving fifteen cents.

But Grandma Sylvia did have one heirloom that meant the world to her: Her mother's diamond ring. Sylvia never actually wore it but always kept it close by. I can remember her showing it to me as a little boy and then staring at it for a good five minutes while telling me some story about how her mother had obtained it. She actually did this many times and added a bit more hyperbole with each telling.

Since I was her only grandchild, and because my mother was AWOL, Sylvia left the ring to me and hoped one day I would give it to the woman I loved. I never told her about Clarissa because it would have caused premature death if she knew her perfect Jewish grandson was dating a Chinese woman. After all, to Sylvia, Chinese women were good for cooking, maybe manicures, definitely for laundry, but certainly not for procreation.

When I returned home from the funeral, I placed the ring in my personal drawer, next to copies of old tax returns, and subsequently forgot about it. Out of sight, out of mind. I had meant to put it in a safety deposit box, but never considered it an urgent matter. Unfortunately, I never informed Clarissa of the ring, either, which made things extremely uncomfortable when she found it.

I remember it like it was yesterday. I came home on a random Tuesday afternoon holding my foot-long from Subway, when I noticed rose petals stretched from the front door to the bedroom. Curiously, I followed them to find Clarissa wearing the naughtiest thing you could imagine from Trashy Lingerie. A bustier that made her pert 32Bs pop like they were D cups. A thong so stringy that you could floss your teeth with it. She had even curled her hair in these long spirals to make herself look extra vixinish. Now, I knew I hadn't sent her flowers that day and wondered why, after weeks of not fucking me, she decided to suddenly become my own personal slut.

Then, she moved her left hand to her knee. The glint of the diamond from Grandma Sylvia's ring almost blinded me.

"I know you were probably planning to give this to me at dinner or overlooking the ocean, but I found it, and all I have to say is YES."

I couldn't move. Not only was this a huge misunderstanding, but she had gone through all the trouble of spreading the roses, buying the lingerie, and waiting to fuck me once I got home. But just when I thought I actually could mutter the truth...

"And tonight, I'm gonna give you the one thing you've never had."

Anal. I knew it was anal. My brain became a measuring scale: the truth and freedom on one side, the ol' no-no hole on the other. Again, there was a reason I hated myself. Clearly, I went with option B and I'd paid for it ever since. Ironically, I couldn't even fit in her ass, it was too tight (though, trust me, I tried. Oh, did I try). I couldn't take the ring back after she'd weathered my numerous attempts. E for effort, after all. And to add insult to injury, by the time we were finished, my chicken parm foot long was cold and virtually inedible. And, thus, that is how our engagement was born: Because she found a ring that I improperly hid and because I was a dirty pervert (or just a guy.)

It had been three weeks since I'd returned from Sweden and, still, not one word from Saga. In fact, her face, the one that was once clear as crystal in my mind, started to become

fuzzy around the edges. I couldn't remember all of her features, all of her personality, as she was starting to become a
distant memory. Due to this, she almost reached mythical
status in my brain, as I completely forgot about her faults,
her secrecy, her brashness, and everything Bryan had suggested. So, naturally, while I sweated away my sins at the
gym, every song on my IPod reminded me of her:

"**Left Behind" by Aqualung:** Because I left her behind.
"**Dancing Queen" by ABBA (don't judge me):** That
one for obvious reasons.
"**Have You Ever Needed Someone So Bad" by Def
Leppard:** Apparently not.
"**Karma Police" by Radiohead:** Because of the lyric
"for a minute there, I lost myself."
"**Pretty Woman" by Roy Orbison:** Because she was a
pretty woman.
"**Human" by The Killers:** Because she was human.
"**Breathe" by Prodigy:** Because she breathed.

And while lost in the rhythm of the elliptical, I had a
recurring fantasy that always put me at ease, even though
the chances of it happening were less than remote. I supposed that's why they called them fantasies.

I pictured myself leaving work for a simple lunch at Subway, fully intending to lose myself in a flatbread chicken teriyaki, but instead of going, I'd have an epiphany (the kind where I'd stop in my tracks, arms akimbo, while I looked off to the side at nothing in particular). It would be brilliant. I'd skip the food, travel to the airport, book the next flight to Stockholm, and revel in the chance I'd decided to take. With only the clothes on my back, I'd walk the streets of the Swedish capital and could even picture the glint of the sun reflecting off the building windows. Everything would be bright, like it was an omen for a great future. I'd walk to that coffee shop by the water with the owner that somehow forgot to die, sit at a table, and wait for her to come. Even if it took days. Then, soon, she'd casually walk in for her latte and stroll past me without noticing. I'd watch her order her beverage from behind and patiently wait. Even while I thought about it, I could actually feel my nipples harden with anticipation. She'd finally turn around, drop her latte to the floor, the golden girl behind the counter would chastise her for breaking her mug, but neither of us would care. And then the first words of the rest of our lives would be said, though I still hadn't figured out what those words would be.

My forty-five-minute elliptical run expired, even though I still had tons of thoughts racing through my head. But the clock struck 9:30 p.m., and I knew I had to get home. After all, the Asian guardian angel no longer looked over us, the Metallica drummer ended his set, and, of course, I didn't want to be in breach of contract.

The Perpetrator

"**G**ood morning, black people!"

It never got old.

"And you toooo, Brandon, our honorary brother," Gladys said with a wink.

I loved the new three-word addition to Gladys's morning routine.

"You got these this morning too," she continued. "This is your fourth one this week! Maybe we should start calling you Brandon Popularity."

I liked that. Maybe BP for short.

Gladys struggled to place the latest orchid arrangement that was so tall it could have started at center for the Lakers. The card read:

Keep on fighting! Your friends at the NAACP.

I wondered if they knew I was actually white.

I really didn't deserve any of the gifts or kind words; all I did was give a stupid quote to a hungry Los Angeles

Times reporter desperately in search of an angle while at the last *Honey Buns* crime scene. Next thing I knew, it was on the front page of the Sunday edition and I had to explain my actions to my annoyed superiors simply because I'd said:

"We will not stand down to this attack against African-American culture. If we take down the billboards because of a couple of threats, what kind of message are we sending to our children?"

Now, the tone in my voice upon speaking the quote was clearly tongue-in-cheek, but even I had to admit that, in print, it seemed like something of a battle cry, which probably explained the flood of gifts from the black community (even Reverend Al Sharpton offered his help). But the quote also got the attention from a lovely sect of white supremacists, who had been kind enough to send me artwork depicting my (black) body hanging from a tree. I supposed I appreciated the effort; I always did like mail.

Due to all of this, I'd become something of an office hero even though the official company line was that I reacted out of passion and the network would reconsider the placement of the billboards. Regardless, apparently this was now my fight, which made me feel guilty because I honestly didn't really care. I had better things to stress over, like Clarissa's latest email:

Brandon,

We need to make a decision on what to serve at the
rehearsal dinner. I was thinking we do a half Chinese,
half whatever you are, you know, keeping a theme? It's
weird that I have no clue what your background is, isn't
it? It's so great that we know each other so well, yet we
still have so much to learn about each other. For the rest
of our lives. Tell me what you think.

Xox

Clarissa

I must have told Clarissa my family heritage the first
sixty-five times she asked over the years. My family was
originally from England, but immigrated to Canada early
in the country's history. I knew I told her this a few times,
because each time the subject was approached, Clarissa
would say "oooh, a Canadian, eh? Get it, eh?" Yeah, I fucking got it. Now please shut up. I wondered what Canadian
cuisine even was? Moose? Bison? Seal? Maybe I should have
suggested all of those for the dinner. In fact, I thought it
would be cool if there was an entire dead, hairy bison on a
cutting board, under a small heat lamp, manned by a carver
who casually sliced it like it was turkey or ham. That would
look perfect next to the General Tsao's chicken or whatever
bullshit would represent her side of the family.

Instead, I just erased the e-mail and answered a work-related query that regarded the future of free KitKats in the break room after Beverly Williams choked on one last week, which unfortunately required a hospital visit. I knew the rehearsal dinner question would be discussed sixteen hundred more times before 11:59 p.m., anyway.

The clock struck 12:15 p.m., and I heard the familiar sound of Bryan sitting on the Everest of Diet Coke, a signal that it was time for lunch.

"Just give me a minute," I said, while firing off the e-mail about the fate of my favorite afternoon snack. I cared more about that than the billboards.

But Bryan didn't respond with his normal "take your time, Jackass" or "yeah, I can wait all day, Princess." Instead, he responded with nothing at all.

I finished the email and turned to ask what he'd like to eat, but though my mouth opened to say words, nothing came out. The reason Bryan didn't respond with his normal "witty" comments was because Bryan was not sitting on the Diet Coke after all.

"So, where do you launch the rockets from?" she asked in her slightly throaty Swedish accent.

Saga.

Holy fucking shit. After all the thinking, the wondering, the hoping. There she was. I had run this moment through my head a thousand times while I tossed and turned in bed next to my fiancée. I had visions of grabbing her, kissing her, and not letting go. It was supposed to be like in a movie, one with a Peter Cetera tune, just the perfect moment. But as my brain attempted to process all the information, it did not feel like the perfect moment. In fact, my first instinct was to shove her in the closet like I did that unwanted Chinese Cabbage Patch doll I was given several years ago.

My boss crossed my desk and noticed Saga sitting straight on the soda. Whatever he was going to ask me was quickly forgotten with the aid of wild gesticulations and a confused mumble. He walked away.

Saga appeared different beneath the fluorescent lights of the office. Perhaps it was the lack of context, the absence of the Stockholm background; maybe it was the fact that she was not draped in the shackles of limited time, but she looked different. And I started feeling indescribable, troubling emotions I'd never felt in my life.

"You really hate phones, don't you?" I said, through a slight stutter.

"So bourgeois," Saga said, while she grabbed a Diet Coke from beneath her. "You don't have Pepsi Max, do you?"

"No one drinks that here," I said, as I still tried to process the moment.

Saga nodded and broke eye contact.

This whole thing was awkward.

I was suddenly stricken with the fear that someone would see her and figure everything out. Like a person could read my thoughts, be confronted with the image of Saga and I fucking, and then would run to tell Clarissa the whole truth. The other troubling thing was the fact that I couldn't feel my feet, as if all the blood in my body found somewhere to hide. I hoped I wouldn't faint.

"I just flew 6,000 miles. Are you going to make me sit here much longer?" Saga asked.

Just then, I heard Bryan round the corner, crooning a rousing rendition of "Camptown Races" I hadn't ever heard:

"Deucetown ladies sing this song dooo deeee doooo deeee, Deucetown races five miles lo—"

Bryan cut his performance short once he finally approached my desk and noticed Saga seated next to me. He made eye contact with her, trying to place why this beautiful girl was casually sitting by my side, all the while fighting the embarrassment caused by the song dedicated to his impending dump. Then, it clicked. Without moving his head, he slowly rolled his eyes in my direction and knew that I had told him the truth. All of it. I broke eye contact and stared at my keyboard with a mixture of shame, fear, and perhaps a touch of pride. All I heard was that annoying, knowing laugh I remembered so well from the donut shop.

"So...who's hungry?" Bryan asked.

I wasn't.

Lunch

"So, a fountain, huh," Bryan said to Saga while he glanced at her mid-section, no doubt in search of a baby bump even though it would have been impossible for one to exist this early. I suddenly really regretted inviting Bryan to lunch even though, deep down, I found his comment humorous. I'm sure I would have laughed if it were at someone else's expense. I also searched her belly and wondered where the nearest staircase might be.

"Don't be jealous," Saga said with a straight face, as she drank her water. Bryan, normally quick with a comeback, just laughed and shrugged.

"Did you tell him every detail?" Saga asked me.

"Only the dirty ones, apparently," I responded, a little embarrassed.

More like scared.

I had picked the Formosa Café for lunch, simply because no one I knew actually went there and it was rather dark.

The last thing I wanted was to explain this situation to anyone I knew, personally, especially one of Clarissa's friends. Bryan proceeded to ask her some questions to which she answered all patiently and, as they were talking, I found myself staring at her. She looked more relaxed than she had in Stockholm; many of her verbal answers were combined with smiles. She wore casual clothes and a light jacket that fit her absolutely perfectly. Her slightly wavy hair was pulled back save for a few strands left loose to frame her face. Her posture was still textbook. Simply put, Saga looked at ease. And beautiful.

"So you guys are gonna get married, huh?" Bryan asked as he elbowed me in the arm.

Saga searched me as if I had an answer.

"Yep," I hesitated as I spoke. "Tyin' the knot," I continued nervously.

As the bill was placed on the table, Saga daintily wiped her mouth with her napkin and excused herself. As she walked toward the restroom, I looked to Bryan for any kind of answer.

He seemed sure of something.

"Yeah, she's trouble."

"Not now."

"See what she did there? The bill came; she walked away. She doesn't have money."

"Then how the fuck did she get here, asshat?"

"Riding a tidal wave of trouble, Broheim," Bryan said. "More importantly, she's cute, but that is not the prettiest girl I've ever seen," he responded.

"Is this really the conversation we're gonna have right now?"

"You're saying she's prettier than my wife? C'mon, her face is a little...I dunno."

"Bryan, dude."

"No way she's prettier than my wife. My wife is way hotter than that. And has better tits."

"Dude!"

"Much better tits."

Even as I considered present company, I couldn't believe I was having this conversation.

"I mean, when I'm home, I feel like the mayor of Titopolis," he confidently continued. "You're gonna be like the town supervisor of Flatopia or something," he finished disgustedly, with a nod toward the bathroom as if he was actually offended by Saga's diminutive chest.

My patience was gone. I drove my fist as hard as I could into Bryan's right arm. He winced and quickly pulled it away.

"What the fuck did you do that for?"

"Why? Because now I have two fiancées, which was crazy enough when they were six thousand miles apart, let alone six miles, and all you can talk about is if she's cuter than your wife?"

"She's not. We just established that."

"Dude!" I said, through gritted teeth, on the verge of completely losing my shit.

"Dude, calm down, what the fuck?"

I sighed and tried to regain my composure. Bryan finally took notice and relented.

"What am I gonna do?" I asked as calmly as possible, while I nervously looked toward the restroom door.

"I dunno. What do you want to do?" Bryan asked. The question was obvious but not simple.

"I have no clue what I wanna do."

"I do know one thing. That..." Bryan said, nodding toward the restroom. "...will never work out."

"Why not?"

"Just tell her to leave. After all, it was only three days," Bryan continued. "How long would it take for her to get over your ass? I'd get over your ass quick."

"Dude, she just flew here from *Sweden* to see me. I don't think she's gonna be all that happy if I tell her 'thanks, but no thanks.' Plus, I don't want to."

"Well, what about Clarissa. Remember her?"

I ran my hands across my face. "I don't fuckin' know."

"You wanna break that off? Why don't you just tell her that?"

"People have killed their significant other just to avoid that conversation. And remember the Runaway Bride?"

"Oh yeah, that crazy-eyed bitch who faked her own kidnapping to get outta marrying that douche?"

"See what people do?"

Bryan was not exactly the most compassionate guy in the world; he actually seemed like the type that killed caterpillars for fun as a child, but he sensed my urgency.

"You want help?"

"*Yes.*"

"I can't believe I'm gonna do this. I'll tell you what, I'm gonna save your life. Well, for three days I will. My cousin owns this really nice bed and breakfast down in OC, in San Clemente. Right on the beach, and he owes me a favor. I can buy you three days."

"Dude, really? But what the hell do I tell Clarissa?"

"Just disappear. You did it once."

"I can't. She made me sign this stupid contract and..."

"A contract?"

"Please don't make me go into it...I just need to buy some time to figure this shit out."

"Honestly, I don't really care. Just say you're goin' on a business trip to check out some new billboards. It's far enough away where it wouldn't make sense to commute. Do you want it or not?"

Saga re-joined us at the table. We both looked at her curiously. She turned to me.

"So, what next?" she asked.

"I wanna show you my favorite place in SoCal. Ever hear of San Clemente?"

Just Your Average Phone Call

"Hey Clariss, it's me."

"Hey Sweetie! I'm so glad you called. I've got some terrible, terrible news."

"Everything OK?"

"No! It's awful! My aunt and uncle from China can't come to the wedding anymore. Something with their visas and an anti-American protest they took part in like twenty years ago, can you believe that?"

"No."

"So, now we have two open spots! Is there anyone you might want to invite that could come last minute?"

"I don't think so."

"What about that guy? What was his name again? Anton?"

"Anton?"

"Yeah, your college roommate! Remember you mentioned him the other day for some reason? At my promotion dinner."

"Oh, Anton Chekhov? That might be difficult."

"Why? Just call him."

"I can't."

"Why not!"

"He died."

"Oh, that's horrible. How?"

"Tuberculosis, I think."

"Really? I didn't know anyone got that anymore. So crazy."

"He actually got it a long time ago."

"Is that why you brought him up the other day?"

"Something like that. So anyway…"

"OK, maybe I can fill the two seats with clients or something. I know Brittany Snow told me once that she adores weddings. Maybe she'll come. It'd be great to have her in the wedding album anyway, she's so pretty, don't you think?"

"Who?"

"Ugh, Brandon, when will you take my job seriously? It's important to me that you know these people."

"Ok."

"Great! I'll give her a call."

"Yeah, so something came up."

"What? I can't deal with bad news, don't tell me bad news."

"It's not bad news."

"Well, what is it?"

"I have to go out of town for a few days, for work."

"What? Why? You never have to do that."

"I know. It's crazy. They want us to actually scout some of these billboards in like the OC, San Diego area."

"Really? Since when do you look at locations?"

"Since people have threatened to bomb them."

"Oh. Well, why do you need to stay down there?"

"'Cause its far."

"Where will you stay? What if I need to get in touch with you?"

"That's what cell phones are for."

"But where are you staying? I have to admit, Brandon, I don't like this. We still have so much to do and remember the *love contract*. We need to mutually agree on trips."

"You were just out of town for two days on that press junket for that new shit Matthew Fox movie."

"That movie is not shit."

"I'm sure it's *Citizen Kane*."

"You'll see when he wins the Oscar for it."

"I don't really care."

"So where are you staying?"

"I don't know."

"What do you mean you don't know?"

"I don't know, some place."

"Brandon! It's not like I'm gonna come down there and bomb the place. I just like to know where my fiancé is in case I need him. The *contract*, Brandon."

"Fine fine, hold on, let me look…it's called the Sunrise Clemente Inn. In San Clemente."

"So it's just three days? But we have a meeting with Mitzy tomorrow to go over the color of the table cloths again."

"I'm sure you can handle it. Are you going to be around tonight? I need to pack some stuff."

"No, I have the premiere of the Matthew Fox movie. You knew this."

"Oh, right. The shit one?"

"Brandon."

"OK, well, then I guess I'll see you in three days, OK?"

"I wish there was a way you could get out of this."

"Me too. There's not though, and you know, the promotion, right? But I need to go. I'll be back in three days though."

"Brandon!"

"Yeah?"

"Aren't you forgetting something?"

"Tell Matthew I said hi?"

"Oh, I totally will, he'd love to hear that; he's so nice. Plus, he finds any excuse to talk to me. I think he has an Asian fetish."

"What red-blooded American doesn't?"

"Isn't there something else you want to tell me? Something you are going to tell me every morning for the rest of our lives?"

"Oh, I love you."

"Aww, I love you too, Pookie Bear. OK, I'll call you tonight after the premiere. I bet it will get lonely down there all alone, and I know you'll miss your little angel."

"OK. Bye."

Saga in Southern California

My future was something I always pondered as a nebulous, perplexing matter that I'd somehow figure out with proper preparation and guidance, until I heard the commencement speech delivered at my college graduation. The school claimed the speaker was a successful author, though I had never heard of him, nor did the old lady at Barnes and Noble with the bird-patterned sweater and reading glasses fastened to a chain around her neck (judging by her appearance, I figured she knew her shit.) This author gave some canned speech that regarded the value in knowing one's future and actually posed the question of whether or not we'd like to know our future if he could provide a glimpse. But before we even had time to consider the options, he answered his own query and informed us that we would definitely not desire to know our future years because, then, there would be nothing left to live for as all the future excitement and pain would have been undercut with the already-obtained knowledge. But what this author, who was so famous that he transcended notoriety, did not consider was that even if he showed me my exact future, who's to say I would have even believed him?

Let's say I were to take the speaker up on his hypothetical offer and forced him to show me my life in ten years. After his general bullshit disclaimer, he'd drive us both to the airport and park near the international terminal so we could board a flight. The discovery of my future taking place in a foreign country would have excited me, considering I'd never been anywhere at that point in my life. Though, perhaps, it would have been possible that he just wanted to show me my eventual, exciting career with the TSA.

But, alas, we'd board a plane to Sweden and, once we had arrived, we'd travel by train to some small town where the author would then drive me to an elementary school, walk me down a hallway filled with children's paintings of Vikings or meatballs, and inform me that he was about to show me the woman I'd one day propose to. He'd carefully approach a classroom and point through the window in the middle of the door. I'd notice a young woman, about my age, relaxed in a chair reading Pippi Longstocking to her class that quietly sat on the floor. I'd smile and wonder what the circumstances would be that would lead to our meeting. What about her would make me fall in love? Perhaps it would be her gentle nature; she was an elementary school teacher after all. I'd ask the incredibly talented and famous writer her name, to which he'd laugh and say: "No. No. Not her…Her."

He'd point a little to the left, at a blond, pig-tailed girl seated on the floor, fast asleep with her head in her hand and drool dripping from her wide open mouth.

And that would be my Saga.

And no matter how much he insisted that this was my certain future, I'd never believe him. Not even for a second. I'd probably laugh, tell the author to get fucked, and escape to go find some chocolate or a Saab dealership.

Point being, if recent events had taught me anything, it's that planning for your future is a fool's game.

Saga stared in the mirror and moisturized every inch of her body that wasn't covered by her tank top or short skirt, while I sat on the edge of the bed located in the center of a quaint room that overlooked the beach from the sliding glass door of the bed and breakfast. Much to my surprise, the room was exceptionally nice and provided a romantic atmosphere that I hadn't anticipated. I had no doubt that people opted to make love rather than fuck in a room such as this. On the drive down, I doubted Bryan's taste and thought we might end up in a motel that saved money by not washing the sheets, but the way Saga nodded as she entered assured me that Bryan's favor would not go underappreciated.

As I watched her routine in the mirror, my eyes were drawn to a small scar on top of her right foot that I hadn't noticed in Sweden. As I searched further, I discovered a small tattoo of what appeared to be a half moon, with a jagged side facing right, on her left ankle. I couldn't help but feel intrigued and sick at the same time. I really knew nothing about this girl and what really compelled her to travel across the Atlantic to see me.

I lay on the bed to gather my thoughts, stared at the ceiling, and pictured Clarissa's body. I knew it by heart, as well as I knew my own. I knew the tiny mole three inches west of her bellybutton, the faded scar from an appendectomy, I even could picture the arch of her foot, the result of hundreds of foot massages while we watched bad movies on television. I had forgotten how much I liked those moments and actually cracked a smile. There was, at least, something somewhat comforting with Clarissa. Something safe. I mean, after years of apprehension, I didn't feel embarrassed to take a shit in front of her, and she in front of me. I could fart as loudly as I wanted to and it would often produce a chuckle from fiancée number one. But I didn't get the impression that would fly with Saga. I bet I would have to pretend I never shat for two years before I got comfortable. I'd be holding in every single fart for the rest of my life. That couldn't be healthy. And who had the energy?

I wondered if anyone knew Saga was here. Did she tell her mother and sisters? Her father? If she did, did she tell them the real reason she had planned a trip to Los Angeles? But these facts didn't bother me as much as not being able to predict how she would handle this situation, who she might tell, who she would be honest with (if anyone) and who she would lie to. She was still a mystery to me. All of her. And while she was exciting and new, I suddenly thought about a marriage and the unpredictability that would come along with it. And I felt panic. It had gone too far.

Saga finished grooming herself and turned toward me.

"What should we do?"

What a question.

"I don't know. Do you want to go to the beach?" I really had no better option. I had never been to San Clemente.

"No," Saga said, while turning back to the mirror to fix her hair.

"OK...well ..."

I really had no answers as I searched my mind for any ideas that didn't rhyme with "har" and "plub." And then it hit me. The perfect idea. I wasn't sure if Saga would be interested, but considering my current warped state of mind, I didn't care.

I knew Clarissa would never go there, nor would any of her annoying friends. I wouldn't be caught. And I thought it might actually be fun.

"I have an idea."

Disneyland

I didn't know there was a surefire way to get banned
from the self-proclaimed "happiest place on Earth,"
but, well, there is.

I had been looking forward to returning to Disneyland
since Clarissa and I had visited early in our relationship.
She never had a real interest in the place, had no childhood
connection to it, and often wondered publicly why a man of
my age loved it so much. But no matter how many times I
explained to her that my affinity was born from the nostalgia of my childhood, she wouldn't listen.

"So weird, Brandon," she'd say as if I were in the minor-
ity. "So weird."

Sometimes I would just look at her.

But, as I mentioned before, the one time we did go, of
course, an incident occurred.

I understood the least fun part of any theme park had
to be waiting in the exhaustively long lines for the rides

that were way too short. Hordes of impatient people, in close proximity, while baking in a hot sun were not the ingredients for a good mood. So it was no surprise that the worst part (or best) of our experience occurred while waiting in line for the Jungle Cruise ride. Clarissa received a work phone call regarding some crap Shia LeBeouf movie and, of course, had to speak sixty decibels too loudly so the people in the parking lot would know that she was doing business with the young, popular actor. And while such a thing might have impressed some assholes, it was California after all, the little boy that stood in front of us, wearing a Captain Jack Sparrow costume, was not pleased by her loud behavior. After sneering at Clarissa for a good two minutes, he decided to play "repeater" with her and subsequently mocked everything she said. His parents actually found his actions amusing (as did I), but Clarissa became visibly annoyed. After the fifth line he repeated, she actually leaned down and screamed, "Shut the hell up, you little snot!"

Of course, instead of repeating the insult, the kid broke down crying and a small argument with his parents ensued. Then, while Clarissa and his mother's voices both escalated, the "little snot" whacked Clarissa hard in the shin with his plastic pirate sword and burst out laughing. And it actually drew blood. Of course, Clarissa threatened to sue because when a retarded, insignificant situation gets unnecessarily out of hand, you have to take the opportunity to up the ante of ridiculousness by threatening legal action. You just have to.

Needless to say, I never got to ride the Jungle Cruise. Instead, we hit the Haunted Mansion where she just bitched the whole time, wondered aloud how any of the "bullshit scared anyone," and pestered me to keep checking for a bruise. And there was one, which I told her several times, so I don't know why she had me keep looking to make sure it was still there.

So, naturally, I held my breath while Saga stared curiously at a small girl in a princess costume that made funny faces at her while we waited in line for the Jungle Cruise. The young girl kept her hands behind her back and swayed in place while her mother chatted away on the cell phone, wishing she was anywhere else but in the line, and clearly ruining the experience for her daughter who probably couldn't sleep the night before in anticipation of today.

"Yeah, I'm at Disneyland with Kayley," her mother said, as she paused. "Yeah, it's totally gay, but whatever, I told her we're leaving soon, but she's being a little baby about it."

I wondered if this woman ran a day care center. If not, she really missed her calling.

Brett Sills

Saga crouched to meet the young girl at eye level.

"You look very pretty in your dress," Saga said to the young girl, who suddenly had no interest in making faces anymore. The girl smiled shyly.

"Isn't it ridiculous?" her mother stated, as she noticed the conversation. "She insisted she put it on, but all she does is complain that it itches."

The mother expected us to laugh alongside her, but Saga looked at her with disgust before turning her attention back toward little Kayley.

"I have one just like it, actually," Saga said, as she looked back toward her mother with disdain. "But don't worry about the itch. Pixie dust always does that."

Mother: Horrified.

"You know, you need a lesson in minding your own business," the mother said, clearly ready for confrontation.

Saga easily shrugged the comment off.

"You need a lesson on how to be less of a bitch," Saga responded, as calmly as could be.

Kayley smiled.

What we didn't realize was that Kayley's tattooed biker for a father was standing ahead of both of them. The inked image of a kitten being strangled by a boa constrictor on his neck suggested that he didn't like to settle disputes with diplomacy. At the sound of the mother's gasp, the father snapped into action and threatened *me* (what the fuck did I do?) with a fate that sounded as bad as that poor kitten's. Because I needed to look brave, even though I was a second away from pissing my pants, I actually said, "What'cha gonna do about it?" in my toughest voice and inches away from his gross beard that still had bits of curly fry in its depths. I figured there was no way he'd kill me surrounded by children, and I was right, though he flashed me a grin that suggested we'd settle up later. I wondered how much the Goofy masks cost at the gift shop.

Needless to say, I didn't get to enjoy the Jungle Cruise that time either.

Just as with Clarissa, we soon ended up on the Haunted Mansion line where I half expected to hear Saga complain about Kayley's mother and father. But she never did. In fact, it was as if she had forgotten the entire incident. It was actually eerie that a confrontation like that had no effect on her at all. She might not have wanted to discuss it, but I, for some reason, did.

"That was some bullshit back there, huh," I said carefully.

Saga shrugged harmlessly.

She looked away from me in a pensive moment, and then back toward me armed with something to say. "When I was a young girl, I grew up in a small town along the sea. Very quiet and peaceful. We grew up poor; my father worked for the government, and my mother stayed at home and she would often sit us in front of the TV and show us these old Disney movies. You know, Cinderella, Snow White. Then my sisters and I would go outside and run into the forest in such a hurry to pretend we were Snow White looking for the dwarves, apples, trees that looked like witches..."

Saga looked away again and gently smiled to herself at the memory, as she fidgeted with the rope that separated the lines. I was relieved and happy that she also shared a childhood connection. But though it was a nice image, there was one word in her anecdote that stood out above all others: poor.

Fucking Blomax. Deep down, my instincts told me that her feelings were genuine, that she was actually enjoying our day together, and she flew all the way to the United States because she was in love. But I also knew my instincts were normally wrong. I had to be asshole Sherlock Holmes. I scratched the back of my head in an attempt to look casual as I probed.

"So, the dinner between our fathers. I found out what it was all about. Get this. Your father is sending mine into space," I said.

"I hear it's nice there this time of year," she replied.

"That doesn't surprise you?"

Saga shrugged. "Men do strange things," she said.

"Strange things? Eating pasta with mayonnaise is a strange thing. Sending someone into space is a little more than strange," I contested. "Did you know about it before the dinner?"

"No."

I hesitated with my next remark. "So, why were you there?"

Saga eyed me curiously. She either really had no clue why I was giving her the third degree or she was a good actress.

"My father asked me."

"But you don't get along with him."

"Neither do you and your father, but you flew six thousand miles for that same dinner."

"He said he'd make it worth my while."

"Did he?"

"Why does it matter?" I answered, a little taken aback.

Saga stared for a moment.

"I went because my father asked me," Saga said, matter of factly, but certainly not in the cheeriest of tones.

The next few minutes were spent in silence. I snuck glances at her a few times to find she never looked back at me. I wanted to know why she was curious about whether or not my father actually paid me off. I hated Bryan for planting this bullshit in my obsessive head. But I also wondered what she meant by her last comment. Did she often do things her father asked her to do?

We passed the introduction to the Haunted ride (that chamber that seems to get longer even though it's just an elevator leading you to the buggies on the ground floor) with similar silence. Once in the private buggy, we ascended into the dark house and concentrated on the narration blaring from the nearby speakers, though I was too preoccupied with my own thoughts to really pay attention. Once the buggy leveled off and the ride displayed images of ghosts, possessed clocks, and floating candelabras, I felt Saga's hand grab mine and squeeze it tight. But not out of fright or nervousness, it just appeared that she wanted to hold my hand. I noticed her staring at me without a smile or frown. As the ride continued past shaking coffins and disembodied voices, she leaned over and kissed me. Then kissed me again, this time not letting go. And even though I had been on edge all day and felt nervous (and even wrong) to touch her, this felt right. Among the faux scares and death, a weight was lifted from my shoulders, a weight I wasn't sure was even there. I was happy she kissed me and wanted her to do it for as long as she possibly could.

She inched her body closer to me until she maneuvered herself on top of my lap and lifted her skirt as we descended farther into the dark ride. I immediately got hard against her as she unzipped my pants and carefully pushed me into her. She ran her hands through my hair, over my ears, and gently bit my top lip. I grabbed her ass as we passed the ballroom where the phantoms danced to a macabre orchestra. I assumed this was nothing they hadn't seen before; it was a dark ride after all. Saga moved faster against me, and I softly lifted her up and down as we continued into the graveyard. The buggy rocked and I was half afraid that it would tumble off the track and into the display. But it held true.

And that is where things got interesting.

Out of the corner of my eye, I could see straight into the buggy adjacent to us because of the way the vehicles curved on the track. And even in the dark, I could clearly recognize the riders: the Chatty Cathy mother, Zoo Tattoo, and the little princess who was now immersed in dirty crash course on the birds and the bees (though I'm sure it wasn't quite as educational as Fuck You, Asswhores 35). Kayley's father must have noticed my eyes bug, because his arrogant grin suggested that he had caught us and we were fucked (no pun intended). He leaned forward and reached for one of the dancing graves.

As soon as he touched it, the ride halted and the house lights illuminated, showcasing Saga's ass to the entire ride. Gasps drowned out the voice on the loud speaker, informing the riders to remain seated, but no one seemed to notice the warning since they were too busy staring at us. Saga and I bristled at the numerous stares while my hard dick remained inside her. The house lights doused and the ride continued. Saga laughed nervously as she disembarked from my body and sat beside me. Embarrassing yes, but no harm, no foul, so I thought. In fact, I hoped that colorful asshole would get in trouble for his successful attempt to disrupt the ride.

As we exited the Mansion, we walked hand in hand into the glaring sun only to find two security guards staring us down. One held out his finger and motioned us toward him.

Now, apparently, this is what happens when you fuck at Disneyland:

We were taken to a holding room where the bushy mustached head of security, that appeared as if he just got off his shift in the 1880s Old West (the real one), sat us down while trying to impress us with his ugly scowl. The silver hair and shiny star badge suggested experience in law enforcement, probably his past career before entering the friendly confines of the Magic Kingdom. He even walked with a slight limp; perhaps a bullet wound in the ass caused him to quit the force, or maybe he just faked it to demand respect. Either way, it looked like he took his job entirely too seriously.

He placed his face inches from mine, and I reflexively leaned back.

"You know why you're here, don'tcha?" he asked, while he peered at me with only his left eye. He even sounded like he should have been an animatronic character in one of the rides.

"Is there a problem?" I asked innocently.

"Well, we heard about what happened in the Haunted Mansion and no one, I mean no one, messes with my Haunted Mansion, ya hear?" he said, while he quickly tried to intimidate Saga with his practiced look of death. She didn't flinch.

"We weren't the ones who touched the grave, Sir," I said.

All the security officials within shouting distance laughed.

"One thing you have to learn about this here place is that we are always watching you," he said, as he pointed two fingers toward his eyes, and then back in our direction. "We. Are. Always. Watching. You."

The John Wayne clone snapped his fingers, and an underling quickly grabbed a remote control and flipped on a monitor that showed our little Disney porno. And this wasn't some infrared, grainy picture. This was clear as day and in fucking color. I had no clue how they accomplished this in a dark room, and I was impressed, but well, there was no denying any of it. It was so clear that I winced as I realized I needed to, at least, trim my scrotum hair. Wyatt Earp pointed at the screen and waited for one of us to say something.

Neither of us did.

"Well?" the security guard demanded. "What do you have to say for yourselves?"

I turned toward Saga and shrugged.

"Well, I always wanted to be in a Disney movie," Saga said.

And that's when we received our ban. A lifetime one, though I wasn't sure how they could keep track of such a thing. I figured it wasn't a good time to ask either.

However, I did ask the security guard if they would make an exception if an actual child was conceived while on the ride, but he just pointed to the door and actually asked me to *let* it hit my ass on the way out. And not that politely, I might add.

I had never actually heard someone say that.

Another day of firsts.

Laying, Laying and Laying

After our second foray into criminal activity (in two different countries, no less—sweet!), in one month (baller!), Saga and I returned to the bed and breakfast with plans for a nice dinner, followed by a day at the beach before I had to return to Los Angeles for work.

But we never actually got out of bed.

I couldn't remember if Clarissa and I ever had such a day where we'd rather just experience each other than attempt to enhance our time together with forces from the outside world. We once took a vacation to the Caribbean, which I had expected to be nothing short of a sexcapade, but after a couple of hours of rolling around naked, we got hungry or bored and spent time at the beach, receiving massages, or playing horseshoes with some fellow vacationing senior citizens. In fact, I'd asked more than once if she minded if

I strolled the beach alone to gather thoughts. She didn't and, in hindsight, the solitary walks might very well have been the highlight of the trip. It always surprised me how quickly we got bored of each other, yet we continued as if it was fresh.

Saga and I had an entire beach just behind the sliding glass door at our disposal, but I had no plans to walk on it alone. I had no desire to even get something to eat and was happy to rely on room service for the entire day. In fact, I had little interest in even putting on a pair of pants. And since we didn't actually get to finish during our carnal ride through the Haunted Mansion, we spent nearly every second since making up for our failure to complete. Frankly, after the ninth time, I was tired and scared that my dick-hole might scream "timber!" just before the entire thing keeled over like a dead tree.

My phone must have buzzed with multiple text messages and phone calls and, though I had answered each and everyone the day before, I didn't return any of them over the next twenty-four hours. I just didn't care anymore. And the one text message I did check, which said "Brandon! The contract of love!" just pissed me off even further and gave me the impetus to ignore the rest.

We had the room for three nights and decided that I would come back down to the bed and breakfast for one more evening after my day at work. I promised I'd find a way to leave early. I was good at faking illnesses anyway.

I propped my head on my hand and studied Saga as she peacefully smoked a cigarette while in bed. Her body was near perfect. She had a beautiful long neck that sat atop small shoulders tickled by her light blond hair. Normally, I was a guy that loved to be smothered by a set of big tits, but I couldn't keep my hands, nor my mouth, off her perky B-cups that featured nipples so perfect it appeared as if she had handpicked them to correctly fit her shape. Her stomach was toned, but not manly, and curved perfectly with her tight ass. My eyes scanned her long, lithe legs down past the small half moon tattoo to the scar on top of her foot. They held on her battle wound, and I couldn't put my finger on why a small, jagged blemish intrigued me.

"I once took classes on how to walk in high heels," Saga stated while she indicated the scar, obviously noticing that I had been staring at it. Apparently, she actually *did* take classes on how to walk.

"I see the Swedish educational system has its priorities in order," I said flatly.

Saga playfully hit my shoulder and smiled.

"So, why did you have to learn how to walk? Did you wear leg braces like Forrest Gump or something?"

Saga sighed.

"No. My legs are just fine, as is my back, thank you. My friend made me take a modeling class with her for a year, don't ask, and learning how to walk a runway is more difficult than you'd think."

"It took you a year to figure it out? Perhaps you're like Forrest Gump in other ways too."

Saga shot me a completely deserved look of disapproval.

"It might be complete bullshit, but trust me, it's difficult. I was a little bit of, how do you say it, a tomboy?"

"That explains the violent streak."

"I never dressed in heels growing up. My instructor was so frustrated with me. 'Saga, stand straight!' 'Saga, more elegant!' 'Saga, you walk like a man!' After it was over, the straps of the heels dug into my foot so badly that I needed eight stitches," she said as she lined the scar with her finger.

"Why'd you stop?"

"Cause I was bleeding. Why do you think?" she said.

I smiled.

"No, why'd you stop the classes?"

"My hips had a problem with my relationship with chocolate."

Fair enough.

"And this," she continued, as she gently touched the small bump on the bridge of her nose, "is the result of my sister and a golf club. An accident, so she says."

"Did you want to kill her?"

"Of course. Though I did nothing. But I ran over her foot with a car years later, by accident. Karma. It's weird, though. I once had a dream where the small bump was gone, and I couldn't recognize myself in the mirror."

"I have a recurring dream where security guards at my old high school kill my baby polar bear."

Saga shot me a curious look. "Why do they kill it?"

"I don't know."

"What do you think that dream means?"

"I don't know. What do any of them mean?"

"I suppose nothing," Saga said as she shrugged.

My eyes met her ankle once again.

"And what about the tattoo?"

Saga acted like she forgot it was even there. She scrunched her forehead and looked toward the ceiling.

"That was just something stupid. You know, just being young."

Saga propped her head on her hand and turned to me, as if a mirror image. She placed the tip of her nail and traced nothing in particular across my chest. I watched her gentle hand glide over my skin and wondered what was preoccupying her thoughts.

"I'm sorry about being short earlier. When you asked me why I went to the dinner. I wasn't trying to be glib."

I wanted to ask her more, but couldn't think of a way to formulate my question. It didn't matter. Saga subtly bit her bottom lip and looked at me with a vulnerable expression. I had seen it before: when she walked to the subway in Gamla Stan. While at the museum. At the airport. But when I narrowed my eyes as if to question her, she quickly looked away.

"Is it possible for you to skip work tomorrow?"

I wanted to know what she was trying to figure out, but I decided to let it go. Plus, when it came to me avoiding work, anything was possible.

"Why?"

"We should go to Vegas."

"Vegas is fun," I said, as I mentally considered, but full well knew I couldn't go.

"And get married."

I knew Saga and I had been engaged and, as romantic and stupid as the entire thing was, I never actually considered the fact that engagement led to marriage. With Clarissa, our engagement and wedding planning had been the most arduous process of my life. We had our sham of an engagement coupled with our failed attempt at anal sex, then had to call everyone we knew, set a date for a wedding, have the engagement party, argue over a venue, the menu, and so on and so forth. It felt like it took more preparation than a space launch (and I didn't have to work for NASA to know a lot was involved in such a task.) Regardless of how I felt about Clarissa and our pending marriage, there was something normal about it. Something that felt kind of right even though it was so wrong. When Saga suggested Vegas, I naturally tensed, because it felt nothing short of surreal, and even if I wasn't to be married to a small Chinese woman, wedding a taller Swedish one wasn't something I was prepared to do either.

"I...I can't. Not now," I stammered.

"Why not?"

"It's just too soon."

"Are you having second thoughts?"

"No. No...it's just, you know it's busy at work and I just...I don't know, need things to slow down for a minute."

"We should do it."

I pondered her insistence.

"The sooner the better, I think," Saga continued.

Why did she need to get married right here, right now? Bryan's voice pulsated through my head again. Money? Maybe citizenship? An agenda? Shit, maybe she was pregnant.

I didn't like where this conversation was going.

"What's the rush?" I said with the hint of an accusatory tone.

Saga looked into my eyes, but I won the staring contest. She averted her gaze to the sheets, while she fiddled with them, and shrugged with her free shoulder.

If anyone could read my thoughts, I knew they would shake me and loudly ask why the hell I wanted to marry Clarissa. In my warped mind, I did not want all the wedding planning to go to waste. I didn't want to disappoint anyone. Plus, and for some reason this seemed plausible in my head (perhaps it was because we resided in Los Angeles), I thought we could always divorce in a year, as if that was as easy and as emotionally painless as selling a coffee table on Craig's List. When you're entrenched in a long relationship, sometimes it becomes impossible to see life outside of it.

I rationalized that I would have time in my life for Saga if Clarissa and I got married and it didn't work out. But, simply put, I was scared to change my life for the unknown. Perhaps I'd had too much unknown crammed into the past month.

Saga searched my eyes for answers, like she was attempting to locate a breach in my defense as if we were playing air hockey again. Her demeanor had changed from comfortable to timid, as she knew I'd never go along with her suggestion.

"I'm going to take a shower," Saga said. "Are you coming?"

I needed to be at work in a few hours and still hadn't had an ounce of sleep.

"Yeah, just give me a minute."

I watched as Saga walked away and was suddenly very glad she took that year-long walking class. Worth every penny. I heard the squeak of the shower knob and the subsequent ambient sound of water hitting the bath. I laid my head back on the pillow and ran my hands over my face. I listened to my heart pound as I finally started to realize the gravity of my situation. I tried to breathe deeply to calm myself, but I knew the nervousness caused by my inability to decide anything would not cease. I was empty. I scanned the floor, walls, blank television for any sort of answer, but clearly found none. But then, I looked at the bedside table and saw the corner of Saga's red Swedish passport peeking out from underneath a magazine. I gave a cursory glance toward the bathroom and could now hear the shower water inconsistently hit the acrylic of the bath, a clear sign that Saga was already inside.

I quickly grabbed her passport and propped my back on the headboard, as if prepared to read a novel. I nervously opened it, not sure what I'd find, and was greeted by a terrible picture of Saga that actually made me smile. Perhaps she should have taken another photograph where both her eyes were open, but maybe she actually enjoyed the silly picture knowing she would have fun each time a customs agent searched it.

But then I realized why I'd been so apprehensive to open it in the first place. For the first time, I saw her full name: Saga Gräslund. I saw her birth date: April 18th, 1988. I saw her place of birth: Lund, Sweden. And suddenly things materialized. I could imagine her excitement upon waking up every April 18th. I had never been to her hometown, had no clue where it was, but as silly as it sounded, I now knew she came from somewhere. There was proof of a history. I wasn't sure how to pronounce her last name, but I loved the two dots over the "A." Saga officially became human to me. And, for whatever reason, any doubts I had about her, whether warranted or not, had slipped away. I loved that human. I looked back toward the bathroom and smiled as I hid the passport back underneath the magazine. I shot my naked body out of bed to meet her in the shower.

Ugh

The ride to work from San Clemente felt like it took forever, which was just fine with me because I liked cruising when I was in a decent mood. Mood elevation also came as great relief for my iPod selection, as it caused me to actually like my songs, instead of cycling through the shuffle while shaking my head and never settling on a tune until I was at my destination.

Even though it was probably misguided, I finally felt as if my current predicament had found some direction.

But all of that was about to change.

While singing along to Bon Jovi and minutes away from work, my in-car performance was interrupted by yet another text message from Clarissa. I finally decided to answer one to let her know that I was alive, but most of all, so she would stop texting me. I grabbed my phone, opened the text, and proceeded to feel my heart sink like the Titanic.

—Brandon, I'm on my way to see you. I'm worried about you. The love contract—

I looked away from my phone and quickly noticed I was only a few feet from colliding with the car directly in front of me. Instinctively, I slammed on my brakes, causing them to scream like banshees, but fortunately I stopped only a few inches from the car's back bumper. That didn't help my already racing heart and rapid breathing.

Scenarios ran, no, stormed through my head like soldiers once had stormed Normandy. Maybe I could turn around, push my car to epic speeds, and beat Clarissa to the OC, but I didn't know when she had begun her journey to ruin my life. If she started from home, she had a fifteen-minute head start on me. Plus, sometimes, her text messages would arrive twenty minutes after she sent them to my phone (fucking AT&T!), so, in actuality, she could have been halfway there already. It was times like these that I wished I had a flying car.

Perhaps I could call Saga and tell her to vacate the premises. I could tell her, fuck, no excuses that sounded even remotely plausible came to mind. I watched my hands shake uncontrollably, like I was suddenly inflicted with Parkinson's. If I had decided to jerk off right then and there, I wouldn't have had to exert one ounce of voluntary effort.

I didn't believe in God, but I found myself staring toward the sky for guidance.

As I pulled into a Starbucks parking lot only a block or two from work, I cursed myself for giving her the actual name of the bed and breakfast. As mentioned, I sucked under pressure and it never really occurred to me that she would use the information. I should have made something up, anything, but I knew Clarissa and, if she had discovered the hotel was not real, she would have exploded like Krakatoa. *But still, fuck, why did I give her the correct hotel?* Sometimes I really felt like I hadn't earned the right to continue living.

I hated conflict. And regardless of all the unusual drama of the past few weeks, I didn't really feel like seeing my life fall apart. Yes, maybe I wanted out of my engagement, but I wanted out on my own terms, and I didn't want the reason for my exit to beat the shit out of me (we all saw what Tiger's wife did to him, if we could all take one lesson from that embarrassing incident, it's don't wrong a Scandinavian girl. They once married Vikings after all). I felt I only had one option: Scratch, claw, and beg.

I decided to call Clarissa, apologize profusely, and beg her to turn around as if my life depended on it. And, in some ways, it actually did. But upon dialing her phone, it went straight to voicemail. *Mother fucking shit.* I tried again. Same thing. I tried again. Fuck, she *always* had her phone on. Why the fuck was it going to voicemail? Had she arrived already? Had she found Saga? Was there a catfight (I wondered who would win. Swedes are tough, but maybe Clarissa had karate in her blood)? My breathing rate increased; this was worse than before. I didn't even know what I was more afraid of, Clarissa's reaction, Saga's reaction, or just the humility and embarrassment of being caught. Perhaps the mixture of the three was the perfect storm for someone not used to so much emotional trauma.

I couldn't feel my left arm. I felt tingles on every inch of my body; this had to have been like the moments before discovering the results of an AIDS test a month after you fucked a toothless hooker in the ass without a condom. I closed my eyes, breathed deep, and pressed Clarissa's name on my cell phone one last time. Voicemail.

"BAAAAAALLLLLLLLLLSSSSSSSSS," I screamed, while I slammed both hands on the steering wheel, causing an inadvertent honk that went underappreciated by the Starbucks assholes who felt inconvenienced because the sound of my car caused them to lift their heads from their laptops and foamy lattes.

"Fuck you! Fuck you! FUUUUUUCCCCKKKK YOU," I screamed at them even though I knew full well none of this was their fault. I was in my car anyway, so they wouldn't have been able to hear, though perhaps they saw both my middle fingers standing tall through the glare of the windshield. That showed them, I'm sure.

But just when I thought I'd *completely* lose it, I pulled out of the lot and drove down the road to my office to find a horde of people standing behind police barriers. Hundreds of people. Worried people. A dozen police cars formed a perimeter around the building as uniformed men screamed to the questioning public with bullhorns. What the fuck was this? I couldn't understand what anyone was saying, but by the looks of the faces in the crowd, I could only feel extreme concern in the atmosphere. The expressions on the cops' faces mirrored their feelings. And was that a SWAT team? Outside my office building? Cool! But then I quickly remembered my problem and that I still didn't have a solution. I tried Clarissa's phone once more, but still got voicemail. I slammed the phone on the passenger seat in frustration, though I was extra pissed when it bounced up and hit me in the face.

There's nothing worse than only having yourself to blame.

As I searched the crowd again, I noticed Bryan's gargantuan cranium stick out like a hot air balloon in the distance. He knew my situation; perhaps he had the answer to my problems. Maybe he could tell his cousin to have Saga leave the hotel? Tell her it was a bomb scare or something.

That actually sounded like a good idea in my current warped mind. I quickly found a parking spot and bolted toward Bryan, who stood on his tippy-toes in an attempt to see beyond the police.

"Bryan!" I called to get his attention through the mass of people.

"Dude, there you are! Can you believe this shit?" he responded with a mixture of surprise and worry.

"Dude, I got a fuckin' problem, Dude. A big problem, and I need your help. Right now."

"Dude, I know, but at least we're not in the office, everything will be fine."

"What are you talking about?" I asked, with the patience and petulance of a five-year-old at his mother's hair salon.

"What are *you* talking about? Dude, do you know what's going on here?"

"No, and I *really* don't care at the moment. I need—"

""Dude, there's a guy in our lobby with a *bomb* strapped to his torso."

Like a bucket of cold water had been dumped on me, my body snapped to, in order to process both my own problem and the current one afflicting the office.

"Wait …The guy who made the threats? Are you serious?"

"I'm fuckin' dead serious! There's people in there and everything. Hostages, Dude! He's threatening to blow up the entire building if we don't take down all of the *Honey Buns* signs right now."

"Are you serious?"

"Can you believe it?"

"What the fuck is wrong with people?" I asked, as if the answer would somehow help me figure out the meaning of life.

"He's been in there for half an hour now."

I moved my head past the shoulders of the crowd in front of me for a clear view of the police barricade. I saw a man dressed in some ridiculous protective suit that I assumed could withstand a bomb blast and a multitude of other officers hiding behind their doors with rifles aimed at the front of our building. Numerous men in business suits discussed strategy with each other and constantly looked at the building with the expectation that it would explode at any moment.

And suddenly, through the commotion, I felt silence. Perhaps that was the sound of complete helplessness. I was fucked and I knew it. Perhaps a miracle would occur and the two would not cross paths, but I full well knew Saga had planned to do nothing but sleep all day. I could picture Clarissa knocking on the door. I could picture Saga opening it. And I realized I needed to do something to make that all go away. Anything. For once, I wanted the happy ending. I didn't want failure to win. I didn't want Clarissa's over-aggressiveness to win. I didn't want this asshole with a bomb strapped to his chest to win. For once, *I* wanted to win. It was time to press the panic button.

So I did.

"Bryan, I need a favor."

After the second incident of vandalism in Little Ethiopia, I stared at the ruined billboard and wondered what could possibly drive a man to such extremes. What could be so definite and so horrible that he actually considered not seeing his next days? What could instantly drive a man to insanity? And it had dawned on me: I completely understood.

"What?" he responded, clearly in no mood to do me a favor.

I handed him my cell phone.

"Right now, Clarissa's phone is going to voicemail. I need you to call her until you get an answer."

"What? Why? No."

"Please, just do it."

"Why don't you just call her? Dude, we have bigger things to worry about right now."

"Can you just please do it?" I said in a serious and urgent tone.

Bryan could see the desperation in my face.

"You OK? Because you look like shit."

"Thanks," I responded, as I turned my attention toward the building again.

He relented and grabbed my phone.

"What the hell do you want me to tell her?"

"This."

I quickly snaked my way through the rows of people until I reached an opening that led toward a blue police barrier that set the perimeter. I closed my eyes and thought over the stupidest things I'd ever done in my life. In second grade, I taught the entire class the word "cunt" during indoor recess and got suspended for a day (childlike innocence stupid). In Junior High, I uncapped a stink bomb during the student body government debates, but accidentally spilled it on myself, making it pretty simple for teachers to find the moron who had set it off (adolescent stupid). In college, I was pulled over by a cop who suspected me of driving drunk and, when asked to produce my license, I accidentally presented him my Captain Video membership card issued to John Stamos III (reckless college fun stupid.) And, of course, I had proposed to two women who were both ready to marry me as soon as possible (really stupid). But none of those came close to this.

I slammed my fists on the police barricade to energize myself and, after I quickly scanned the officers to make sure no one was looking, I hopped the fence, burrowed my toes to the ground, and sprinted as fast as I could in the direction of the building. I pumped my arms and legs harder than I ever had before and released a battle cry loud enough that it could warn boats of incoming fog. Halfway toward the door that felt like it was getting smaller, even though it was growing larger, I heard a cacophony of yells and screams from the surrounding policemen that made no sense in my muddled mind. Their cries from the bullhorn only increased my speed. I squinted, prepared to even take a bullet, but as I reached the steps of the building, none came.

I hopped up the stairs, three at a time, and blasted through the door to see a plethora of innocent bystanders hunched to the floor, holding each other, scared out of their minds. They watched me with fear, confusion, and every other conflicted emotion a human could feel as I instantly located the one man standing in the middle of the room with a long black coat. I could barely make out facial and body features as I only saw red; the adrenaline coursing through my body obscured all my senses and only allowed me to see basic shapes. All my energy was focused into my legs, arms, and shoulders. In that moment, I was not human. I was an animal. Like a rabid gorilla. An insane, rabid gorilla.

I dashed toward the cloaked man quick enough for him only to start to turn around when I slammed into him, shoulder first, like a middle linebacker on a 4th and two in the Super Bowl, and sent us both flying to the floor, a few yards from where I initially hit him. We landed with a crashing thud that temporarily knocked the wind from both of us.

My instincts (who knew I had any for a moment like this) hit overdrive and I quickly noticed a trigger in the hand of his extended left arm that connected to a dynamite contraption tied to his torso. Completely disoriented, I reached my hand to meet his and squeezed it as hard as I could to prevent his thumb from plunging the trigger. I felt our bodies struggle against each other, our legs tangled, our chests tensed as I held his hand like he was the one thing preventing me from falling off a cliff. I could feel commotion around me, but I did not know the source. The bomber kicked me hard, but my hand was a badger's jaw protecting the trigger.

And then I felt it. A burning sensation in my lower torso that I couldn't decipher. I yelled loudly from the feeling that didn't quite hurt but also sucked the energy from every part of my body, except for my hand, which clamped so hard that the trigger released from his grip.

And that's when I felt bodies grab and surround me. My eyes could barely stay open as my mind vacillated between cogency and delirium. I felt arms, legs, and bodies twist me over while they held my hands at my side. In a moment of clarity, I opened my eyes to find cops and medics hovering over my body; one medic tending to a bloody wound on my stomach. I turned my head left to see another officer looking over a knife, which in my altered state, appeared the size of King Arthur's sword. And, finally, I noticed the man I had hit. My threatening penpal. He kneeled with his hands behind his head; two officers pointing guns at his torso while another cuffed his wrists. The man had a long grey beard. Wrinkles. He had a large nose. Beady eyes...and a yarmulke on his head with a Star of David chain wrapped around his neck. Clearly, a senior citizen Jew.

And that was the sight that temporarily made me sane.

"Fuck!" I exclaimed in frustration. But not from the pain.

"Great, you're here. Do you understand what is going on?" the medic said with urgency, as he flashed a small light in my eyes to determine whatever it was he needed to determine.

"Yeah, I owe Blomax twenty dollars."

I hated when he was right.

The medic paused, utterly confused.

I passed out.

The Hospital
Where My Life
Ended

(So It Seemed)

I wished, for once in my life, I had thought something through.

The good news: my plan actually worked.

The bad news: everything else.

I woke up lying in the hospital with a foggy head and a sharp pain in my side. As it turned out, and I know this is hard to believe, being stabbed was not as sexy as it sounded. But lucky for me, the blade narrowly missed any organs and, with the aid of some stitches, I would be completely healthy sooner than I ever figured. In fact, my doctor informed me I would be good enough to walk down the aisle as scheduled. When I asked if it meant I couldn't exert too much physical energy (jerking off), he patted my shoulder and assured me that I'd be lucky enough to dance at my wedding.

"It's really only a messy flesh wound," he said, as if I was complaining about hangnail. "Pretty lucky, all things considered."

He clearly didn't know me at all. But, believe it or not, the pain and hospital stay were not the reasons I regretted my actions.

Somewhere in between Clarissa's original message about driving to San Clemente and storming my office building like a kamikaze pilot, I had completely forgotten an obvious angle to my "heroic" actions: this was the media's wet dream. Another little fact also slipped my mind under duress: Clarissa worked for one of the most powerful publicity firms in Hollywood and was a complete attention whore. As I watched the story of the "Hero Groom" (they couldn't come up with anything better? Brandon Popularity was so much better) on the local five o'clock news, while surrounded by hundreds upon hundreds of flowers that littered my hospital room, I knew I had completely fucked up. I had somehow solidified myself into a loveless marriage. Think about it. If I chose to run, I would go from "Hero Groom" to "Asshole Groom" in record time. I'd never be able to show my face anywhere without judgment.

Not to mention, Mr. Chang would probably kill me by ripping off my appendages, one by one, and then beating my
bloody stump of a body with my detached limbs.

Also, technically, I was a criminal. After all, I had endangered the lives of hundreds of hostages, not to mention the
structure of the building, had the bomb detonated. And
yes, the bomb was actually live; that old Jew meant some
serious business. But since the explosive was never triggered, and the hundreds of innocent bystanders were saved
by my utter stupidity, the Mayor of Los Angeles insisted
that the city immediately drop all charges and declare me a
hero. Sensing an opportunity to bring attention to herself,
Clarissa and her partners found an angle, notified all the
media outlets, and informed them that I was to be married soon. In the eyes of these gutless douchebags, I was
even more of a hero since I put my future happiness on the
line to save faceless innocents. And the story took off in
minutes.

Within hours, we already had three networks offer us
a reality miniseries that would document our wedding and
the days leading up to it. When I initially woke up for the
first time after the stabbing, and was greeted by Clarissa's
smiling face as she held my hand, she asked me if I'd be
interested in the show idea. It was actually her third question after "how are you?" and "that's so nasty, does it hurt?"

I told her I would be completely interested, but only if it ended with me climbing a mountain and throwing myself off of it. She actually instinctively muttered, "We can make that happen," before realizing what I had actually said. I wasn't a hero. I didn't want the attention. I didn't want a media circus. You know what I was? An asshole that did something stupid in an effort to make his problems disappear.

And all I wanted was for Saga to forget how to turn on a television.

After dozens of people came to visit, including my entire office (my boss gave me the finger guns and commented on how nice it was outside), Bryan (he just wanted his twenty), and Clarissa's parents (who still didn't seem impressed, Mr. Chang asked how I could support his daughter while lying in a hospital bed), I begged my doctors to clear the room so I didn't have to look at all the annoying faces (though I just said I needed rest). When they told me that Clarissa could stay and hold my hand for the entire night, I declined. All I really wanted was peace and quiet, which I supposed was true, though I just didn't want to see Clarissa since I internally blamed her for all of this, even though it was completely my fault. After I asked Clarissa to get home and sleep ("for me, please"), she kissed my forehead and told me she would be back bright and early. I couldn't wait.

And finally everyone left. I wished they'd never come back.

I stared at the closed door thankful that Saga never walked through it, and at the same time, couldn't have blamed her if she never did. I knew this couldn't end well. She either saw the news telecast and that awful photo they kept showing of Clarissa and me in straw hats from our Caribbean getaway, or she was pissed at me for standing her up after not returning to the bed and breakfast like I had promised. Either way, it didn't look good.

As I rested alone on the hospital bed, pumped full of painkillers, I turned on CNN to discover that I was now officially national news. The big time. And for the first time, I saw the raw security camera footage of me pummeling the old Jew into the ground and the wrestling match that ensued. All I could think about was how pathetic I looked. It was quite the struggle, and the wrinkled man really held his own. I couldn't believe I didn't have the ability to kick the ass of a senior citizen. Really, fuck the gym, no seriously, fuck it hard.

I gently poked at the red and purple mess that was my stitched wound and closed my eyes to concentrate for the first quiet moment in what seemed like forever.

And then the door opened.

And my nightmare was about to come true.

Saga walked in.

It was inevitable, I figured.

I smiled.

She didn't.

Without words, she slowly looked at all the flowers that had been delivered, even picking up a few cards and reading them without so much as a reaction. I couldn't say anything either. I could only watch her as she casually walked to the chair beside my bed and sat. She clasped her fingers and waited for me to speak.

I immediately recalled our first game of verbal chicken while we strolled the streets of Gamla Stan after the dinner with our fathers. I would have given anything to be back there with her; it seemed like so long ago. I told her that night that if I could talk to the fifteen-year-old version of myself, I'd tell him to do it all differently. I still believed that.

We stared at each other for two straight minutes without so much as a word, a smile, or anything that resembled an expression. I could tell by the heaving of her chest that we were breathing in the exact same pattern.

I cleared my throat. It was time to do what I did best: take a fucked up situation and make it worse.

"Why did you want to marry me?" I asked.

Beautiful start.

Saga's face didn't even so much as twitch. It was as if I never asked the question at all. I waited for an answer, but never received one. Of course, because I enjoyed pain, I couldn't let it go.

"It's a simple question," I said.

"How can I answer that?" she finally said.

"With words would be nice," I responded. I had no clue why I was being an asshole. Perhaps a defense mechanism where I attempted to make it seem like it was her fault. I didn't want to do that; I don't know why I tried.

After I officially recognized the consequences of my words, I figured that instead of stopping, I'd continue being a complete moron. "Were you trying to get pregnant?" I accused.

She ignored my question, but remained calm.

"Remember what I asked you in the airport?" she asked.

"If I had any gum?"

"No," she said without a hint of emotion. She was a robot.

I knew what she meant: The question about the color of the sky.

But I didn't care about her question. I needed an answer: "Why did you want to marry me?" I asked again.

"Well, I clearly know why you wanted to marry me now," she said, as she nodded at the television. I guessed she remembered how to turn one on after all.

341

"If that's what you believe, you really don't actually," I responded, knowing full well that maybe she was, at least, partially right.

"And you can't even apologize," she responded.

I broke eye contact.

"It's just curious that you'd agree to marry someone you barely knew," I said, as if the whole thing had been her idea.

Saga shrugged.

"You asked me."

In case I needed the reminder.

"Yeah, but I resigned myself to forgetting about it. You came and found me."

"So now this is my fault."

"I just want to know why you wanted to marry me."

The more I asked the question, the more I desperately wanted the answer.

"Does it have anything to do with my father?" I accused.

"What?"

"My father. The fact that he won the lottery."

And now all the cards were on the table.

Saga leaned back in her chair and shook her head as she drew her eyes to her lap. She absent-mindedly tucked her hair behind her ear; God she was beautiful. When she raised her head again, there were tears. I immediately regretted the accusation.

"So that's what this is about?"

"Well..."

"Brandon, I didn't even know that about him."

I wasn't sure if I believed her.

"But if that's true, he needs to buy some nicer shirts."

OK, maybe I believed her.

"And kick the orange eating habit."

Fuck. I hadn't even realized my shoulders were tense until they fell like bricks. I softly dropped my hands to my sides in some sort of surrender.

"I just don't understand why someone like you would want anything to do with someone like me," I said, as I looked away like a child. It was something I had felt, but wasn't quite sure I actually believed. It just seemed like something I'd normally say.

Saga breathed quickly through her nose in what appeared to be a short, dismissive laugh and shook her head.

"I just don't need to hear it," I said.

"You have no clue what I came here to say." She gathered her things.

"Whatever." It was the best I could come up with.

I guessed there was nothing left to be said. I couldn't even look her in the eye, although I felt hers on me. I can't even imagine what I looked like. It certainly wasn't a mature adult.

"Fine," she said. She had no energy left for me. I couldn't blame her.

She vacated her seat and walked to the door, but as she twisted the knob to leave, she turned to me one last time.

"You look really pathetic right now."

I gulped.

"I guess I don't have a future in modeling hospital gowns," I said, as I grabbed a piece of the paper garment.

"You don't need one. You're completely covered in your own bullshit."

And with that, she left.

I sighed and slammed the back of my head against the pillow like I was the limb-less cripple pounding Morse code from *Johnny Got His Gun*. *Fuck it*. I wasn't going out like that. I tried to raise myself from the bed, but doubled over in pain from the movement and stumbled on to the floor.

"FUCK!" I yelled at the top of my lungs, not caring who heard. I could feel the cool air against my exposed bare ass as I remained motionless, defeated, with my cheek pressed against the sterile linoleum.

Seconds after my exclamation, the door opened and I prepared my apology to the nurse for disobeying orders and mooning her. But when I finally managed to look toward the door, all that stood before me was a protruding belly and surfer riding a gnarly wave on a Hawaiian shirt.

My father held out his hands and smiled.

"My son, the hero," he said, as he laughed and helped me back into bed. I shrugged him off and painfully crawled back over my sheets.

For some strange reason, I was only slightly irritated by his presence. It sounded ridiculous, but other than Bryan, Helga the stripper, and the Segway attendant, he was one of my only human connections to Saga. There was strangely some comfort in that.

"How ya doin' there, champ?"

"Sore."

"Yeah?"

"Yeah."

"That's some serious shit you pulled today."

"Yeah."

"Why in the hell would you do that?"

"For the children."

My father kept his eyes on me as he sat down in the chair next to the bed and pulled out a fresh orange.

"Would you fuckin' quit it with the stupid oranges."

"Brandon, they're my thing."

I supposed that was the least of my problems.

"So you're still gettin' married, eh?" he asked, while he looked toward the door.

Shit, he had entered my room only moments after Saga had left. Had he seen her in the hallway? I wanted to change the subject.

"Aren't you supposed to be in Russia?"

"I'm going up in a few days. It's really exciting stuff. You should see the training these Rooskies go through. Those Commie bastards really know a thing or two about putting your old man in orbit."

I didn't give a shit. "Then why are you here?"

"I came back to talk to you," he said, suddenly serious. "You know you're a real asshole when it comes to returning a fucking phone call."

"What about? I really don't care to deal with your bullshit if you die up there."

"You know, you can be an insufferable prick."

"Thanks."

"But that's not what I wanted to talk to you about."

"Then what?"

"You don't have to do this," he continued, while waving to the air as if it encompassed my entire life. "All this bullshit."

"All what bullshit?"

"You know what I'm talking about."

"What? And end up like you?"

"What's wrong with ending up like me?"

He waited for an answer from me that was never going to come. I think he was finally sick and tired of my baby routine when it came to discussing his life. I was actually sick of hearing myself perform it.

"I won the lottery, traveled the world, had experiences most people only dream of while fucking the most beautiful women culture has to offer. I'm about to go on a mission, an actual space mission. I can't think of anything more exciting than that. And guess what, I smiled the whole way through," he continued.

"The crazy thing is that you honestly think you're happy," I said, as I folded my arms like a child not getting his way.

"And why do you think I'm not?"

"Because people don't behave like you do unless they are seriously deranged."

"Is that right? Says who?"

"I don't know. People."

My father smirked slightly and nodded.

"Let me tell you something about *people*, Brandon. People fight wars for, really, no reason other than they can't get along. People let millions of their fellow men go hungry while they gorge themselves with hot dog eating contests. Humans are the most imperfect, dishonest organisms this planet has to offer."

"What the fuck is your point?"

"My point? These same *people* created 'normal.' They tell you what's right and what's wrong. They tell you that you should grow old, get married, have a family, and that is the key to happiness. Let me tell you something about people. People don't know shit."

I didn't have a response.

"Let me tell you something else. If I could replay the last four years of my life, since I won the lotto, I wouldn't do a thing differently. I wish I could do it forever."

"And you flew back from Russia to tell me this," I finally responded.

"Yes. You're my son."

I was. But I didn't want to be like him. In fact, I'd marry Clarissa for no other reason than to spite him.

"Get the fuck out of my room," I said, as seriously as I've said anything in my entire life.

He nodded and breathed heavily from his nose, as if he expected that exact answer. Like this was his last attempt to get inside my head and it had failed. I didn't want to listen to him anymore. All I wanted to do was lay in my own misery. I wanted to think about Saga. I wanted to think about the wedding and how I'd get through it (or out of it). I wanted to think about every single moment of the rest of my life and how much I didn't want to hate it. And I didn't want to think about him.

As he walked to the door, he turned around one last time.

"In the next few days, you're probably gonna hear some shit about me, OK? Just know it's not *all* true."

I had no clue what he meant; I didn't care enough to ask.

And that was the last time I ever saw my father.

Simpler

You could often hear a pin drop after dusk on the streets of the typical suburban town in which I was raised. Since I was old enough to look after myself, I'd take long walks during the late hours of the night just to hear the soft rhythm of my shoes against the concrete, while the leaves rustled slightly in the cool breeze over the distant sound of a train's horn that made the night feel as if it were the first page of a children's book.

But even though the town was far from magical, the easiness of the area provided a cloak over the wicked that so easily seeped through the cracks of our consciousness. As if the metaphorical white picket fences in our town warded off pesky details like reality, leaving its citizens to worry about "serious matters" like litter on Lake Road, or rumored bags of weed left in the shaft of the replica Civil War cannon that stood guard in the center of town. While I'm sure my neighbors had secret problems like domestic disputes and financial shortcomings, I never once felt a sense of true despair, and I honestly believed that only appeared on the news, in movies, or in some far off land I would never see.

And, believe it or not, my parents, despite my father's absences, might have been the prime example of the delighted, committed couple who honestly believed that true love could help you navigate any uncharted path. With their respectable jobs and dinner dates, their Sunday mornings passing the *New York Times* crossword back and forth like a hot potato and Sunday nights watching *Murder She Wrote* with hands clasped tight, you would think they could have authored the latest edition of *Marriage For Dummies* and maybe even have earned an *Oprah* appearance. Now, I was left to wonder how Jerry Springer bided his time.

I never thought about reincarnation, but if I opened myself to such beliefs, I could easily be convinced that my childhood occurred in a completely different lifetime.

My first date took place when I was twelve years old. The fall. I was a short, braces-faced, pathetic wisp of an excuse for a boy, but for some reason, Tina Riscotti, who must have been a foot taller than me, took a shine to my younger self and demanded that we go out on a date. That's right, demanded. She actually tapped my shoulder during lunch, while my mouth was full of turkey and potato bread, and told me—no insisted—that I liked her and that we'd be seeing *Teenage Mutant Ninja Turtles* at the Cinema Six that weekend. She waited, not so patiently, for my response with her head cocked to the right and arms akimbo against the waist of her burgundy Z. Cavaricci's, while her two friends stood behind her with their arms crossed to provide intimidating support. There was a rumor that she had paid those two girls to hang out with her. I wasn't sure if it was true, but Tina wasn't exactly the friendliest bully in the world, so I assumed they stood their ground in fear as well. I actually never gave her a second thought before that proposition and was rather afraid of her, which is probably why I agreed. I always wondered what would have happened if I had declined. I couldn't picture Tina welling up and burying her teary eyes in the shoulder of her friend's Francois Girbaud top, but I supposed it was possible. A more likely scenario involved, at best, future harassment until I relented or, at worst (and more probable), a bruised shin and perhaps a bloody nose.

On the night of my date, I must have tried on about sixty different outfit combinations to impress Tina. I actually don't even know why I cared, but it just seemed like the thing to do. After I finally decided on my prized purple Hypercolor shirt and a pair of Skidz my mother had bought me only a week before (which had no business ever gripping the waist of a short, twelve-year-old Jew, or anyone for

---

that matter), my father entered my bedroom, sat down at my desk, and nodded toward me as if I'd done something that might have impressed him.

"You know, your life is never going to be the same after tonight," he said, as sure as he'd ever said anything to that point in his life.

I didn't quite understand what he meant. After all, we'd just be seeing a movie about talking turtles with a penchant for kicking ass; it wasn't like I was headed off to my wedding. At least I didn't think so; Tina's fists were quite persuasive when she wanted them to be.

"Trust me, while I'm sure you've liked girls in the past, from this moment forward, pretty much every decision you make is so you can continue to have nights like this. Even if tonight's bad, even if the next one is shit, or if the one after that makes you want to kill yourself, something in you is gonna keep trying to make it work. One day, you'll be cursing to the world, wondering why you put yourself through something that hurts you more than a llama's kick to the nuts, but you'll keep doing it. You'll gladly stand in back of that llama again and again, begging it to kick you in the jimmy just one more time."

It's probably the truest thing he'd ever said to me, though I wondered if he'd actually been kicked in the testicles by a llama. Then he patted me on the back, handed me twenty dollars, and told me not to buy Jujyfruit because it was impossible to pick out the licorice ones in the pitch black theater. Sound advice.

And then he set me free to the rest of my life.

Tina's mother dropped her off in something I had never expected to see: a dress. She actually looked like a young woman; she was kind of pretty with her edges smoothed. She wore eyeliner and blush. I could picture her mother helping her put on makeup for the first time. And she looked nervous. Tina, who once punched Mr. Colotta in the ass (a solid jab to the right cheek) during fourth grade recess and threw Alex Zambito in the garbage in the fifth grade version, looked vulnerable standing in my foyer only minutes before we were to walk to the movies. She liked me and just wanted to be liked back. It was that simple. It was a feeling I hadn't experienced before and I knew my father was right. I remember I looked toward him before I walked out the door, and he nodded to me, while silently commenting on our height difference with his hands, which strangely made me feel as if I had his know-how and could easily store it in my back pocket in case I needed it.

As we prepared to leave and refastened our jackets, my parents, with arms around each other's backs, watched us walk out the front door and down the path to the sidewalk with huge smiles on their faces. My mother called to us, and Tina and I turned our heads back just in time to see the flash of my father's camera.

I don't know if he ever developed that photo, but I hadn't seen it.

My parents made love seem so simple. I obviously did not witness their courtship, but much of my childhood was spent looking at their smiles. I do remember some fights, but I also recall their heartfelt apologies, always punctuated by a soft peck on the lips. Going out on my first date just seemed like the first step of a journey along the same path. I was nervous, but it didn't seem difficult; it felt like something that would just happen. I never would have thought their love lives would get so mutilated and also never figured mine would one day rival their complexity.

I can still picture Tina and me walking to the movies on that cool night. Me kicking errant brown leaves that lay dead on the grooved concrete. Her picking up solitary rocks and throwing them at distant trees in an attempt to display some sort of accuracy. No real words spoken. My neighbor walking his golden retriever and patiently waiting for it to pee. Crickets chirping loudly in Mrs. Hendrickson's bushes. Just two kids going to check out some freaky humanoid turtles.

And then nothing was ever simple again.

Life seems so effortless when it exists in snapshots.

PART FOUR

The Lamest Bachelor Party Of All Time

The minute I got engaged, one of my first fears was that someone would demand that I have a bachelor party. Normally, I understood why the groom-to-be looked forward to this rite of passage more than any other in his life. I comprehended the appeal of multiple strippers (eight boobs are always better than two), the stories that were born from both the retarded shit said and done by the friend that had way too much to drink, and, of course, the multitude of bonding moments between friends that would be discussed, from that day till the end of eternity, in hushed tones, so women would never be able to understand the code of brotherhood. It was the one last secret a man could keep before marriage. I'd seen *The Hangover*, twice. I got it. It did sound fun, but the problem was I just didn't have too many friends. Or any, really.

I once did. Back in high school and in college I had several, but I lost many to bouts with time and geography. And, unfortunately, about six months before I left New York, my two closest friends died in a car accident on an icy road on their way to see *Brokeback Mountain*. I had never been so glad to be turned off by the sight of two dudes kissing because they had invited me to go along. An Oscar-caliber film, they claimed. Ebert said it was a "revelation," one of them told me minutes before they got in the car. I still declined, as I had little interest in seeing two cowboys bang while tending sheep or whatever they were doing.

I'd often think about what they might have discussed moments before their car hit the icy patch and skidded into oncoming traffic. I wondered what song they were listening to. Perhaps they were singing Journey's "Separate Ways" at the top of their lungs in between gasps of laughter. They had a habit of this after all. I just hoped they were having fun and that the end was painless.

There are so many jokes that I supposed could be made and had been made by people who knew of the incident, but weren't close to either of them. They were my best friends and, while I was an asshole that normally was not above poking fun at tragedy, it was still a subject I could not touch. In fact, it was partially the reason I had moved to California.

It's hard to meet new friends when you're a twenty-something that moved across the country without knowing a single soul in an entire strange city. When I first arrived in Los Angeles, I did meet a couple of people here and there, you know while playing basketball at the park, at a sports bar during NFL football games, and at my first crappy job, but I had met Clarissa soon after that and, from that point forward, most of my free time was spent with her. This was not a knock on Clarissa, but I depended on her for companionship and she depended on me because she was needy. Soon, those minor relationships I'd forged had quickly disintegrated and left a black hole that was really only filled by Bryan, my only real current friend. And since I had no siblings or any cousins I actually had any real contact with, Bryan really was the only one who could possibly mention a bachelor party.

And, of course, he did. "Dude, you don't know how bad I need Vegas. This is the only excuse I'll ever have that'll make sense to my wife," he practically begged.

"I'm not feelin' it, dude."

"Dude, Vegas."

"I dunno, dude, I'm still feelin' iffy from that whole incident."

"Dude, it's a flesh wound."

"Well, it fuckin' hurt."

"We're going."

"Dude, it's my bachelor party."

"We're going to Vegas."

"I don't want to go to Vegas."

"Dude, Vegas."

And that was that.

When I told Bryan that I didn't know enough people to fill a credible bachelor party, he claimed he could easily round up six guys who would be happy to go in a matter of fifteen minutes. "Dude, you have no clue of the desperation among dads at Daycare," he assured me.

He was wrong. It only took thirteen minutes to compile six eager men hungry for an excuse to get away from their wives and children. There are lots of depressing things in the world. Death is depressing, bankruptcy is depressing, cancer is really fucking depressing. And while all those tragedies were universally recognized as devastating, I couldn't help but feel that, in that moment, nothing could be more depressing than introducing yourself, for the first time, to 84 percent of your bachelor party.

And though I consistently resisted, Bryan promised me that once we started winning at blackjack, shoving twenties into strippers' pussies, and drinking until we passed out, I'd have the time of my life. Well, five hours into the party, I was down two hundred, fifty bucks, vomited what I thought might be my spleen, and was fancied only by an overweight stripper that appeared to have been fit to birth calves and not human children. Worse off, her enormous tits only reminded me of Helga, the over-the-hill stripper in Stockholm, which naturally reminded me of Saga. Which naturally reminded me of marrying Clarissa. Which naturally crushed me. Which naturally caused me to temporarily remove myself from the bachelor party area so I could sit in the corner and think; even though it was particularly difficult to ponder my thoughts while the sound system loudly pumped Ace of Base throughout the entire strip club. Strippers danced to the strangest shit.

I could say that the conjured memory of Helga was the first time I'd thought of Saga since she left me, but that would be a lie. I thought of her every second. And because I often analyzed my thoughts just as much as I produced original introspection, I tried, once again, to figure out why she had such an effect on me. After all, even though I had spent memorable time with her, they only amounted to about four or five days. I figured Saga represented an escape. It wasn't her as much as the idea of stepping out-side of my body, Los Angeles, the United States, and everything I knew. I remembered that when I fantasized about Saga, the ruminations always were set in Sweden. In the brief moments I dreamt of a family with her, I pic-tured walking our tall (with luck) children along a river in Stockholm, never along Santa Monica Boulevard or 6th Avenue in New York City or the main street of some town in America where I'd possibly one day reside. And yes, I also recalled her passport, her body, her thoughts, thinking of her as a complete person instead of some beautiful ideal whom I constructed in my pea-sized mind. But though I recognized all of those thoughts and facts, I couldn't quite reconcile them.

With Saga, rationality was often forgotten and all I had left were my feelings. And my feelings suggested I missed her. I knew I'd never see her again, that she would only exist in my memory. And that was something I figured I'd have to be OK with. It probably was better as a dream any-way. I knew, in reality, there was as good a chance I'd be as miserable in her arms as I was in Clarissa's.

While I watched Bryan and the six guys I didn't know (I knew one of their names was Henry because I found it odd to meet someone under thirty named Henry) fondle and chuck money at the strippers, I knew that I wanted to be anywhere but there. Without any of them noticing, I walked out of the second-rate club and out toward the parking lot where my car was parked.

I got in the car and rested the back of my head against the headrest while breathing out a sigh that was meant solely for self-dramatic purposes. I placed both my hands on the steering wheel and contemplated turning the key and driving away. Bryan and his buddies wouldn't know I was gone for hours and, while they may have been pissed if I left, I bet it would soon become a legendary story that they would one day tell: the bachelor party where the bachelor left us at the strip club. Maybe they'd go home with some of them and have a large gangbang or something. See, I would be doing them a favor. It was Vegas after all.

Restless, I checked my glove compartment simply because I was fidgety, had nothing else to do, and thought maybe I had left some Altoids in there even if they were over a year old. But while I searched through car paperwork, manuals, and receipts I was too lazy to throw out, I found an old credit card statement that was probably meant to be discarded long ago.

The bill was already three years old. I reviewed the purchases and shook my head at the incredibly appropriate memories: A sixty-dollar charge to a decent restaurant on La Brea called Amalfi. That was my third date with Clarissa. I had picked that restaurant because it was within walking distance of my apartment and I figured it would be easy to lure her there after dinner in the hope of a good fuck or two. And it actually worked. We had plans to see a movie afterward, but I slyly asked if I could stop by the apartment to grab a jacket, to which she agreed, and of course once we got inside, I suggested we just watch a movie on cable instead, which led to a heavy make-out session and, eventually, my penis in her vagina. And while I pondered that memory and tried to recall the other purchases on the statement, I couldn't believe how much time had passed. So much had changed, but it felt like nothing had changed at all. I closed my eyes to picture the memories and tried to recall exactly what I felt like at the time I paid that bill three years before. It had to have been a lot different than this. Or maybe it wasn't.

There was an address in the corner of the bill where the payment was meant to be sent, a random place in Vermont. I thought of the envelope traveling from sunny, busy Los Angeles to the peaceful countryside of Vermont. I imagined a long road surrounded by trees, maybe a barn or two, perhaps a cow taking a dump, mountains in the distance en route to the mundane office complex where the credit card company did business. I pictured the bill tossed with many others just like it, rolled through the hallways in a huge bin, and then given to a few workers who would be in charge of opening the bills and logging them in some boring computer program. A machine couldn't open and read the bills, right? It wasn't like they could hire a robot to sort the checks. It was the job of some nameless, faceless human who had a basic nine-to-five. And, suddenly, I became very jealous of that employee. It might have been a boring, entry-level job that barely required a high school diploma, but I would have bet that it was the easiest, most stress-free job in the world.

I gripped the steering wheel again and imagined myself following a similar path as my credit card payment had done three years before. Across the country, over the Rocky Mountains, through the great plains, past New York City, Boston, until I arrived in pastoral Vermont. I'd drive along that wide-open, empty road with my driver-side window cracked so the clean autumn air could consume my car with its sweet smell and rushing noise that would drown out the song on the radio. I'd breathe it in deeply, so I could taste it as I watched the bright sun dance along the mountaintops on the horizon. It would just be me on the way to work. To log those bills. I could do that. I could escape and start a completely new life.

But, instead, I removed my hands from the steering wheel and knew I never could. I exited my car and walked back toward the obnoxious neon lights at the entrance of the strip club. I'm sure Bryan and his friends never knew I was gone.

My Wedding Day

I woke up alone on the day I was to be married. I realized then it probably would be the last time I'd wake up without a warm body next to me for some time. It was an eerie feeling. Sure, I thought about marriage and a life with Clarissa for months, a year even. We had done the stupid rehearsals, pored over the minutiae of every detail of both the ceremony and party. But, regardless of all the preparation, there was nothing quite like opening your eyes for the first time on the day you commit yourself to another for the rest of your life.

It made me feel old. And stupid.

I rubbed my stomach, unsure if it tumbled due to nerves or a bad experience from the rehearsal dinner the night before. Unfortunately, there was no bison or seal, or even Chinese food for that matter, as a local Italian restaurant offered their services for free after they heard about our bullshit media-hyped romance. I found it amusing that so many people claimed we had real love simply because some old Jew stabbed me. It made absolutely no sense. I didn't run into a burning building to save Clarissa; I ran into a building filled with complete strangers due to momentary insanity and the fact that, at the time, death seemed like a better option than marrying her. It probably still was. Their logic didn't make sense, but I understood people needed to fabricate happiness any way they could to escape their own miserable existence. Having said that, I guessed we would have been foolish to reject a free meal that would have otherwise cost well over three thousand dollars. I chalked up the gurgling in my stomach to the karmic eggplant parmesan.

I had three hours to kill before the town car was scheduled to pick me up for the ceremony, and I really had no clue what to do with myself. I figured I'd finally watch some of the shows that had been clogging my TiVo, anything to get my mind off of the huge mistake I was about to make. I laid my tuxedo on the bed and ran my hands across the dark fabric, in part hoping that my hand would sink through the blackness, like it was a magical rabbit hole, and lead me to an alternate universe where I didn't have to get married.

I wondered if when Clarissa was younger and dreaming about her perfect wedding, she had ever considered what her groom would be doing the morning of the ceremony. I doubt she figured her Prince Charming would be jealous of *Alice in Wonderland* or even the chick held captive in *Silence Of The Lambs*.

And just as I delved further into this daydream, my phone rang.

A blocked number. I thought to skip the call, but then remembered I was getting married and felt that it would be wise to answer all calls in case there were any last minute changes. Like my bride calling it off.

Then, suddenly, Saga popped into my mind. Wouldn't it be poetic if she called on my wedding day? She had a sixth sense for bullshit like this. It had to be her.

I picked up.

"Hello?"

"Is this Brandon?" a definite male voice asked.

My shoulders slumped. No such luck.

"Speaking," I said unenthusiastically.

"Are you watching TV?"

"Why?"

"Turn on Channel four, please."

"Who is this?"

"Apologies. My name is Martin Simon. I am your father's attorney. I'm afraid I have some...well, I think you'll want to turn on Channel Four."

I reflexively turned on the television and was greeted by the vision of plane debris floating in the ocean. The crawl at the bottom of the screen claimed that a private jet had crashed in the middle of the Atlantic and all passengers were currently missing. The pieces floated calmly in the still ocean despite the commotion of boats and helicopters that surrounded it.

"Yeah, so?"

"Are you watching the news about the plane crash?"

"Yes."

"Your father was on that flight."

Jesus.

I sat down on the bed without taking my eyes off the TV. I felt an honest twinge of sadness. I had known he was flying back to Russia for the space mission, but I never figured it possible that he would actually die on the way to the most dangerous thing he would ever do. I think Alanis Morrissette wrote a song about this exact thing.

"Oh." It was all I could say.

"I know you two had a rocky relationship. But I am truly sorry for your loss."

"Thanks."

"Why don't we just take a moment of silence for him," the lawyer said.

Weird.

Though a plane crash was beyond his control and ironic in its own right, it was hardly shocking that it happened on the day of my wedding. One more way to distract me from the act he never approved.

I kept the phone to my ear and listened to the lawyer as he breathed. His breathing was so loud, it sounded like he had ham sandwiches shoved up his nostrils. I'd bet a million dollars that he was a fat shit.

"OK, this is weird. I'm done," I said.

"Your father requested that I show you something on the day he died. Could you meet me at his mansion in an hour?"

I had never been invited to my father's mansion. I actually had never even seen it other than in obnoxious photos he would send on occasion to taunt me and brag about his money.

"No."

"No?"

"I can't"

"Ok...But I think you will want to."

"I'm getting married today."

"Oh, right! The hero groom. I'm a fan."

I would normally have hung up, but for some reason, I didn't. As I sat alone in my room, staring at wreckage on the television, I couldn't help but see the metaphor. I was a Christmas ornament in April. But not lonely, so much as abandoned.

"Well, I suppose we could do this tomorrow, if we must, though your father specifically said the day he died. He even told me to beg."

"This doesn't make any sense. My father had no clue when he was gonna die, so what's the difference when you show me?"

"Do you want me to beg?"

"No, I want you to tell me why it has to be today."

"It's just what your father wanted."

"I never really cared what he wanted."

"OK, then, I have to beg."

I looked at my tuxedo and thought three hours of Tivo held much less interest than my father's mansion. After all, I was curious to find out what was so important.

I relented.

"Fine. What's the address?"

Donned in my tuxedo (just in case I ran out of time), I pulled my car on to a winding street deep in the heart of Beverly Hills and drove past numerous gates in front of palatial estates nestled in the distance. The grass beside the faultless sidewalks was as bright as an unused light-green crayon fresh from a box of sixty-four. The trees were perfectly manicured. Not a piece of garbage in sight. Actually, there was not even another human or vehicle in the entire area; the neighborhood appeared to be in a lovely slumber. Most would say an area such as this would look "dead," but the color, cleanliness, and opulence suggested it was anything but.

I double checked the address and approached a large white gate with my father's initials emblazoned on the center of the doors, as if he was Richie Rich. As soon as the front of my car broached the property, the intercom set in the bushes crackled to life and informed me to follow the path toward the circular driveway in front of the house.

The gate opened like arms of a hug and I carefully drove past the pristine lawn that featured fairway-like green grass and continued over a small bridge that sat beside a fountain that appeared as if it had been transported from Ancient Rome. But instead of the diminutive cherubic creatures spitting streams of water, he had constructed large-breasted women that squirted liquid from their oversized nipples. This was the perfect example of what insane people with too much money did to amuse themselves. Normal people just jerk off with cock in hand; rich people masturbate with a pen and checkbook.

I still had two and a-half hours until I committed myself to a lifetime of miserable slavery. Clarissa hadn't called. No one called. This, for no good reason, made me feel safe.

As directed, I pulled through the circular driveway in front of a house with several white pillars gracing the entrance. I exited my car and found Martin Simon waiting for me by the front door. He actually wasn't fat at all, quite slim really, but he had an unusually curved nose that resembled Lombard Street in San Francisco. It appeared to have been pummeled many times, like he was a former boxer, but one who lost far more than he won. But judging by his hunched stature, I assumed he had no pugilistic ability at all and was just naturally ugly. The curved nose might have clarified why he breathed like a ninety-year-old man after a marathon, though it didn't quite explain the permanent expression on his face that suggested he had just sniffed a hellaciously offensive fart.

Martin waved enthusiastically, entirely too happy of a greeting for someone who had just lost a parent.

"So you must be Brandon. I've heard so much about you."

What a guess.

Martin led me inside the house that was as gaudy as it was impressive. After exiting the foyer that was four times the size of my entire apartment and actually decorated with tasteful art (was that a Picasso?), we crossed a small bridge that was built over an indoor stream that seemed to span the entire bottom floor.

"Your father bought this house from an investment banker shortly after he won. He claimed he always wanted a house with a river that ran through it. So he built this. He'd often sit in a floating tube and relax as the current took him throughout the house. It runs through every room on the ground floor. It was his Amazon."

I tried to show disdain, but I admitted to myself that I thought it was pretty cool. The main portion of the house was a healthy mixture of museum-like standoffishness combined with a hint of comfort. It was different than I had imagined.

"Follow me, please."

I followed Martin into a study with red painted walls, a fireplace, tall bookshelves complete with a rolling ladder to reach the books on the top shelf, and, the coup de grace, a ten-foot-tall, crudely-painted portrait of my father with a George Washington-esque wig and a Napoleonic uniform. His two raised thumbs and his protruding tongue set the tone for both the painting and his entire life.

"That's actually a self-portrait," Martin said as he pointed.

"It's horrible."

"He worked on it for a long time."

375

"He wasn't very good."

"Yes, well...yes," Martin muttered.

Martin approached a large antique desk and pulled out a manila envelope and a DVD from one of its cavernous drawers.

"This was your father's study. He spent much of his time in here," Martin said, like a tour guide. He pointed to the large bookcases that reached the ceiling and surrounded the room, which was strange because I never took my father for much of a reader. The only novels I even remembered him discussing were the John Grisham books he read while he tanned his rotund stomach on the Cape Cod beaches during weekend family getaways. Those seemed like lifetimes ago. And as I looked at the room and most notably the self-portrait, I was pretty sure that it actually was.

"He never read a single one of these. Not one. Just had them ordered specially to look old. Felt as if it gave the room character."

"Why?"

"I think he just loved rolling along the ladder like it was a ride at a carnival."

I shrugged.

Martin readied the DVD on a flat screen in the corner of the room. He handed me the remote control and patted me on the shoulder.

"He told me I couldn't watch this. Just press play when you're ready. I'll be right outside if you need me."

I waited until Martin had left the room and breathed a long sigh when I was finally alone. I walked over to the desk where I expected to find some kind of business papers or something official like a stack of leftover twenties he might have used to burn in the fireplace. But all I saw was a yellow pad with mediocre doodles of various animals like ducks and panda bears. There were a few trinkets, things like snow globes from London, a clay cup, probably from Africa or India, and other little pieces of crap to remind him of his travels. And in the corner of the room, on a small end table next to a recliner, rested a black and white picture: the picture of Tina and me from my first date. I couldn't believe he had it. My father, the romantic. I wondered how long the picture had been sitting there. Perhaps he had placed it there knowing there was a chance he wouldn't return from his space mission, but the dust around the edges of the frame suggested it had been undisturbed for quite some time.

I figured Martin was pacing behind the door, so I finally decided to watch the DVD to ensure he wouldn't keel over and die from too much exertion and heavy breathing.

I had seen these sorts of things in movies: someone doesn't feel like writing a will so, instead, they videotape themselves giving instructions on who gets what and what goes where. I never really wanted anything from my father but suddenly thought it might be cool to inherit his large estate.

I pressed play and stood in front of the television.

Black screen. Only a date in the corner: July 2002. 12:35 p.m.

The screen remained dark and the faint sounds of a song eased its way from the speakers hidden in the nooks of the study. As it incrementally got louder, I finally recognized the tune.

"Groovy Kind Of Love?" Phil Collins?

I really had no clue of what to expect.

The black screen pixilated with color. Slowly. As the color gently morphed into definite shapes and sizes, my face soured as it actually appeared like...a porno. Much like a scrambled porno I would watch when I was a teenager in the hopes of seeing a green boob through the wavy, multi-colored lines and swirls on an adult cable channel my parents didn't order. Was this so important that it needed to disrupt my wedding day?

But as the music continued and the picture became clearer, the oxygen suddenly left my body and I took a step back to gather myself.

The angle of a woman's face that was indecipherable, in absolute pleasure, getting banged from behind by a fat hairy stomach and droopy man-teats. After a good two minutes of his stomach fat slapping the woman's ass, she turned toward the camera with the man's protein shake dripping down her cheeks. And that's when my life would change forever...again.

Remember the last scene of the music video for Pearl Jam's hit song "Jeremy?" The shot of the horrified class, with their blood-covered hands protecting their eyes from the image of Jeremy blowing his brains out?

I felt like one of those students.

The woman was my mother.

The man was not my father.

And so it continued.

A montage of various positions, various men pounding the shit out of my mother's privates, all dated from before my parents separated. Do you have any clue what it is like to see your mother getting slammed against a wall by the next-door neighbor that used to offer to mow the lawn? It all took place in my parents' bedroom and occurred during times my father must have been at work. I couldn't watch anymore. In fact, I wanted to poke my eyes out like Oedipus did after he discovered he had fucked his own mother. I had seen enough. More than enough. I didn't care if I didn't see anything else, period, for the rest of the day. Maybe even for the rest of my life. He had made his point. There was no room for denial. This is what he'd been trying to tell me for years. It was the first time in my entire life I hoped I'd never have to see my mother again.

I quickly pressed stop and sat on an all-too-comfortable, hand-carved Victorian sofa. This must have been what it felt like to discover the world was not flat. My father was an asshole. A big obnoxious asshole. He thought he ruled the world. The way he ejected my mother out of both our lives was classless and vicious.

But for the first time in four years, I understood. It now made a lot of sense. While trying to find the restaurant to meet Gustav and Saga in Stockholm, my father mentioned loving my mother more than anything in his life. At the time, I thought it was callous and bullshit. I now thought that might actually have been the truth. I now knew he stayed with her for the wrong reasons, but it must have been painful, watching the love of your life, not just fuck numerous other men (in, ugh, so many positions), but to literally watch her slip from your hands like desert sand. He must have been humiliated. I'm not sure how hard he tried to rekindle the romance, and though I could blame him for thousands of things, I couldn't blame him for being upset. I couldn't blame him for being driven into delirium. The more I considered it, I really couldn't blame either of them; perhaps it wasn't meant to be. I still, however, could blame him for his horrible Hawaiian-themed wardrobe choices.

Martin knocked on the door, and I softly told him to come in.

He entered.

"Well, I hope that DVD brought you some kind of cheer in this difficult moment."

I laughed once to myself.

"Yeah. Guess again."

Martin pursed his lips and shrugged.

"Well maybe this will."

Martin handed me the manila envelope he had taken earlier from the desk.

I feared to find out what was inside. Still pictures of my mother's privates being penetrated by someone else's thick, hairy schlong? I concluded that my father wanted to torture me after death too. If he couldn't be a ghost, at least he could provide me haunting information that already etched itself as new crevasses in my brain.

I opened up the envelope and pulled out a check in the amount of two million dollars. Two fucking million dollars. I held it in disbelief; I'd never seen so many zeros in my life.

"He told me he had spent it all."

I did nothing, nothing at all, to deserve it. Then again, it's not like he really earned it either.

"He did," Martin responded.

"So, what is this, fake?"

"No, he sold the house a few days ago for that amount."

"Why did he sell his house?"

"I don't know."

"And isn't this place worth more than that?"

"It's worth twenty. He took it for two because the buyer could pay that amount right away in cash. A last-minute decision before he left for Russia."

"Oh," I said, with a hint of realization.

"I tried to advise him against it, but you know your father."

This was his gift to me. But the money wasn't the only thing in the envelope. I reached back in to grab a small sheet of paper folded into what appeared to be a sad excuse for an origami swan, but that was just a guess.

"He really tried embracing his artistic side," Martin noted of the swan.

I unfolded the swan to see the following address:

Engelbrektsgatan 44

Stockholm, Sweden

I didn't even have to think it over for a second. I knew exactly what that was. I knew he saw her in the hallway that night in the hospital. I fucking knew it.

"Is everything OK?" Martin asked.

I looked over the check again, all the zeros and the possibility it brought. I could do everything I ever dreamed of with that money. But instead, I gripped the top of the check and tore it in two. I didn't want it. I couldn't take it. Martin gasped at the sound of all that money being denied.

"Brandon, that was a very generous gift he left for you."

"So give it to a charity or something. I don't want it."

"Are you sure?"

I didn't answer him.

I folded the address and placed it in my back pocket. I knew what my father wanted me to do; I knew it was what I wanted to do.

Martin clapped his hands once in finality.

"OK well, that's it. And congratulations," Martin said, as he extended his hand for a shake.

"For what?"

"You're getting married today, remember?" Martin asked, as he pointed at my tuxedo.

"Oh yeah, right."

I shook Martin's hand.

Before I walked back to my car, I thought about the absurdity of everything that had just taken place. My father insisted that I see Martin the day of his death, which coincided with the day of my wedding. He had sold his house only a few days before his trip and wrote me a check for everything he had left. I turned around to ask Martin one last question. Something wasn't right.

"The last time I saw my father he told me I'd be hearing things about him and that not all were going to be true. Do you know anything about that?"

"No," Martin shrugged genuinely. "I'm sure people will say lots of things about him though."

I nodded, not satisfied with his answer.

But as I looked at the sunshine pound the bright grass, like it was my own spiritual traffic light, I felt reborn. Though I was still questioning my father's lifestyle, motives, and current situation, at least I finally had an answer to a question that had plagued me for four years. Perhaps there were more answers to come. Perhaps my father was actually right.

But I knew one thing for sure: There was no fucking way I was going to get married today.

At the Airport Again

Since my departure from Sweden, I had the vision of spontaneously returning and experiencing a ridiculous romantic fantasy that could only exist in the cheesiest of movies. The thought was asinine, the act would have even been more asinine, but if there was ever a time in my life to do something beyond asinine, it was now. Why not? I was so up shit's creek, I felt like I was playing with the house's money anyway. Plus, I always wondered what it felt like to be kicked in the nuts by a llama.

After speeding toward LAX, like I was racing in the Daytona 500, I perused the flight board to see which option would best fit my soon-to-be maxed-out credit card. I booked a Delta flight that arrived in Stockholm at ten a.m. the next day, local time, and hoped this one wouldn't crash in the ocean.

With the address placed on my lap like a sleeping infant, I felt a twinge of melancholy while I waited at the same gate I had on my last trip to Sweden, before all this. I recalled walking toward my snoring father and all the dread that stewed in my body. I felt guilty; I almost felt the need to wear a disgusting Hawaiian shirt in his honor, maybe one with a fat-island dude playing a ukulele, but then I remembered I was always a sucker for nostalgia and I was better suited clearing my head of such nonsense.

I noted the time: 1:00 p.m. Clarissa's limousine had probably just collected her and her bridesmaids. I hadn't seen her dress, but I knew it was pure white like untouched snow. I could imagine her bridesmaids, all clothed in an honest pink, surrounding her like flower petals around the stigma, or maybe like tentacles sprouting from the body of a squid, or the balloon knot-like ripples of skin that bordered the anus. All seemed appropriate.

I wondered if she tried to call me. Maybe she attempted to text me something like "I love you," or "I can't believe we are doing this." But the only thing that might have read the text would have been an empty Jack In The Box cup in a public trashcan in some Beverly Hills park because that is where I tossed my phone after I left my father's mansion.

And it was that pathetic image, coupled with the thought of Clarissa's eventual tears that inspired an idea that really seemed genius at the time. I swore I knew the perfect thing to make Clarissa happy. It would fix everything. She would forgive me and soon, well maybe ten years later, we would enjoy a cup of coffee and laugh about the entire thing.

I remembered my mother once told me that, if you cannot attend a wedding, then you have to send a gift. This is the sole reason people invited everyone they fucking knew to weddings, and the only reason people tracked down the address of their great uncle Harry, whom they had never even met. They are fully aware many will decline to spend ungodly amounts of money to travel to the bullshit party, but will reap the benefits of a gift they have guilted the prospective guest into sending anyway. Humans could be so obviously conniving, and the worst part is, you can't accuse a bride and groom for being greedy. It's probably bad luck. But since I knew I was traumatizing a girl's entire life (even though I was probably doing her a favor in the long run), I figured I'd make it up to her somehow.

I asked the man next to me if I could borrow his laptop, opened up a web browser, and quickly typed: RONALD FONG, ATTORNEY into a Google search. Within seconds, the webpage for his firm appeared on the screen. I clicked on his name and was greeted with his brash Chinese face as it peered over his Armani-suited shoulder like you caught him in a candid moment, much like the actors looked during the opening credits of the original *Beverly Hills 90210*. I bet he convinced juries his clients were innocent just using that killer stare alone. I would have wagered anything that he was a great boyfriend. And I figured, despite the stereotype, he had a big dick. Robust. And as I looked into his pixilated eyes, I could see he'd make a great father. Father-of-the-year type shit. Their little, full-Chinese kids would brag to the others at school about their daddy and his successful law career. They would tell their classmates that Daddy could build anything in the world as they rode their newly constructed bikes down a perfect street in a plush California suburb. They'd even brag about their daddy's big dick. They would actually make him those stupid coupons and pray he'd use them so they could serve their daddy with fifteen minutes of cleaning dishes. Yeah, I was definitely doing Clarissa a favor.

Using a payphone, I called his number and prayed for an answering service, which I thankfully got.

"Fong, Kiick, and Delgado. How can I help you?" the woman said in a shrill voice with the enthusiasm of someone about to get a tooth pulled. She sounded like she had saggy cheeks that needed a bra and a pair of those ugly-ass glasses that had half lenses and sat at the end of a beak-like nose.

"Hi. I need to get in touch with Ronald Fong, esquire," I said casually.

"Mr. Fong is only to be contacted in an emergency. Is this an emergency?"

Sure, I thought so.

"Of course."

"Because your tone does not suggest an emergency, Sir."

"No? What does it sound like?"

"Like you're ordering a pizza."

Pizza sounded good.

"What kind of tone do you suggest I use?"

"One that sounds like it's an emergency."

"OK. If I don't speak to Ronald Fong in the next twenty minutes, one of his clients is going to attach jumper cables to my already sensitive nipples and start the engine," I said, as calmly as someone thirty minutes deep into a shiatsu. "And I'd like a large pepperoni."

"Hold please," the woman said, unfazed.

I'd finally go toe to toe with the great Fong. But as the phone rang, I hadn't prepared a game plan. The idea suddenly seemed really fucking dumb (probably because it was in the first place).

"Ronald Fong," the Chinese Tom Cruise said before I could hang up.

"Mr. Fong?" I stuttered in only a way that I could stutter three syllables.

"Yes, the answering service said it was an emergency, may I ask who is calling?"

"Umm, well, I'm Clarissa Chang's fiancée."

A pause.

"I heard you were getting married today."

"Yeah, well, that's not going to happen," I said, as I fiddled with the phone cord. I actually felt comfortable.

"Does she know that?"

He knew me too well. If I were Robert DeNiro, I'd shake my finger at him and tell him he's good.

"Not exactly."

"Perhaps you should tell her."

"Well, that's what I wanted to talk to you about."

And over the next four minutes, I laid out my brilliant plan for him. I told him he should drop everything, buy a tuxedo (I even recommended a good shop), and attend in my place. He could walk down the aisle, maybe even wear a veil for a big reveal (I got excited when I told him that part. I felt it would help sell it). Everyone would be happy. Mr. Chang would have to call the *Guinness Book of World Records* to inform them he'd finally smiled. It was the perfect plan, and the more I discussed it, I was convinced it could actually work.

"I knew Clarissa and you had something. So I'm giving you this opportunity," I said. "A gift really."

Ronald gave a long pause. I tried to picture him on the other end of the phone. Maybe he was dancing silently, like Carlton did in the *Fresh Prince of Bel Air*. Exactly like that, actually. Or perhaps he opted for the knee lift and fist pump that is normally punctuated by a loud, extended "YESSSS!" But as I gathered other reactions in my crowded head, my concentration was interrupted by the sound of a dial tone. I looked at the receiver as if it had wronged me.

"That went well," I said to myself, as I shrugged my shoulders.

I really should have cared more about my reckless behavior. But I had my sights on something else. And if all went well, perhaps I'd never even return to see the damage I had caused. Just me and my tuxedo setting sail on a new life together with the girl I figured I was in love with. And it was a rental, no less. See the chances I took? Though I figured the store wouldn't deal with the hassle of contacting Interpol to locate my whereabouts over a cheap tuxedo.

"Hey look, it's the hero groom," a random stranger said, like he just found Brad Pitt. "I'm a big fan, but hey, aren't you supposed to be getting married today?"

"Think so," I responded.

"Oh...what?"

The airport PA came to life:

"We'd like to commence general boarding for Delta flight 87 with non-stop service to Stockholm, Sweden. We are boarding all rows, thank you," the kind flight attendant said over the loud speaker, like she was a boxing bell that saved me from an awkward conversation.

I raised my eyebrows toward my biggest fan and proceeded to the gate.

I had fifteen long hours to figure out what to say to Saga. I pulled out my father's yellow pad, the one with the drawings, and grabbed a pen out of my pocket that I'd earlier found on the floor.

I needed the perfect speech.

I approached the gate and handed my ticket to the smiling flight attendant with teeth and lips perfect enough for a Crest commercial. A good omen, I thought.

"You look very nice today, Sir," the friendly stewardess said in reference to my tuxedo. "What's the occasion?"

"I was supposed to get married today," I said as I shrugged my shoulders. "But I decided to fuck it."

The flight attendant's face briefly contorted like a disrupted television signal before it relaxed into a stale smile. I bet they had to take classes on how to smile during any situation and that was a level-one grin.

I, however, smiled genuinely: A level-five. I confidently walked past her and toward the plane. I felt like I had just outrun the police to the state border during a high-speed chase and was home free.

Flight 3

Draft one: The Self-Deprecating Draft.

Saga –

Wait, don't shoot. I know, I know. I fucked up. I should have been straight with you the entire time. I'm a jerk, what can I say? Remember that little kid that always had to stay after school because he was too stupid to figure out math problems during normal class hours? That was me. I'm a little man. Little and pathetic. I need direction in my life, and the only direction I can think of is you. Like I need to drive down the Saga highway of love. Because I'm little. A little man.

Not so sure about that one. Moving on…

Draft two: The Romantic Draft

Wait, don't shoot. Just hear me out. I know you weren't expecting to see me. I did a terrible thing. A terrible, terrible thing. It's true; I was supposed to get married. Yesterday, actually. But I realized I just couldn't do it. Not even at all. Because as I pictured myself walking down the aisle, all I could think of was you and how much I wished you were at the end of that long road waiting for me. I know this sounds insane, we have not known each other for that long, but I want to spend the rest of my life with you. Desperate to. And I will be on my knees every day, every goddamn day, asking for your forgiveness if that's what it takes.

Survey says? I SUCK. Moving on...

Draft three: The Humorous Draft

OK, so I know you weren't expecting to see me, but stop if you've heard this one before, OK? What's the opposite of Christopher Reeve? Remember *Superman*? Any guesses? No? Christopher Walken! Haha, get it? You know, cause of his legs? He was paralyzed? No? And Christopher Walken... because you know, his last name has the word walk in it?

No? You know, Christopher Wal—No? Well, OK never mind, but that's only one of a number of jokes I can—

Let's just stop that one right there. Moving on…

Draft four: The Truth Draft

Fuck.

I had nothing.

Not. One. Damn. Thing.

I checked the time. Seven hours till Stockholm and I couldn't find a way to put the maze of thoughts in my brain into an endearing sentence. *How the hell can I have NOTHING*, I thought. And to think I fancied myself a writer. I supposed there was no secret why I could barely find work in that field. Then again, I always thought I was better at comedy, so if pouring my heart out to Saga simply consisted of fart jokes, perhaps I would have had an easier time of conjuring something. I didn't want it to sound cheesy, but I didn't want it to be too serious. I needed it to sound like something George Clooney would agree to say in a romantic comedy. It needed to be something cool, but meaningful. But, most of all, I needed it to be perfect because, in my head, it was to be the perfect moment. It had to be. I had left my entire life behind in pursuit of the moment, even if my entire old life rivaled a steaming pile of horseshit in a smelling contest.

I felt a short nap was in order, just an hour, if I woke up refreshed, I knew I could figure out something. I only had one shot at this, though I wouldn't blame her if she slammed her front door right in my face like I was an annoying Jehovah's witness.

But I wouldn't go down without a fight.

I looked at the address again. Thank God my father had seen her in the hallway.

Why couldn't I come up with something?

I slammed my head against the headrest and threw a copy of *SkyMall* to the ground as if that might inspire.

But it only inspired the person seated next to me to tell me to calm down.

By the way, tuxedos make horrible airplane attire if in search of comfort.

I wanted to be comfortable. I couldn't quite get there.

I couldn't imagine a flight more agonizing than this.

Stockholm: Take Two

The doors of the airport rail shuttle opened, and I could see glimpses of Stockholm through the spaces of the train station. With a few steps I would be engulfed by the city and unable to turn back. I sat on the bench in the station, for a brief moment, and took in the sounds of the city. I felt like if I didn't move, I could remain in a protective cocoon that would shield me from reality just for a few more minutes. There was excitement, but also immense fear.

The idea of sweeping Saga off her feet originally seemed romantic and honorable, but now that I was faced with actually walking toward the address in my hand, the comfort of time was gone and I was afraid. But, fuck it, even though my nerves were shattered, I knew there was zero chance of me re-entering the train, traveling back to the airport, and returning to America with my tail between my legs. So, I figured I might as well confidently trudge forward into the uncharted waters and do my best not to drown. It all sounded so good in my head.

After exiting the station, I was greeted by bright sunshine complimented by a cool breeze that was a touch too cold for my Los Angeles trained body. But it felt good. As I looked at the row of modern buildings in front of me, all sided with glass, the reflection of the sun glinted the same way I pictured in my daydream. But, unlike the fantasy, I wouldn't have to wait in a coffee shop for Saga while receiving questioning looks from the old broad behind the counter. This was probably a good thing because I'm sure I'd get restless, drink tons of coffee, and have to piss every five seconds.

I glanced down at the address again as if to make sure it hadn't changed. I felt exactly like my father must have during our first trip. Nervous. Constantly searching the address as if it had a secret code. I even wondered why the damn street names had to be so damn long.

Pedestrians eyed me curiously. I'm sure they wondered why a man just stepped out of the train station in a wrinkled tuxedo with the bowtie out of place. I probably looked like the drunk guy from a wedding who took the open bar a little too seriously, yet I wondered why this sight was any more peculiar than the guy dancing on the flatbed of his truck in traffic.

I returned to Stockholm to find it exactly how I remembered it. Clean. Brisk. But, at least, this time more familiar. I gripped my tuxedo jacket tightly around my body to protect myself against the stiff breeze. I could feel my rock hard nipples chafe against the stiff cotton blend of my undershirt.

And with each step I took, I felt more confident. I passed some of the landmarks we had visited during our time together. I strolled by the mall and wondered if the same Segway attendant was on duty, and if his horrid zit had retreated back into his oily forehead. Perhaps he'd like me to say hello so he could punch me in the face. I passed the movie theater Saga and I had crossed while walking through the quiet city at night, though the ridiculous poster with the dog and the priest was gone. And, of course, the fountain. It felt like my fountain. Like I was a dog that pissed on it. Other people might look at it, they might take photos in front of it, but I did the ultimate thing inside it.

The walk took me past department stores, fast food restaurants, and though I knew it was only a few minutes away, each step felt like it was a mile and my heart pounded a little harder and faster as the distance between me and Saga's place became shorter. I'd never done anything like this. Not even close. Once in college, I met a girl at a bookstore who lived an hour south, and I agreed to visit her for a date. But, a week later, I got lost in country roads and corn fields on the drive down to her house and decided to head back home because I was an hour late and didn't feel like it anymore anyway. I never called her, though I had no doubt she got over it quickly. She was five inches taller than I, so even if we were destined to be together, I, at the very least, avoided an awkward moment if we ever decided to do it doggy style.

I was always lazy in my relationships. Clarissa hated that about me. But for Saga, apparently, I'd chase her around the world.

I finally came upon the street, Engelbrektsgatan. My heart damn well near stopped.

And it looked familiar. The picturesque street actually bordered the park where we watched the two men argue over a bocce call. I was surprised Saga didn't mention her residence when we walked through the park. One would think it would have come up while she was explaining the history of other buildings in the area, but I figured it hadn't slipped her mind.

I continued down the street as if I was being watched. Careful to search the faces of every blond head that passed by. And there were plenty in Sweden's homogenous population, so my head was constantly on a scanning swivel like I was the Terminator.

I wasn't sure exactly what I'd even do if I saw her on the sidewalk. I wasn't prepared for a public greeting. I'd probably do something stupid, like tell her I just happened to be in the area, as if Stockholm was Santa Monica, and suggest this had all been one great coincidence. Of course, she wouldn't believe me, but I'd stick to my story as I get unusually stubborn when things don't go exactly how I planned.

I carefully approached the residences and inspected the first one for a numbered address. A gold plate on the immaculate façade displayed the number 22. The distance of twenty addresses provided me some sort of security. I breathed a quick sigh of relief and took in the row of buildings; the entire street was encapsulated by a quiet opulence. I bet the insides of all these buildings were beautiful. I guessed I would find out.

I methodically moved down the street, now only lifting my head to take note of the escalating addresses: 32. 36. The world became silent, save for my thoughts and the cadence of my rented black shoes hitting the pavement. Clunk clunk. Clunk clunk...38...40. I swallowed hard as I hit 42 and stopped. I eyed the next building, which I assumed to be 44. Flowerbeds, much like the one my father robbed in Gamla Stan adorned the front windows, just beside a stone staircase that led to the enormous front doors that appeared as if they comprised a drawbridge. I hoped she wouldn't slam that mammoth door in my face because it probably would have led to a concussion.

I searched for illuminated lights inside of the house, but the angle of the sun prevented me from confirming any sign that someone might be home. I peered down at my clothes and suddenly felt like a complete idiot. Was dressing in the suit I was to be married in really the smartest choice of attire? Of course not. I was a fucking moron, but I supposed there was little I could do about it.

And then I had doubt.

Natural doubt.

You know what would have been easier? If I turned around. If I forgot any of this ever happened. If I went back to Los Angeles. If I walked back to my apartment. The idea of facing Clarissa's parents even seemed less daunting than surprising Saga. Even if Mr. Chang pounded me in the stomach with nunchucks while her mother popped my head off as easily as she would untwist a soda bottle cap; it sounded less intimidating than what I thought I was about to do. The idea seemed so much easier while sweating on the elliptical wrapped in the comfort of a six-thousand-mile buffer.

And I still didn't know what I'd tell her.

Saga and I shared shit. Like real shit. This should have been a cinch. Really, what did I have to lose, other than pride, which I had so little of anyway?

But as I stood at the bottom of the staircase, listening for movement in the house even though it would have been impossible to hear, I knew I couldn't back out.

Fuck it.

I marched up the stairs, two at a time (yeah, that's right), and placed myself in front of the door like I was a taxman coming to collect. I gripped the large silver knocker and banged it against the solid wooden door three times.

BOOM BOOM BOOM.

I stepped back like I'd be ready to pounce and took comfort in the fact that the door had no peephole. This was better as a surprise attack.

I waited.

And waited.

Where the fuck was she?

I shuffled my feet and cleared my throat. My heart was still pounding, I felt like I could almost see the breast pocket of my suit move in unison.

I knocked again.

And waited for what seemed like forever, even though it was probably five seconds.

Still no answer.

Well, fuck. This wasn't part of the plan. I could feel my adrenaline slowly drain from my body as my mind drifted to the consequences of a surprise visit. I hoped she wasn't on vacation.

I turned toward the street, annoyed like a child who didn't get what he wanted for his birthday. I resigned myself into thinking that I might have to wait for her, but where? Would I really sit by the doorstep like a homeless boy begging for shelter? Maybe I could find a restaurant to kill time in and try again a couple of hours later. I couldn't believe I left my fiancée at the altar and flew all the way to Sweden to stand like an asshole outside of an empty house; this was not how it happened in the movies.

But then I had another idea. I'd just see if the door was unlocked. This was Scandinavia, after all; people trusted each other here, or so I figured. Maybe she was in the other room and couldn't hear the knock.

I plunged the handle on the old, metal door and, much to my extreme fear, it clicked and slowly opened with a gentle creak.

Oh shit, now what?

I inched my way inside, like I was a teenager sneaking in after a long night, and was glad I had opened the door just wide enough that it narrowly missed the tin umbrella holder just alongside it. The immaculate house was warm and appeared different than I had expected. The furniture was antique, as were the rugs and the curtains that grazed the shiny hardwood floor. Unlit candles stood on a few of the end tables, while ornate lamps and pictures sat by the others. It just looked too nice for a girl of Saga's age. What address had my father given me? Was this another joke?

I tiptoed farther into the room and noticed a photo of a little blond girl placing her finger up the nose of what I presumed to be her grandfather. Her smile was bright. I'd never seen someone so happy to do something so oddly objectionable. And I never saw a man that pleased to have a finger jabbed up his nostril.

And then I heard a sigh. No, more of a gasp.

I saw her. Saga. Her hair as bright as the sun. A red turtleneck that looked a little too Christmasy for early November. Tight jeans that she immediately placed her hands in the back pockets of, a nervous gesture. She tensed, her mouth open as she looked back into a room I couldn't see. She tried to say something, but couldn't. At least she didn't pull a gun.

I immediately put down the picture like I was caught in an attempt to steal it. She hadn't moved. I hoped she was happy to see me; I took her silence as a good sign.

I still hadn't thought of anything to tell her. Not a word. But as we stood together in that uncomfortable moment, I finally mustered my first one.

"Hi," I said. *What an opening*, I thought. Classic. Simple. I shrugged harmlessly when she did not respond. The door was still open, and I knew there was a chance to escape. I could run out with the knowledge that I'd made some kind of effort, but, if I ran, I knew I'd literally find a way to kick myself in the ass every time I thought of it; this would not be a repeat of my trip to Los Angeles when I was a teenager. I didn't want her to be the one that got away. I closed my eyes and knew I had to think of something.

And then the muse finally struck me.

And the words poured out like verbal vomit: "I know you weren't expecting to see me. Especially after everything that happened," I said uncomfortably. She stood frozen, but I could tell that she was listening.

So I continued: "And I'm sorry for that. I am. But, honestly, the moment I met you…I knew I couldn't go through with that other thing. It was never real, something stupid that just kinda happened until it became so big I didn't know what to do anymore."

I paused again for some kind of reaction. Nothing. I don't think she even moved a muscle. No "go on" or a head nod that suggested I should. Not even a "shut up, just shut up, you had me at 'hello.'" Shit, maybe I should have actually started with "hello," instead of "hi" to have ensured that possibility. But I just continued.

"And there's so much I want to tell you. I want to tell you exactly why I rushed to Sweden, found your place, which is quite nice by the way, though not very girly...but I digress ...and just...it's because...because..."

She looked so vulnerable. She didn't appear to be the same girl that had stolen a Segway. She was scared and helpless. Impotent.

"Because...To put it simply, you're smart. Really smart. It was the first thing I noticed about you, actually, well, other than your lightbulb blond head, but I know it's rare."

I felt like I finally released a piss I'd held in for hours. It was all just flowing uncontrollably.

I continued: "And Because...Japanese people wanted to touch your eye. I mean, what does it say when someone finds something so beautiful that they don't trust their sight, but instead need to touch it to confirm it's real? It's because, you're beyond beautiful."

Her face finally cracked. She smiled slightly. But said no words. I stammered. I wanted to continue.

"And because...because...you're stubborn and secretive and because I don't even care that you are. I like that you are. You've experienced things. Things I want to experience. And I just want to experience things with you. Because you make me do things I only imagine doing. You make me say things I only imagine saying…"

She swallowed hard and placed her hand against the wall. I took a step forward and looked her directly in the eyes; I saw tears welling in her stare.

"Because…you are always on my mind. And you always make me smile. And because I love that. And because well…just because…"

I paused. And then I loosened my bow tie. Then I took it off.

I was unsure if I wanted to go through with what I was about to do. But why not, I thought. Go for broke. Make a statement. Or go down in flames. Whatever.

I unbuttoned my shirt, quickly, until it was completely undone. I pulled it out from under my pants so the wrinkled bottom hung over my waist. I clumsily removed both my jacket and shirt, revealing my under-toned bare torso that I quickly sucked in (a Jew is never too stressed for vanity), and unbuckled my belt. Unsure of exactly how to unbutton the tuxedo pants, I just ripped them off like an amateur Chippendale's employee and kicked them to the side. I noticed Saga's eyes widen as she watched me in just my boxers. I held out my hands as if to say "yeah, that's right. This is what I'm doing."

And then I dropped them. The Full Monty, baby. And there I was, in front of Saga, in her warm, immaculate house, completely naked.

There was nothing to hide.

"I remember the last thing you said to me," I said, as I pointed at my entire naked body. "I'm not covered in bullshit any more. It's just me."

I locked eyes with her once again.

"Because...I love you," I finished.

And I waited for an answer. An eternity for an answer. She had to say something. I wanted her to rush into my arms. I wanted her to bury her head in my neck so I could smell her intoxicating perfume. I wanted to lift her off the ground and twirl her moments before we fucked, no *made love*, right then and there, in the center of that room.

And then I heard footsteps. She had to have been walking toward me. But I was in such a trance, nerves coursing so hard through my veins, that I didn't actually see her walking in my direction, though I heard footsteps getting closer.

I shook.

And then I heard one solitary footstep that was way too loud. It was from a heavy shoe. Like a boot. But Saga wasn't wearing boots, or UGGs, or anything like that. In fact, she remained still. Like someone with no power or soul. And then it occurred to me: That was a man's shoe.

Oh fuck.

And behind her was the surprised face of her father: Old, enormous Gustav, who looked ten times bigger standing up. He offered no barreling laugh this time. Not even a smile. My mouth dropped. My testicles retreated into my body; they must have been as embarrassed as I was, but I obviously didn't look down to see my pathetic wobbly bits in all their shriveled splendor.

I quickly considered the décor of the house; I knew it was too adult. My father couldn't have warned me that this was not Saga's house, but her father's? Perhaps I should have figured that part out myself.

"Brandon?" he asked in disbelief.

I thought I responded with a customary "hello," though I couldn't be sure.

"What are you doing, Brandon?" Gustav asked in a tone I felt was all too serious. I had zero answer for him. I didn't really know anymore.

"What do you think you are doing?" he said a little angrier.

He looked at Saga, but she might as well have been catatonic. This was not good. I wished he would see the humor in this; it was at least a little funny.

And then I discovered why.

My eyes slowly moved past Gustav to another male face. A taller face. A younger face. A much more chiseled face, perfectly chiseled, like it was made from granite. But most of all, an angry face. A livid face. I could see the emotion quickly rise through his body and redden his perfect face until he appeared like Mephistopheles himself. I half expected sharp horns to protrude from his forehead and a long, pointed tail from his anus as he barked something horrible in Swedish to both Saga and Gustav.

Saga, unable to actually utter audible words, just shrugged and shook as she tried to mumble. But before she could speak a coherent sentence, the chiseled face turned back toward me with unmatched fury.

This was not going to end well.

He took a step in my direction.

"Oh fuck," I said under my breath.

And like a bull released from its holding pen during a rodeo, the muscular beast pushed through Saga and Gustav, and charged me with the full intent of killing me. This stud was eight feet tall if he was an inch, and he was bearing down on me like a locomotive that had no brakes.

I backed up, holding out my hands as if to suggest a misunderstanding, but when I instantly realized that gesture would be futile, I did the next best thing: I rushed my bare, naked ass out the still open front door and into the brisk Stockholm afternoon.

I could only imagine what the nice family across the street must have thought. I'm sure the young couple figured it was a lovely day to walk through the neighborhood with their twin girls, probably to enjoy the changing of the leaves and the brisk autumn breeze. They'd share laughs and perhaps stop at a local café for a few treats. I doubt they ever dreamed that they'd see a completely naked American, penis flopping like a flag in a hurricane, as he dashed down the street with a large Swedish man of similar age chasing him, like he'd just stolen the Hope Diamond. I wondered how they would explain this to their children.

I kept looking back, suddenly glad that I had less clothing to weigh down my body; it would have been impossible to escape in the tuxedo. He was getting closer, I could see his well-toned muscles undulate through his shirt and, if he wasn't insistent on ripping my body to shreds, I would actually have been impressed with his physique and might have even asked him for some workout tips so I could earn a decisive victory the next time I wrestled a seventy-year-old, Jewish man.

But all I kept saying to myself was "run faster, you fucking idiot, run faster." I felt my legs kick into second gear.

I raced across the street, dodging cars like Frogger, and entered the park where three kids on the half pipe immediately slipped off their boards due to the unexpected sight. I didn't stick around to find out if they were OK.

I'd often heard people say that during a near-death experience, your entire life flashes before your eyes in a cinematic tale. I had a similar moment as I could feel the cool concrete below me scratch the soles of my feet. But it wasn't my life that flashed before me as much as every possibility of who was chasing me and why. I wishfully thought maybe Saga had a very protective brother or cousin she had failed to mention. But it wouldn't explain why he was *so* angry. I knew who it was, but I didn't feel like admitting it to myself.

I thought about Saga the night we met. The way she smiled and denied me when she turned toward the subway entrance without so much as a word. She might have returned to her house that night and got in bed next to the rabid juggernaut (who was gaining on me) and watched her life pass before her, similar to how I would when I looked at Clarissa in calm times. She, too, probably wasn't ready for that future and decided to break into my hotel room just to see what would happen.

It was all supposed to be innocent.

Like me, I assumed she could never have predicted the outcome. Or maybe she could have. Maybe she was desperate. She did, in fact, fly to the United States and ask to marry me in Vegas. She wanted a way out, and I was it. I couldn't blame her. The guy did seem like he had a shit temper. And it also explained why she was so public with her affection during my first trip to Stockholm. Maybe, deep down, she wanted to get caught. So she, too, could dig herself out of the hole she was currently buried in, even if it meant embarrassment and pain. She once told me she loved to live in moments, and perhaps I was just a moment to her. Just still time, like the picture in the restaurant.

I wasn't even angry. She had used me as I had used her. In fact, it further cemented our bond. But now I was the one who wished we could live forever in our painting.

(On a side note, if ever looking for a way to beat the cold, try running for your life, buck ass naked, while being chased by a psychotically angry man four times your size. It's like emotional flannel. You won't feel a thing.)

And as I peered back and noticed he was closer, the gravity of the situation settled in. I knew this would end. And end soon. And not favorably. And even if I miraculously outran this enraged man, I had no clothes, no money, no passport, no nothing. No matter what I did, I was completely fucked. I looked back for what I figured would be the last time, and it was.

But not because he caught me.

When I turned my head forward, a forearm immediately met my face and knocked me parallel to the ground, until I landed with a thud that scratched the hair off my poor, naked ass.

And as I looked upwards at two uniformed policemen, I didn't even bother trying to get up. I had had enough.

One of them yelled something in Swedish to which I could only reply: "what?" He rolled his eyes and gestured to his partner as if to say, "Can you believe this shit?"

He looked back toward me. "You think you can wrong a Swedish Baron and just get away?"

"A baron? That guy?" I said, defeated.

I expected a verbal response, but only received a punch in the face. Hardly necessary. But hey, only a few hours before this, I watched video of my mother getting pounded by numerous men in numerous holes. Trust me, no punch could hurt me more than that.

By this point, dozens of locals stood on the opposite side of the park path to watch the shit show. The Baron finally caught up and paraded around me like a gladiator would before cementing his kill. He leaned down toward my face and breathed heavily as he death-stared deep into my eyes. I sat up and looked straight back, helpless, I suddenly felt cold.

I really just didn't give a fuck anymore.

"Hi," I said, resigned.

He swung his arm back and clocked me across the face. I felt my cheek instinctively and sighed with exasperation.

"Was that really necessary?" I asked through extreme pain.

Apparently, it was.

"You expose yourself in front of *my fiancée?*"

He had to be kidding.

"Oh come on, Really? Fiancée?" I said in surprise. "I thought boyfriend for sure, but fiancée? Dude…"

His boot slammed against my ribs as if to answer my question. I lay down on the sidewalk in surrender, my pale white, curled, cold naked body displayed for the world to see. I didn't even bother to hold my ribs as the pain was partially obscured by the irony of the entire situation.

I heard the crowd across the street gasp as I tried to catch my breath. But as I lay my head down on the con-crete, I tried to find Saga in the crowd, but to no avail. In my sick mind, I still thought this situation could actually be rectified in some way.

The Baron's boot stepped directly in front of my line of sight. His pant leg was caught against his sock, probably due to movement caused by the unnecessary swift kick to my midsection. It wasn't like I had any chance of fighting back. And that's when I noticed it:

A half- moon tattoo. With a jagged edge. Facing left.

And I bet it fit perfectly with Saga's like one of those God-forsaken broken heart chains young couples once bought at Spencer's gifts. And for whatever reason, that, of all things, made me feel violated.

And I got primal. *Animal Planet* primal. I obviously couldn't see my eyes, but I could imagine them red, like a werewolf. I yelled as loudly as I could, a scream a Viking could be proud of, and sunk my teeth into his calf, like a lion securing its prey. Right in that fucking horrible tattoo. I could feel my teeth penetrate his skin. I could taste his blood. I felt strands of his leg hair infiltrate the tiny gaps between my teeth like it was dental floss. I wanted to destroy it. Like if I bit hard enough, my whole world would turn back to normal. I'd wake up from this horrible nightmare. It was my last, stupid stand.

But the bite didn't quite have the same effect as Dorothy clicking her red slippers. All I heard was his loud scream, and I figured that might be it for me. I felt a subsequent kick in my midsection from one of the guards which caused me to taste blood again, though, this time, I couldn't be sure if it was the Baron's or my own.

I felt my consciousness start to fade.

I disengaged and my head fell to the concrete of the sidewalk once again, completely exhausted. My energy was 100 percent sapped. But just before my eyes closed, I saw past the numerous legs around me. Past the row of people just beyond my beating. Past all the commotion.

I finally saw Saga.

Her face was soft among the horrified and bewildered expressions of the others. She locked eyes with me and shook her head. I hoped it was some kind of apology, but I honestly could not tell. She opened her mouth to speak. I squinted to concentrate on her words as the world became silent.

And that's when I felt the needle of the tranquilizer pierce my neck.

I could see Saga's lips move, but couldn't decipher her words. I needed, more than anything, to hear what she said. For her to tell me this was all a joke. That the candid camera was just around the corner. This had to all be a joke. It had to be a dream.

But I couldn't understand her words.

"What…"

Seconds.

"Did she…"

My eyelids were anvils.

"Say…"

I passed out.

Flight 4

See page 1.

Detained

The tranquilizer had finally worn off by the time I was brought to a windowless holding room in the depths of LAX airport, which caused me to wonder what other menacing places were hidden in the mess of terminals. Members from the Swedish Embassy sat beside numerous American officials at a long table while I slumped on an uncomfortable stool that I constantly swiveled just because it was fun. It really shouldn't have been, but apparently it's a big deal when you bite another country's royalty like you're a rabid dog. Who knew? I hoped they wouldn't put me to sleep like they would an insolent canine, though if they had, at least I'd finally get some rest.

Normally, ten pairs of stern eyes glaring in my direction might have made me nervous, but perhaps there were residual effects from the sedative, or maybe it was because my head had been pounded like pizza dough, but I figured there was nothing they could possibly do that was worse than what I'd already been through over the past few weeks, which had ten times more action than my previous thirty years combined. I always claimed I wanted a more exciting life. I should have been careful what I wished for.

One of the cue-ball bald American officials cleared his throat, the universal sound of commencement. His perfectly trimmed mustache and the manner in which he crossed his hands and tilted his shiny noggin made me think that he should have been conducting the interview in a military uniform with tons of those crazy, colorful bars attached to the chest of his jacket. I always wondered what those signi-fied. But, alas, I apparently wasn't important enough for a plethora of bars. Not even one bar.

"So..." he said, getting down to business. "You're the Asshole Groom," he continued with a knowing, slow laugh.

I knew it!

I pointed both thumbs at my chest. I guessed Brandon Popularity was long dead.

I sighed as I touched the numerous wounds on my face and body. They all still hurt like a bitch.

"You got a lot of balls starting shit with...what do they call him again?"

"The Virile Viking," a Swedish official confirmed, like he was promoting the man's fighting career.

"The Virile Viking?" I asked, not quite believing it. "Seriously?"

"Yes."

"He the Swedish Wilt Chamberlain or something?"

The Swedish representatives didn't seem amused.

"He's the top boxer in his weight class in Sweden. Cruiserweight," the American official said. "Undefeated. Wrong guy to pick a fight with. Especially naked."

"I noticed," I said, as I threw my arms up to show I really didn't give a shit. "Though let the record show he needed help to keep me down and I did draw blood. Not bad I'd say," I continued while wagging my finger as if I had made some kind of point.

The Americans watched with pity. In contrast, the Swedish officials viewed me with disgust. To them, my crime was as horrible as murder. Apparently, no one ever exposed themselves in front of the fiancée of royalty before. I was a trailblazer.

"What do you have to say for yourself?" General Mr. Clean asked.

What a loaded question, I thought. But all of my queries consisted of shit they couldn't have cared less about. I wanted to know about Saga, though I figured the Swedes might have shot me in the face if I had asked.

Instead, I just shrugged my shoulders. Apparently, I had nothing to say for myself.

And the rest of their interview was really boring and, by the sound of the questions and their frequent giggles, I had a feeling this wasn't as important as protocol made it seem.

We were all just wasting time.

I supposed we had to fill it with something.

So I just nodded until I thought they might let me go home.

The Second Walk
Down The Hall

After a quick call to Martin Simon, it was obvious the American and Swedish officials had better things to worry about than a pathetic thirty-year-old, brokenhearted Jew that only really posed a threat to himself. Apparently, that mouthbreather of an attorney had some serious clout. They let me go with a simple slap on the wrist, under the condition that I never step foot inside Sweden again. Not necessarily because they feared I might do something irrational, but instead thought the royal family might rip me into ten thousand pieces. That was fine, that didn't sound too fun anyway. Plus, I had no intentions on ever going back there, really. What was left there to do? Find that Ikea I never quite located? Have more explosive diarrhea? Maybe pee on the King? Somehow, I figured I could live without ever having those experiences, though I'd regretfully have to cope with the fact that I'd never be able to visit the much-anticipated ABBA museum once it opened.

I should have listened to that dude in the donut shop. Or David Lee Roth. Both of them, I guessed. On a positive note, the Swedish government let me keep the clothes they provided, which I found generous, because what a keepsake the oversized garments splattered with my own blood would make. I was shit out of luck with my rented tuxedo though; they claimed they couldn't find it. I thought Saga's fiancé (it still hurt to say that) might have eaten it, though in reality, I'm sure they never bothered to look for it. I wouldn't have.

So there I was, back in my apartment elevator, back at home. And this time, everything *really* felt different. And for good reason too. Because, at least last time, I figured I knew what I might come back to. This time, I had zero clue. And I was just too tired and out of it to really deal.

The elevator door opened and I walked down the hallway, barely awake enough to lift my feet off the ground. I stopped in front of the hallway mirror to watch myself, much like I did upon returning from my first trip. My face was still puffy, bruised, and wore every second of the past few weeks. My battle wounds, if you would. It was the first time I'd seen my mangled face, or the first time I was cogent enough to really take it in. I looked like absolute shit.

I glanced toward my apartment door, the apartment I'd shared with Clarissa. The apartment where we watched hundreds of movies on the couch. The apartment where we consummated our engagement. The apartment where we simply lived.

I thought about our wedding ceremony and how it might have evolved: Clarissa off in some hidden room as one of her bridesmaids tied a floral arrangement in her hair. She probably stood in front of a mirror and looked absolutely beautiful, her dark eyes and straight black hair a perfect contrast to her white frilly dress. Her numerous bridesmaids standing beside her in a moment that was impossible not to smile, not that they would have fought the urge anyway. Clarissa would hold back genuine tears of happiness. She had looked forward to that day more than any other.

Then I thought about the person who would be forced to deliver the bad news. Maybe it was Bryan. She would immediately know something was wrong. He'd be unable to hold eye contact as he'd inform her that he couldn't find me, and was unable to get in touch with me. Clarissa would ask if he had tried my cell, to which he'd gesture in an obvious fashion that he had. She'd let loose those tears she tried so hard to withhold; he'd suggest I was an asshole; her bridesmaids would call a code red, and that would be that.

And then I thought of what might have made the situation even worse: if Ronald Fong had actually showed up. What if he had taken my asinine advice and arrived at the wedding in full tuxedo, in front of more than one hundred, fifty guests, most of them with no idea who he was. Perhaps the only two people cheering in the entire party would be Clarissa's parents. How would Clarissa explain that? How would she even feel about that? Utter humiliation. An embarrassment beyond comprehension. Not only did I skip out on our wedding, but I actually tried to replace myself with someone she had left years ago.

Or maybe I flattered myself and she wouldn't give half a shit. I somehow doubted that possibility.

And while I looked at my mangled face in the mirror, I wondered how anyone could possibly love that. That disgusting face. Even if the bruises were healed, the eyes normal, the lips regular sized, I didn't see how someone would want to kiss me, let alone love me. But she did.

And then I thought of my mother. On *that* day. And I remembered the sound of her stiletto heels as she escaped her embarrassment through the silence of over two hundred onlookers. And then I imagined Clarissa as she fought tears, grabbed the front of her dress to lift it from the ground as she ran to anywhere that was out of sight, wishing she could transport herself in either geography or time. Sobs so big that she might have actually choked on them.

And then I realized one of my biggest fears was actually my reality. That fat, old, dead fuck was right. I was his son. We not only shared blood, but also sensibility. I was the same as him. And I'd spent the past four years pretending I wasn't. But here I was, doing the same bullshit he had. Maybe even worse.

It might not have seemed like it, and it was clear that I could have handled it in a more mature manner, but I did Clarissa a favor. It would have never worked. Not in a million years. So, instead of fearing the worst, I decided to consider the best possible scenario:

Clarissa laid her eyes on Ronald and realized she actually did love him and that she'd been mistaken all these years. They walked down the aisle while Mrs. Chang raised her hands in praise and eclipsed the sun. Everyone would be happy as Clarissa and Ronald danced to Jared Leto's sweet, sultry voice while he sang that Bryan Adams song. They would look like Baxter and Jennifer. Maybe the performance even earned Jared a job.

That sounded better.

I approached my apartment, still uncertain of what I'd find.

And what I found made perfect sense.

Because there was nothing.

Everything was gone.

I threw my keys on the counter, which caused an echo that only appears in emptiness, and approached the indentation in the carpet where the TV stand used to be. I stood in it. Our Ikea coffee table was gone (she could have our child; it was the least I could do), the couches, the loveseat, the dishtowels, everything. It reminded me of the day I moved into that apartment, one of my first in LA. It was so full of hope. A fresh start. A new beginning. Exciting things were supposed to happen to me. And I supposed they did.

I entered the empty bedroom and smiled, as I saw the one object Clarissa left for me: That stupid John Wayne Gacy print. I had thought she'd thrown it out. I sat down, Indian style (can I still say that?), cross-legged (if I can't) in front of it and stared at the misery in the lines and color. It was all appropriate. I rolled my back against the carpet, gently laid my head on the floor, and held out my body spread eagle.

For the first time, maybe in my entire life, I was completely alone. My best friends had died. My father had died. My mother was gone. Clarissa was gone. Saga was gone.

No one would walk through that door. No one would call on the phone I no longer owned. All I had was the silence around me.

And, for the first time since God knows when, I thought I actually felt OK.

Finger Guns

A few days later, after the swelling in my lips subsided and the color of my eyes had improved from black to yellow, I returned to work and found a note on my computer screen that summoned me to my boss's office for an impromptu meeting. While I approached the waiting area beside his door, I noticed Bryan already occupied one of the chairs. I actually hadn't seen Bryan since the rehearsal dinner and knew he would insist on some sort of explanation. He obviously had no inkling as to the events of the past few days, but as he noticed the scratches on my fading multi-colored face, I figured he probably had an idea.

He smiled.

"I don't even wanna guess," Bryan said.

"So don't," I responded.

Of course, Bryan took that as a challenge.

"That'd be too easy. OK, let's see..." he said, as he rubbed his hands together. "Your Dad tried to stop you from going to the wedding, you had a violent fight, and then ran off because you thought he actually might have been right?"

"Dad died the morning of the wedding in a plane crash."

"No shit?"

"Yes shit," I nodded.

"Well, I'm sorry to hear that."

I shrugged.

"Did you get any money?"

I nodded.

"How much?"

"Doesn't matter, I ripped up the check."

"Really?"

"Really."

"Wow."

Bryan paused. Perhaps a moment of silence for my money. "So you went to the funeral instead of the wedding?"

"Not exactly."

"Then what?"

"It's a long story."

"Does the story include why your face is so fucked up?"

"Yes."

Bryan paused, not sure what to make of my blasé nature. "Well are you gonna tell me about it?" he asked

"It doesn't matter."

"You gotta give me something."

"No, I don't."

Bryan smiled and leaned back. Both his attitude and tone changed. "Did you speak with Clarissa?"

"No."

"Wanna know what happened?"

I did actually. I really, really did.

"No," I said.

For once, Bryan didn't press me. And for the entire exchange, my eyes remained forward, fixated on one of those framed black and white photos of a bunch of construction workers sitting on a metal beam, eating lunch, while on break from building a skyscraper. I wasn't sure what feeling that picture attempted to convey. Perhaps it was motivational. Perhaps it was to remind us that, even though we hated sitting at our shitty computers for nine hours a day, it was better than eating ham sandwiches while suspended forty stories off the ground. I bet Saga would have found beauty in it. Or maybe she wouldn't have. Regardless, I kept trying to.

I felt Bryan's eyes finally look away.

"Any clue why we're here?" he asked. "I feel like I'm waiting for the fucking principal."

As I shook my head, our boss opened his door and motioned us into his office. Bryan and I sat in the chairs opposite the desk as our boss relaxed in his leather ergonomic chair, threw his feet up on the desk, and held his clasped hands at his belt.

He looked me over with a sour face, like he'd just eaten a lemon.

"Does the other guy look worse, Brandon?" my boss asked.

"I'm fairly certain he looks just fine, Sir."

My boss nodded and smiled uncomfortably, probably didn't expect that answer.

"You guys know why you're here, right? It's promotion time."

I'd actually forgotten all about that. Bryan suddenly improved his posture as if a stiff, upright back improved his chances of earning this death sentence that I was certain had already been determined.

"I know both of you guys worked hard, gettin' the word out. Our shows are doing decent numbers, especially in the urban areas. So everyone is very happy with your work. But you know times are tough, and there's only room for one manager position. So me and the fellas made our decision."

Bryan eyed me nervously. I don't think my expression changed a bit. Plus, it hurt to move my face.

"And we decided that Brandon's heroic acts have shown us a new level of commitment. I'm not sure what exactly about *Honey Buns* made you run into that building; perhaps you enjoyed all the plot twists and cliffhangers from this past season, but you did. And not only did you save the office, you brought us good publicity. You believe *Honey Buns* went up two entire points in the ratings? Crazy, I know. So congratulations, Brandon, you've earned it."

My boss held out his hand for the congratulatory handshake.

Bryan leaned back, ran his hand over his hair as he gripped it from the roots in a poor attempt to mask his frustration. He needed that promotion. More than anything. He had a kid who played in puddles of piss. He had to feed the little fucker somehow. I didn't have a little fucker to support. Plus, I could probably have lived off Subway for a while, you know with the five-dollar foot-long and all. I'd said many times the world made no fucking sense, and this, too, made no fucking sense.

So why not try to make some.

I declined the handshake, kicked my feet up on the desk, and morphed my hands into finger six shooters.

"I really don't want it," I said.

And I really didn't. My boss was clearly offended and completely unable to understand why anyone would want to turn down such a shitty opportunity.

"The decision has already been made. This is a great opportunity to grow within the company, Brandon."

"Great, give it to Bryan. He deserves it. Trust me, I couldn't give a shit about *Honey Buns* and *Honey Buns* was not the reason I ran into that building. It wasn't even in the top hundred reasons. Or thousand! Now, Bryan, he probably would have run into the building if it meant that he'd get that promotion."

"Fuck yeah I would have," he concurred. "Really, I'd run in twice."

"The only reason I even took this job is because my ex-fiancée—wow it feels weird saying that—made me take it. But I left her at the alter a few days ago, so I figured I'd leave this too."

My boss shook his head, confused.

"So why the hell did you run in there?"

"Many reasons, but the main reason, Sir, is that I'm an asshole. Just ask Blomax over here."

I patted Bryan on the shoulder and, without so much as another word, rose from my seat and left the office.

As I passed by the reception area, I knew I'd never hear Gladys greet the black people in the morning again. I'd miss being singled out. I'd miss being the exception.

"Goin' to lunch, Brandon Popularity?" Gladys said with her trademark smile. At least I still had one fan.

"Something like that."

She had no clue what I meant, but smiled and nodded anyway.

"You gonna be OK, Brandon?" Gladys asked. It was probably the most sincere question I'd been asked in a long time.

I'd miss her.

I had no plans to ever come back.

My Return Home

I exited the building and walked toward my car on a picturesque Southern California day. Though most parts of the country were well into autumn, the seventy-eight-degree sunshine felt comforting to someone who just released himself from arguably his last shackle. As I approached my car, I realized my legs felt great and I wanted, more than anything, to keep using them. I didn't want to sit. I didn't want to wait at red lights. I didn't want the frustration of idle traffic, and trust me, there's always some traffic to be found in SoCal. I wanted to use the greatest tool I owned: my body. So I walked passed the car, returned my keys to my pocket, approached the street corner, and figured I'd walk home. It was only five or six miles anyway. I didn't really care about the car; I knew I could always retrieve it later on.

I strolled down Santa Monica Boulevard, something I'd probably never done in the middle of a weekday. The streets were jam packed with cars and I wondered what they were all doing if not working. Where were they going? Where did these people with odd schedules have to be?

As for me, I had nowhere to be. Nowhere.

Before I moved in with Clarissa, I used to have a Sunday night ritual that involved a long walk down Third Street to a Coffee Bean that was about two miles away. It became so regular that the girl behind the counter prepared my order the second the hanging bells chimed to announce my entrance (yeah, I was that predictable). I'd often do my best daydreaming along this walk while I tried to predict what my future held. Each time, the fantasy included a writing career, the ability to work from home, and a whole lot of money. I'd think about possible women I would meet, but the images of said females were always fuzzy. And no, I did not dream about meeting Nicole Eggert again, though if she wanted to have a go, I doubt I'd kick her out of bed even to this day.

But sometimes I'd think about the past. Calm moments of my past. Moments where I felt free. Most specifically, I'd conjure the following memory:

I attended college out of state and, since I preferred to have use of my car, each fall and spring I'd drive over fifteen hundred miles to either campus or home. The year I graduated, I managed to score a job I figured would be perfect for me, and even better, I had a month off between graduation and the planned start date. On the ride home, I'd always make at least one overnight stop and, on that particular trip, I decided to spend the evening in Toledo, Ohio. But this was not an ordinary night. No, it was the season finale of my favorite show at the time, *The Sopranos*. Season three: The episode where Jackie, Jr. was shot in the back of the head after leaving the crackhead's house. After I exited I-80 and settled on the surface streets of Toledo, I only had one goal in mind: Find a motel that had HBO. Couldn't have been simpler, right? One would think locating a motel with the most popular premium cable station would have been an easy chore, but maybe the Home Box Office slept with Toledo's wife or something, because finding a motel that met my requirements was akin to a quest for the Holy Grail. I searched that excuse for a city far and wide, past the numerous chain restaurants and rundown storefronts, and finally found a crappy Days Inn, with only a smoking room available and about an hour to spare before the show was scheduled to start. I bought a chicken sandwich at the adjacent Denny's and watched the incredible finale in that smoky, shabby room that had probably borne witness to a number of sexual transactions. I felt as content as a human possibly could. I didn't even care who had

used the sheets and comforter before I had or what dried
fluid might be on them.

And I realized now that *that* moment, that quick tour
of Toledo to find a TV, was arguably the best moment of my
life. That's right. The best. Because, at that exact moment,
I only had one worry in the entire world. One solitary problem that wasn't a real problem at all: find a motel that had
HBO. I was done with school, had mutually agreed to end
some bullshit college relationship, had a good job waiting
for me in a month, and I even had just taken a physical and
was declared in perfect health. The day existed as a buffer,
a limbo period, between my old life as a student and my
new one as an adult. It existed in a vacuum that could not
be touched. For at least one night, I felt no burden at all. A
complete fresh start. And I couldn't remember a time when
I had ever felt that way.

Until now.

Yes, there were people I missed and things I should
have done differently. But, in regards to Clarissa, I felt like
I had ultimately done the right thing. And, as for Saga, at
least I had tried. It might not have worked out the way I
wanted to, but I showed up and was literally beaten within
an inch of my life. I earned the E for effort. And I missed
her. I wondered about her. I still wanted her, though I knew
it was utterly ridiculous that I felt that way. Once upon a

time, I pondered the rest of my life married to Clarissa. Having kids. Living a life I knew I'd hate. Downtrodden with a consistent, yet heavy dose of reality. Then I pictured a life of fantasy in Sweden. Having beautiful blond children. It would be like Christmas every day. I knew that was too good to be true; none of it was real. Though I still wondered.

As I reached the halfway point of my walk between my now former office and home, I took note of my surroundings. I could see the rotating tower atop the Grove parking structure and thought about all the time I'd spent there. The number of times I had eaten at its restaurants and the number of times the Changs rode the stupid trolley. I passed the La Brea tar pits and recalled I had never once visited them, even though I lived so close for so long. I walked by the Subway where I knew every Sandwich Artist by first name. The Starbucks where Clarissa and I had our first "date." There were many memories; a lot of shit can happen in four years.

I breathed the dirty air of Los Angeles and savored it like it was a strong cup of coffee. I knew it would be one of the last times I ever tasted this dirty city.

"Hey look! It's the asshole groom!" a fellow pedestrian excitedly exclaimed to his friend. He smiled and patted me on the shoulder. "Whoa, brother. Whooooa brother," he followed with a knowing laugh.

Whoa brother, indeed.

I figured it was time I forgot these past four years ever happened.

I figured I'd go back to New York.

THE END AND
THE BEGINNING

"Pizzzzzzza! Pizzzzzzza!"

Two young children jumped up and down while screaming those beautiful words, while their exhausted mother finished her coffee in the dead of winter at a downtown Manhattan café. I loosened my recently purchased winter jacket and watched the snow fall outside on the mid-December day that was a perfect precursor for the upcoming Christmas holiday.

I somehow knew all great stories started and ended in New York. I felt as if I was experiencing both simultaneously.

I held in my hand something that intrigued me from the moment I ran into the FedEx man just outside my new building. I certainly hadn't been expecting anything priority mail. In fact, I didn't know anyone actually knew my address. The only person I told I was moving was Bryan, and I wasn't sure he was even smart enough to fill out a FedEx label properly. I still didn't have a job in New York City, but with the money I had in savings, I had bought myself a few weeks before I'd have to consider a cardboard box outside of a church.

I examined the return address on the thin envelope, which was distinctly Russian. I thought that perhaps the Russian space program was simply returning some of my father's documents, though I couldn't imagine what could be useful. I wasn't sure how they had obtained my address, but I'd seen *Red Dawn* and lived through the '80s, and I knew the KGB was capable of much greater than finding a single apartment in New York City.

But when I opened the envelope, it contained no letter, no trinkets, only photographs. Black and white photographs. From space. I sifted through the pictures of various parts of the shuttle and couldn't, for the life of me, understand why they'd been sent. But as I kept flipping through, my questions were soon answered. Because the tenth picture featured a very familiar face standing between two Russian cosmonauts among a sea of what appeared to be Froot Loops freely dancing in the zero-gravity environment. My father. I stared at it in disbelief as I remembered the words he told me in the hospital: I was going to hear shit about him and not to believe it all. However, I didn't see any oranges floating in the shuttle. Perhaps they didn't keep in space.

I quickly viewed the next photograph: my father in his space suit. A broad smile, ear to ear. Then a photo of him on a space walk along what appeared to be the side of some kind of space station. That fucker actually did it. As I looked at the photos, I didn't even think about why the hell my father had it appear as though he had died in a plane crash. But the next photo might have provided an answer.

A picture of my father floating in space. There was no tube connecting him to the ship. There was no rope, no nothing. I didn't know much about space flights, but I knew that not to be normal. And he was waving. Waving goodbye.

The next photo showed him farther away.

And the next farther, until he resembled a toy in an outer space diorama crafted by a second grader. Since my father had won the lottery, it appeared that he wanted to be a star. Now, he was one.

I placed the photos on the table, in sequence, and ran my hand through my hair while I tried to make sense of it all. And that's when I noticed the corner of a piece of paper sticking out of the FedEx envelope. A medical record. Cancer. He was actually sick after all.

Fuck.

The waitress brought me a steaming latte that had a symbol of a heart carved into the foam. I took my coffee stirrer and gently manipulated it, but not enough to disturb the entire image as I thought about the photos and medical record. I took a small sip of the drink and felt the foam stick to my upper lip a moment before my tongue streaked across it to clear it of any white residue.

I thought about my father's past four years. He constantly traveled; he spent all his money on entertainment. Simply put, he had nonstop fun for about fifteen hundred straight days. This had to be his last hurrah. Maybe he felt it appropriate to fade away in the grandest manner possible. They never found any survivors from his plane crash; they actually never found any bodies, period. And now I knew why: there weren't any. Think about it: if he actually wanted to die in space, the Russians would never let that happen. Could you imagine the international uproar if a Russian lost an American civilian on a mission? He had to falsify a death, though I didn't quite understand why he just didn't fake a heart attack. Then again, it wouldn't have been my father if it wasn't dramatic.

"I love pizzzzzzzaaaaaaa!" the kid screamed while he spun around in circles.

"I know you love pizza," the mother responded with the same enthusiasm she would if she were getting a mammogram.

I continued to watch the two pizza-craving children as they pulled on their mother's sleeve. Their father, or who I presumed to be their father, approached one of them and lifted him high up in the air while taunting him with the promise of pizza.

I thought about revisionist history and if I had gone through with my marriage. I pictured Clarissa and me in those seats, with our little hybrid children bothering her about pizza while she was probably on the phone discussing some bullshit about some new Ryan Gosling movie and how he'd win a million Oscars for it (even all the science and technical awards). She'd chastise our little spawn in the middle of the coffee house while they cried for something as simple as pizza. I bet she'd even drag them home without the sweet taste of cheese, sauce, and pepperoni.

And I thought of Saga. Just Saga. The way she'd roll her eyes. The way she'd smile. The way she said exactly what was on her mind. And I didn't want to think about it anymore. Because I knew, deep down, it could have worked.

I finished my latte as I watched the family gather their belongings.

"OK, you guys ready for some pizza?" the father asked, while he waved his fingers like magic wands.

"YAAAAAYYYYY," the two children responded, as if they had just secured a Super Bowl victory.

And I, too, thought it was a great idea.

Human life is ultimately frail. There's no reason to settle for pain. Companionship, marriage, a "soul-mate" sure looked right on paper, but this was the real world. And in the real world, there are no guarantees. Only random occurrences. But there are plenty of small victories to be had in life; all you can really ask for is some pizza.

I slowly rose and refastened my jacket in preparation for the stiff wind that would belt my face as soon as I left the coffee shop. It was a new day in a new life, and I was prepared to brush away residual sadness so I could enjoy every second of it.

It was time for pizza. And you know what else? A fucking cookie. Maybe I'd even look up Christina Hawkins and demand that I squeeze her tits.

I approached the exit and, just as my hand gripped the cold, metal handle of the door, my thoughts were interrupted by the sound of a porcelain mug crashing to the floor. A sound so loud that it halted the collective restaurant conversation. I instinctively looked back to see the pieces of the mug as they lay still in the quickly spreading puddle of light coffee, coffee that surrounded a pair of black boots.

I followed the boots up a pair of legs, a waist, a jacket, and to a face. And in a second, I knew my father's ending would never be mine.

Because there she was. My Saga. But this time, judging by the mug shards and surprised look on her face, she clearly was not following me. Call it fate, call it luck, but there she was.

My mental library of Saga memories appeared before my eyes as I tried to see through them and to her face. The dinner, the walk, the air hockey, the sumo suit, Disneyland, the hospital, and lying naked in the middle of Stockholm.

Our eyes locked much like they had when I stood in her father's house. But, this time, it felt like less of a duel.

I'm sure everyone's attention was on us, but like Jennifer and Baxter, I don't think either one of us noticed or cared.

I only had one question for her:

"What did you say?"

She knew exactly what I meant.

"I don't want to kill your polar bear."

I hoped she wouldn't.

About The Author

Brett Sills is a multi-optioned screenwriter/freelance ad writer who, self-admittedly, probably saves his best work for e-mails and text messages. Though he resides in Los Angeles, he never takes long walks on the beach, but probably should. *My Sweet Saga* is Brett's first novel.

Brett can be reached at MySweetSaga@gmail.com.
Or check out his blog at http://peelingtheskin.blogspot.com

www.ingramcontent.com/pod-product-compliance
Lightning Source LLC
Chambersburg PA
CBHW031412240626
47154CB00001B/6